Whistle
Down
a Dark Lane

Whistle Down a Dark Lane

a novel

by Adrienne Jones

Harper & Row, Publishers

Library of Congress Cataloging in Publication Data
Jones, Adrienne.
  Whistle down a dark lane.

  "A Charlotte Zolotow book."
  SUMMARY: The summer of 1921 is a turning point for
Margery as the slow disintegration of her parents'
marriage forces her mother, older sister, and Margery
to learn to manage on their own.
  [1. Divorce—Fiction] I. Title.
PZ7.J677Whab 1982   [Fic]   81-48661
ISBN 0-06-023063-0   AACR2
ISBN 0-06-023064-9 (lib. bdg.)

My love and gratitude
to Charlotte Zolotow and Robert O. Warren
for vitally enhancing my view and this book;
to Orianna Mason,
a stellar performer in the original triumvirate;
and finally and especially
to my sister, Doris Meek,
who has shared my whole life
and enlarges and reinforces my memory,
so past and present have greater value.

Contents

Prologue

The past becomes present as I stand at the window. Its panes of glass reveal an old landscape of the heart.

Maybe it is the little girl who has brought back those events leading to that long-ago summer, brought back the summer itself, and an echo of first love and loss and change. The solemn child plays there next door beneath a tree. Her family moved in yesterday.

Memory be green. I whisper the old words.

Suddenly that whole year stands clear in my mind. Its excitements, its joys spring to life; and its times of terrible fear.

Memory be green, I breathe again.

And sharp recall summons the bite of defeat, the balm of victory which marked the end of one era, the beginning of another for my sister Blainey and for me; but most of all for Mother. She had the most to lose and the most to conquer.

Today I watch the little girl through the curtains. She cannot see me. She plays alone except for a doll and a stuffed animal—a rabbit, I believe, lop-eared from much love. The child arranges these friends carefully in the tree's shade. She squats and seems to talk with them. I cannot hear her. She must be about seven, pale haired, skinny, her serious face peppered with small light-brown freckles. It is as though I watch the child that was me, across the years.

But perhaps the child has nothing to do with this upsurge of memories. Mother died two weeks ago in our front bedroom, and it is true, the past seems heavily present when someone dies. Blainey had come to be with her and with me in this last time of crisis, this last departure. We knew this was the final sundering of our staunch threesome. There had been other crises, other departures, but none that shook us as much as the one of that summer long ago.

Mother, toward the end, asked us to read aloud from her worn King James Bible. During the past few years, and especially during the last illness, she had seemed to let go of her Theosophical beliefs, and had reverted to the Methodist religion of her childhood. But, just before slipping into half-consciousness, and finally into death, she winked at us.

"See you on the A.P.," she had said softly.

It was an old bit of humor among the three of us at bedtimes when Blainey and I were little. Mother was speaking of the astral plane, a Theosophical phrase and doctrine. Astral plane: Where the second and invisible body goes during sleep—the only remnant of that sojourn the next morning scraps of dreams, and quickly forgotten. Astral plane: Where the eternal essence of each person survives after death of the physical self. Mother, with a wry and gentle irreverence, had dubbed it the A.P., and tucked us in each night when we were little with the promise we would meet together there in sleep. Astral plane: To us a familiar and comfortable region.

"See you on the A.P.," she had told us two weeks ago. "My dear, dear chicks . . ." She winked, gave a faint smile, closed her eyes.

So at the end, despite the hold of her own childhood and of the Bible and the Methodist church, she had not entirely forgotten the Theosophical colony, Krotona, in the hills above Hollywood, and the strange year that led up to our journey there away from Atlanta and Daddy and George and our summer home, Cloudacres. Leaving everything, everybody. Mother leaving her ten-year love. Going to California.

Susanna Mason Standfield no longer one with Allen W. Standfield. "A grass widow," someone whispered. Yes, going to California.

> *Oh, Susanna!*
> *Oh, don't you cry for me.*
> *For I'm goin' to California,*
> *With my banjo on my knee. . . .*

I remember being struck by the oddity then that the song we sang seemed to be especially for Mother. We changed it, though, to fit the occasion, for *we* were going to California, not Daddy.

The events of that shattering year were caught by the naive gaze of a seven-year-old—by me, then Margery Standfield—all faithfully recorded by a child's mind, the conversations, the whispers, the sighs, the tears, the laughs, even the muffled voice of the Grand Dragon from behind its Klansman's hood, the thrust of the Drag-on's pike hunting for Uncle Franley.

A child's interpretation may be limited or askew, even when the observation itself is accurate, but basic intent is seldom misread. I knew what Noni Shattock was up to the night her warm husky voice came from the dark of the mountain night. Noni with her innocent face and knowing body.

"Beau, honey, no man in hollerin' distance of Rabun Gap got hands like yourn. You be about the mostest fella I ever *did* know. All the girls go wild over you. Old 'uns, young 'uns, even little-bitty ol' runny-nose gals."

"You be about as crazy as they come, Noni, sweet thing." Beau Tulley's laugh was different, somehow, from the one I knew. It made me uncomfortable, and presently, sounds from Noni, sounds with no words, no laughter, made me run away through the dark.

Though I didn't understand what had passed between Beau and Noni, I did know what she was up to. She was stealing my love from me.

Today the little girl outside my window still squats there in the shade, still communes with her doll and rabbit. The late-afternoon sun slants in beneath the branches, but she has used the protection of a low-hanging limb, so from my view she and her silent friends now glimmer in leaf shadow.

She looks up as a car door clunks shut. She leaps to her feet, flies down the drive. A man in a business suit has climbed out of the car. He slips off his jacket, his day done, begins to loosen his tie. The running child cries aloud. At last I hear her.

"Daddy, Daddy! Catch me!"

He drops his coat and swings her high, laughing.

I am overcome with loss.

1

Bless the Tender Girls

Blainey and I argued in later years over exactly when the change began in our family. I insisted it began on Armistice Day 1920, two years after the end of the Great War. She said it was earlier, the year we moved to Greenwood Avenue in 1918. She claimed that was when Mother and Daddy stopped sharing a bedroom.

Before Greenwood Avenue, we had lived in a flat over on Atlanta's Tenth Street, somewhere between Georgia Tech and Piedmont Park. We had taken in roomers then, young interns from the nearby medical college. That was before Daddy's building-supply business began to prosper as the war tapered off. The rising prosperity brought us a new affluence, and when Daddy bought the house on Greenwood Avenue, we stopped taking in roomers.

Our new brick house, with its wide veranda, sat sturdily on its sloping site. There were other houses scattered up and down Greenwood, an agreeable meld of city and country with open stretches of land here and there. The following spring, Daddy purchased Cloudacres. Cloudacres, the place we had rented for several summers up in the tail end of the Blue Ridge Mountains.

None of those years before 1920 are very clear to me. My sister, Blainey, two and a half years older than I, may, after all, have the straight of it. Maybe she's right that the change began the day we moved to Greenwood Avenue. But for me, events didn't begin to connect and form a pattern until the fall of 1920. In November to be exact, the Armistice Day parade.

I realize that, at the time, the change was invisible to Blainey and me. And maybe to Mother, who puffed a little, turned pink from the effort of getting me out of the tub, and from the hurry to have us ready in time for the parade. Despite the rush, her hands were quick and gentle and easy. She smelled faintly of violets.

"Why do I always have to get out first!" I cried.

Blainey chortled, "Now I've got the whole tub to myself!"

She flopped to her stomach, stretched out, kicked the water to a froth. She twisted to her back, floated there in the big slant-end tub that stood high on its clawed feet. Her stomach and chest glistened, white as a fish's belly.

"Just look at her!" My voice rose in outrage. "It's not fair!"

"Hop out, Blainey," Mother said.

Triumph smothered outrage. I felt entirely mollified as Blainey, for once, sprang from the tub with no argument.

"You're usually first out, Margy, love," Mother was saying, "because I like to help you get good and dry."

"Blainey dries herself."

"But you're my baby." Mother kissed my shoulder. "When you're as old as Blainey—"

"I'll never, *ever* be old as Blainey." I ignored Mother's frown at my interruption. "Even when I'm eight like she is, *she'll* be going on—on—"

"Eleven." Blainey's eyes, hazel like Daddy's, sparked as she furnished the number for me. "Eleven, Magpie, eleven."

"Eleven." I threw her a dirty look. "So I'll never, *ever* be oldest! Not *ever* in my whole life!"

"Sh-h-h, little chick. Ladies shouldn't interrupt when someone is speaking," Mother said softly, but forgetting me she breathed, "Oh dear, we're going to be late," then called out, "Allen! Could you help Margy finish drying? Do you mind?"

I clutched the towel around me. Daddy had never dried me before. The prospect of it delighted and disturbed me.

Blainey could manage by herself after bathing. She could manage almost everything, anytime. Except today.

Today was unusual. Today she was performing. So on this morning, Mother insisted that Blainey's chestnut curls would need an extra brushing to burnish their auburn lights.

Today, Blainey was to sing to General Pershing and Marshal Foch, she and every other third grader in Atlanta. Most particularly, the performance was for Marshal Foch, visiting the United States from France in a gesture of friendship. In 1920 we weren't so much one world, and I wonder, looking back, what the Marshal thought, that November day, of all those young American southern accents struggling through his national anthem in French.

"Allen?" Mother tried again.

From the sitting room came the rustle of newspaper.

"Are you calling me, Mase?" Obviously he had reeled in his mind from distant and important events in the news.

"Yes. I hate to bother you, hon, but I'm afraid we'll be late picking up Marian and Mrs. Hewitt. And Blainey will be late for the 'Marseillaise.' "

"Yes?" Daddy sounded willing but vague. He had gone back to reading, for we could hear the newspaper again.

"Would you dry Margy and help her with her shoes and socks?"

"That's not quite in my line." He seemed to be talking to himself. But he hadn't refused.

"Run, little chick." Mother gave me a nudge. "Daddy will help you this once."

Even now I remember his touch that day. Not at all

like Mother's. He did not rub, but patted the towel along my back and bottom. Mother handled us as though we were an extension of herself, her touch easy and quick; his had a deferential air; hers so natural I had no sense of self; his solemn and aware.

I glanced over my shoulder into his eyes, hazel eyes, brown with green flecks, intelligent and intense beneath straight dark brows. Quickly I looked away. Self-consciousness and silence suddenly overwhelmed me. I felt a vague sense that I was overstepping some tenet of ladylikeness, one of those tenets Mother and the ladies of her circle held in such high regard.

Daddy finished drying my back. With a touch he turned me about. The pat, pat continued over my chest and stomach.

"That feels good." My voice managed only a whisper. "I like the way you dry me."

He smiled, said nothing. He blotted under my arms, then worked down each arm separately, smoothed the drops from my hands, the dampness from between my fingers one at a time. He bent to my legs. The faint scrape of his just-shaved chin buffed my shoulder. Next, he sat me beside him on the couch to work the terry cloth between my toes. At last he stood me again, handed me the towel.

"Now you can dry the rest of you, sugar." He picked up the paper, disappeared behind it.

Mystified, I held the towel before me, sorry he was finished, wishing for his closeness, for the feel of his steady hands, wishing that the smell of his tweed suit coat and shaving lotion would surround me again. I longed for his cheek to softly abrade my bare shoulder once more.

He lowered the paper, looked over the top. "Go ahead, hon."

"I'm all dry."

"No. You should dry between your legs. You don't want to be damp when you put on your panties. You might get chafed."

"Mother dries all of me."

"Don't you ever dry yourself?" He seemed surprised.

"Hardly ever."

"Let me show you." He took the towel, stretched it across my shoulders, handed me the ends. "Now pull it back and forth. That's my girl. See, you can dry your back, easy as pie. It works for all the hard-to-reach places. Now, between your legs. One hand in front, the other behind. That's right. No, no, not so hard, sweetheart." He laughed a little. "Girls are tender there, bless them."

My self-consciousness flew away in the joy of having his special attention. How fine to have him teach me how to use a towel. How grand to have him to myself! At last, dry, and in no danger of chafe, I leaned against his knee. He kissed my forehead.

"Run along now, little Margy." He took the towel, wrapped it around my body, tucked the end to hold it. His hands turned me about and sent me off to Mother. Reluctance, regret, stopped me at the door. I looked back.

"I want to go with you and Blainey, today," I said.

"You and Mother and Marian Pickett and Mrs. Hewitt are going to have a great place to watch the parade.

A friend of mine has lent us his second-floor office on Peachtree Street. You'll have a bird's-eye view of the whole shootin' match."

He winked at me, then raised the paper before his face. His voice had turned distant when it came from behind the newsprint.

"Scoot now, sugarfoot," it said.

2

Old Battles
and New Changes

The parade itself marked a kind of watershed for the Standfields and particularly for me.

At the beginning, it was the flash of sun on golden horns that stirred my heart. This dazzle blinded us for a moment as the Marine Corps Band swept around the corner onto Peachtree Street. We could, indeed, see the whole shootin' match from our second-story vantage.

"Here they come!" Marian Pickett's light voice sparkled, an echo of the fifes. It also carried the sound of relief, for the crash of the music ended Mother and Mrs. Hewitt's argument. At least for a while.

"Bravo! Oh, bravo!" Mrs. Hewitt's British accent came in tuba tones, as the Sousa march blared up at us.

"Now it begins!" Mother breathed in my ear.

The music swelled more loudly as the last ranks of the band wheeled around the corner. Mrs. Hewitt's argument with Mother was canceled for the time being, Mrs. Hewitt's old argument about the Revolutionary War, which wasn't over for her in the same way that the Civil War wasn't over for Mother. Each fought the lost cause of ancient loyalties. Despite Mother's allegiance to the South in matters of the Civil War, she hotly defended the entire thirteen colonies when Mrs. Hewitt was on the attack. Despite their frequent clashes, Mrs. Hewitt and Mother remained friends.

Now, the band below was in full swing. The tubas and trumpets and slide trombones and flutes and fifes, the rattling snare drums, the booming bass drums, the poised cymbals, stepped smartly along. John Philip Sousa's "Washington Post March" oompahed and beat and fanfared and sparkled. It reached forward and back, and touched the entire line of the parade and the crowds edging each side of the street.

Behind the band, a company of soldiers swung along, their overseas caps jaunty, khaki jackets and trousers properly creased, woolen puttees neatly wrapped to midcalf, Springfield rifles aslant on shoulders. Applause rippled toward us. The whistles, the hurrahs, the clapping kept abreast of the military men. This swell of sound increased, crescendoed, then diminished as they passed.

In seconds, though, a new and delirious roar swept around the Peachtree corner. Mother leaned forward. Her plump form pushed me before her until my head and shoulders poked alarmingly from our high perch. But her hold on me was tight.

Suddenly she exclaimed, "General Pershing! And look! That must be Foch! Yes, yes. Just like his picture in this morning's paper."

Marian's eyes shone, too, as she glanced at us. She had caught Mother's happy agitation. Her face turned rosy.

"Aren't they the handsome and manly ones though! And so elegant, too."

She and Mother touched hands in delighted communion. They were as close in their friendship as sisters.

But it was not Foch and Pershing who caught my eye. I was entranced by their great brown horses glistening in the sun. High-stepping, dancing at an angle, the beautiful beasts moved to Sousa's metronomic rhythms. They stirred my soul and covered me with goose bumps. In fancy I, too, bestrode a spirited animal, in fancy I bowed to all the people while they cheered. It made no difference that I was only a girl.

Then Mother's voice dragged me to reality. "That's General John J. Pershing, chicken little, the big handsome gentleman. And the small, neat fellow beside him, the one with the fierce mustache, is Marshal Foch, the French general. Without those two the Kaiser might have won the war."

Mrs. Hewitt spoke up, her voice a challenge. "Yes, but Marshal Foch is the real hero. The Marshal was Supreme Commander of *all* the Allied forces in the Great War, *including* the military *finally* sent over by the States under your Black Jack Pershing, there."

She gave a deprecatory little wave. Her precise words made it clear even to me that she had just, in a way, demoted our General Pershing. Mother stiffened but did not reply as we watched the changing scene below.

I felt outside of Mother's and Marian's and Mrs. Hewitt's world. Longing for Daddy seized me. If only my hand were in his strong one, if only my cheek were pressed against the wool of his coat sleeve with the good smell of shaving soap and manliness drifting down to me. I remembered his touch as he dried me, the sanding of his chin against my shoulder. At that moment, my bird's-eye view had no value at all. I did not care that I could see the whole shootin' match.

Besides my yearning for Daddy, I always had more fun when I tagged along with Blainey. Blainey, who never failed to carry drama with her. How miserable that I was only a first grader. Oh, to be in the third. Right this minute Blainey would be with every other third grader in Atlanta, lined on the State Capitol steps waiting to sing to Marshal Foch. And in the crowd, Daddy would be watching, his fine eyes alight with pride over Blainey. How grand to sing the "Marseillaise" in French to a French general!

Blainey had practiced it every night at home for two weeks. Even in those solitary rehearsals she performed with flair. She did the nasal French pronunciation to perfection. I was awed by the marvelous sound she produced, singing through her nose.

Blainey was a born performer. In her kindergarten class picture she had been the only child with one foot crossed on the other knee so her underpants showed.

In the photo her eyes glinted with this knowledge. Yes, she had been a smashing success in kindergarten. That was when she was five. She had had three years' practice since then at wooing the spotlight. Mother found her a handful.

"Weren't we lucky that Daddy borrowed a friend's office so we ladies would have a good view," Mother was saying.

"I'd rather be with Blainey," I said, forgetting that Blainey sometimes teased me to tears, forgetting sometimes I pestered her into fury.

Today I remembered only our fun together, our shared secrets, our closeness; the way I called her Blain in comradeship, the way she called me Magpie with joy and love. Magpie, from the time Mother had said to her, smiling, "Margy's so quiet with most people, but she chatters away like a magpie with you, Blainey love."

So today I repeated, "I'd *rather* be with Blainey."

As though she had not heard me, Mother went on, "See the children down there? They have to be held up for only a glimpse now and then, but we have a box seat."

I settled into sulky silence. A box seat was not as grand a thing as singing to Marshal Foch through one's nose.

After the generals, there marched endless companies of other military men. The Marine Corps Band had passed out of earshot, but the cadence of the hundreds of feet was accompanied now by the Army Band.

Presently, Mother gave me a squeeze of jubilation.

"Look, little chick," she cried, again as delighted as a child. "Now comes the trooping of all the states' colors. Isn't that thrilling? See, the banner in front says, 'Flags of the Forty-eight.' "

The brilliant reds and greens and blues, the intriguing emblems worked into the flags, caught my imagination. I stopped brooding about Daddy and Blainey.

"Mase, dear." Mrs. Hewitt spoke warmly to Mother. "What is your state? Virginia, is it not? Has its flag passed in review yet?"

"No, Elizabeth, not yet. They seem to be marching in alphabetical order. Virginia should be near the end."

Several minutes later, Mother leaned forward again. "There it is!" She pointed below. "After Vermont! Virginia!"

A gust of wind blew the Virginia flag straight out from its staff. The flag bearer looked up at the unfurled banner, grinned with pleasure.

"Explain the emblem to me, Mase," Mrs. Hewitt cried, "quickly before it passes."

Mother's words rushed out, and sudden satisfaction rode high in her voice.

"There are two figures. The one standing is Virtue, the one lying on the ground is Tyranny. Virtue's foot is on Tyranny's neck, you see." She smiled brightly at her friend, and I felt the soft, hidden tremor of her laughter against my spine.

"What does it *mean?*" urged Mrs. Hewitt.

A lady should not be rude nor deliberately start a quarrel. But a lady could certainly answer a direct question.

"Virtue," Mother said, "represents the State of Virginia. Tyranny, lying supine, is Great Britain. The scene depicts the time Virginia joined the other colonies to whup England in the Revolutionary War."

Mother's eyes twinkled as though she were making a joke of it all. Nevertheless, she finished with purpose.

"The Virginia State motto, there at the bottom of the flag, reads '*Sic Semper Tyrannis*,' Latin for 'Thus Ever to Tyrants.' "

Mrs. Hewitt's exclamation came sharp as a sword thrust. "*Oh!*" The flags of Washington, West Virginia, Wisconsin passed. And finally Wyoming. "Humph!" she sniffed at last while Mother innocently fastened her gaze on the next group of marchers.

"Rotarians," Mother said to me.

I noticed that Marian Pickett was quietly convulsed with laughter. She did not look at Mrs. Hewitt either, but leaned forward to concentrate on this next company in their business suits. Each carried a small American flag.

"Yes," she agreed. "Rotarians. But something has slowed the parade."

"What?" I said.

"You mean what slowed the parade, honey?" She smiled at me. "Well, parades just tend to bog down from time to time. It will move along presently."

"I mean what are Rotarians?" But I hadn't followed Blainey's advice again—speak up, Magpie, speak up— and Marian didn't hear me.

Instead, excited, she turned to Mother. "Look, Mase, bringing up the rear. A group of Suffragettes!"

"Well, I declare!" Mother said.

And Mrs. Hewitt forgot her recent defeat.

"When they pass below our window we really must send up a hurrah!" she cried.

"Yes," Marian agreed, "without the Suffragettes we'd never have been given the vote. We certainly must cheer them. Mase, did you cast a ballot in the presidential election this month?" She did not take her eyes from the women below.

"Not this time," Mother said, "maybe next. Though I wonder, is it strictly proper for a lady to be seen in a polling place?" She frowned, then suddenly smiled at Marian, and boldly finished, "Yes, indeed, I may very well vote next time."

"At the end of Mr. Harding's first term?" Marian asked.

"Yes. Allen says he thinks Mr. Harding will be little better than having no president at all."

Mrs. Hewitt broke in. "Of course, I'm not an American citizen. If I were, *I* would have voted. Ridiculous for women not to vote." Her eyes grew large with defiance, her wiry hair seemed to gain extra starch, and she rushed on, "I bloody well wouldn't care if it was ladylike or not, I would vote!"

Mother flushed and was silent. Mrs. Hewitt had overstepped the bounds of decorum with her bloody well. *A lady does not use vulgarisms.*

Marian, undisturbed by Mrs. Hewitt, said, "I voted a week ago Tuesday." Her tone was casual, calm, and she gave a quick polish of her nails against her shirtwaist front. "November second." She fanned her fingers, inspected her nails, smiled at them. "Voted in the presidential election."

Mother gasped. "Marian, you're the most amazing and independent—"

Marian dropped her hands into her lap, laughed, defensive now. "I *had* to vote, Mase, when Mr. Pickett declared himself for Warren G. Harding."

"Your husband voted for Harding!" Mother was aghast.

"I told him he was a traitor to his Southern heritage."

I nudged Mother's arm. "I'm hungry. I bet Daddy and Blain stop at the ice-cream parlor."

But Mother didn't even look at me.

"Marian, honestly, did you really vote?" she said.

"I did!" Marian's laugh trilled again, this time in triumph. "Voted for Mr. Cox and canceled my husband's vote to boot!"

Mother looked at her friend with uncertain admiration. "Marian, you are the bold one. Imagine, casting a ballot this first time around after passage of the Women's Suffrage Amendment. Walking right into a polling place and casting your ballot! And even going against your husband's opinion on how to vote."

Then they were both laughing together, and Mrs. Hewitt's hearty, horsy whicker joined them.

My ice-cream parlor hint was a lost cause, but the parade had begun to move again. With my stomach over the windowsill, I thrust myself halfway out into the crisp November air. Mother's hand absently reached, held the fullness of my skirt.

The Suffragettes were just coming into view behind the Rotarians. They carried their lettered banners on high. Mother read the words aloud—WOMEN'S RIGHTS—SUFFRAGETTES—WE WON THE VOTE!—and kissed the back of my neck. It seemed more of a promise than a warning when the youngest, the liveliest of this last contingent of the parade called up to me where I hung from the window.

"Get ready for some changes, little girl! We've already given you the vote!"

What changes seemed a mystery to me that day.

"Hip, hip, hurrah for the 1920's!" she cried, throwing me a kiss. Suddenly my peeve at being left with the ladies evaporated. True, it was always exhilarating to be in company with Blainey and Daddy; but Mother had a way of making everything comfortable and fun. Now there was my Suffragette to add a fillip of excitement.

Though the stirring music of the military bands had faded away down Peachtree Street, the company of women stepped along with great élan. Some wore their hair bobbed in the daring new style, replicas of F. Scott Fitzgerald girls; their skirts showed a bold amount of leg. Others were as sedate as Mother in high-necked lace shirtwaists, with skirts exposing only a modest glimpse of buttoned shoe and ankle.

With the music barely a whisper, and the glory of Pershing and Foch astride their chestnut mounts long gone, the crowds lining the curbs began to break up. A few people stopped to applaud the determined, smiling band of women. As though this approval lit the fuse of a dark counterresponse, others turned and began to call out insults.

A slender fellow in minister's garb bugled in a voice developed by pulpit oration. "Go home to your children and husbands where ye belong, before Satan claims ye, ye sinful daughers of Eve!"

From the sidewalk directly below our window, a burly man blatted, "A foin pass the country's comin' to, givin' the females the vote!"

A feminine call came, shrill with something beyond anger.

"Hussies!"

Another woman's voice, sweet-sour, jeered from the opposite curb.

"Can't you get a fellow of your own, dearies?"

The man at her side gave a coarse laugh.

"I reckon I know what them babies really need," he said. His voice carried up and down the street. The woman laid her head on his shoulder, giggled at her man's cleverness.

"You could show 'em what it is to be a *real* woman, Harry, luv," she cried. "You could take some of the starch out of 'em or my name isn't Glory Jean."

When I looked at Mother, each cheek had a red spot, darker than her carefully applied soft rose rouge.

"Why do those ladies hate the ones that are marching?" I asked.

It was Marian who smiled reassuringly at me. "They're scarcely ladies, honey," she said, and to Mother, "Isn't it maddening there are always some women ready to cut the ground from under us."

"Us?" Mother sounded dismayed. "Are you a Suffragette, Marian?" Her surprise was genuine, and I remembered she had once told Daddy that Marian had a bit
of an imp in her.

"No." Marian laughed. "But I do admire them."

Below, the ugliness had spread like spilled oil. A dark
mutter arose from some of the people clotted along the
sidewalks. The anger was directed at the marchers, not
at those ladies who were scarcely ladies. Suddenly a
stone whistled past the jaunty contingent. Seconds later
another came hurtling. This one grazed the cheek of
my Suffragette. Her hand flew to the spot. For a moment
her banner dipped. Quickly she swung it aloft again,
two handed, and I could see the slow red run of blood
along her cheekbone.

At that instant a man's voice called out, brave and
hearty and gallant. "Hear, hear for the ladies!"

Moderate cheers began, men's and women's cries sup-
porting the group of doughty marchers. This swell of
approval swallowed the ugly mutters, the rough taunts.
When a final overripe tomato came flying, it was so
wide of its mark, the company of women all burst into
laughter. The merriment spread as this last of the parade
passed below.

Yes, the parade, a kind of watershed for the Standfields. A watershed for me. Even after the ugliness of
the jeers and the catcalls and the thrown stones, my
Suffragette turned once more to look back at me, her
eyes glowing above the streak of blood that marked her
cheek. She threw me another kiss, waved again.

"Remember . . ." she called.

3

The Eavesdroppers

Daddy was settled in the sitting room after dinner when Mother announced to him, "Marian voted a week ago Tuesday. Can you imagine!"

She sank into the rocking chair, embroidery basket in hand. Our tabby cat, Hooligan, captured his favorite spot, crowded between her warm thigh and the chair arm.

Daddy continued to scan the Atlanta *Constitution*. He turned the page, folded the newsprint neatly under.

"Marian's a little forward for my taste," he murmured.

"Read us the funnies," Blainey said, leaning across the sofa arm.

"Not just now, sugarfoot." Daddy smiled at her, kissed the corner of her forehead, went back to reading.

"Aw-w," Blainey began.

"Not now." Daddy's voice firmed. She backed off, scowling.

Mother rested her embroidery in her lap, prepared for a further discussion of Marian Pickett. Hooligan gave her a reproachful look as her elbow bumped his scarred ear. Scarred because Hooligan was a fighter. He was gentle with us, though, and now only drew his head farther down between his paws to escape the offending elbow.

"Marian is my best, my oldest friend here in Georgia," Mother was saying. "She's the only one who goes back to when I first came here. Why, I've known Marian longer than any of my Theosophical Society friends, and certainly longer than any of the Atlanta Women's Club ladies."

"We're in for a bad four years," Daddy muttered, turning a page once more. "Harding doesn't know his left foot from his right, his head from his . . ." and Daddy's voice trailed away into mumbles of pained disapproval.

But Mother was saying, "You remember, she and I met the first week I came down here from Virginia. Do you realize, Allen, I've known Marian even longer than I've known you?"

At the sound of his name, Daddy lowered the paper a bit. "Who?" he asked.

"Oh, Allen. Marian. Marian, of course. I told you she voted in the last election—"

"Yes. Yes, of course. As I said, she's a bit forward. Very nice though. A good friend." The paper started to rise again, but then it stopped as Daddy looked directly at Mother. "Who did she vote for? Not Harding!"

Mother laughed with satisfaction. "For Mr. Cox. Though *Mr.* Pickett cast his ballot for Warren G."

"That's a shocker. Husband and wife on opposite sides. I wonder if giving the women the vote will split up many families."

"Marian has too much good sense to let that come between them. I was saying what a dear friend she's been to me. What would I have done without her at Rich's Department Store? We were friends right away, both new, both working in Notions there. Oh, how forlorn I felt! Away from my family and Lynchburg for the first time in my life."

"You were a tender flower, Mase." Daddy smiled at her for a moment, then went back to his paper.

Mother's jaunty nickname, Mase, came from that short fling at independence in the business world, working at Rich's in downtown Atlanta. Mase, for her maiden name, Mason. Susanna Mason.

"It seems only yesterday." Dreamily, Mother scratched Hooligan's jowls. He closed his eyes to green slits. You could hear his purr clear across the room. "Marian and I, new salesladies at Rich's. How independent I felt!"

"Um-hm-m." Daddy nodded behind his paper.

"Rich's. That's where I met you, too." Mother tipped forward in the rocker, reached, touched his hand. The motion dumped Hooligan. She ignored his gravelly protest. "You were such a charmer, Allen, that day you came into Notions. Your mother had asked you to buy her an embroidery hoop. I do remember that right on the spot, I was taken by your looks and manners." She laughed, the recollection bright in her eyes. "Oh, Allen, you do have a way about you."

It was true, Daddy did have a way about him. He wasn't a big man. But he was a dresser, neat and classy and in good taste. He even wore hand-tailored silk shirts. Women always perked up when he entered a room, for he had a warmth in the way he looked at them, the way he conversed, courtly and easy, his hazel eyes alight with pleasure. We never crawled into his lap when he had on a silk shirt and one of his good English wool suits. It spoiled the knife-sharp crease in the trousers. Mother never worried about us wrinkling her.

Now Daddy glanced up, smiled again, took Mother's hand. They sat for a moment, silent, seeming unaware of Blainey and me and the Parcheesi game we had started. Presently, Mother went back to her stitching, he to his reading.

Her thoughts must have reverted to Marian, for in a minute she said, "I think *I* might vote in the next presidential election." Her tone was tentative and she stole a glance at Daddy.

"Hm-m-m." He looked over the top of his paper, but seemed unalarmed.

Blainey stopped shaking the dice. "*I'm* going to vote next time," she announced.

"Me, too," I chimed in, remembering my Suffragette who had given me the vote.

"How do you know about voting, chicken little?" Mother turned her attention to Blainey.

"The kids at school were talking about it. One of them asked our teacher."

"Didn't she tell you that children couldn't vote?"

"Why can't they?" Blainey challenged with her eyes, eyes so like Daddy's. She set her chin, put one hand on a hip.

"The law doesn't allow it." Mother's voice became a little stiff. Blainey's sauciness since the "Marseillaise" was getting to her.

"I thought mothers couldn't vote either. Only daddies."

"That law was changed." Mother tried for patience, but her needlework lay idle once more.

"Then the law ought to be changed for children, too," Blainey said with finality, as though this feat were already half accomplished.

Daddy laughed, slid his paper aside. Mother's amusement was thin. "It's really not funny, Allen. She's becoming very uppity."

"She does have a point, though," he said, still laughing. "If the law was changed for women, then why not—" But he stopped as Mother snatched up her embroidery again, started piercing the linen with quick fierce little stabs of her needle.

"The lady in the parade said she had given *me* the vote," I told them, but nobody seemed to hear this.

Daddy, serious now, turned to us. "You girls run along," he said. "You have about fifteen minutes to play before we get ready for the Theosophical Society meeting."

"We'd rather play here." Blainey stared boldy into Daddy's eyes, began to shake the dice again. After a moment, under his hard look, her gaze faltered. "We've got to finish our Parcheesi game, Daddy," she said, trying sweet reason.

"Take it down to the playroom. Finish it there." Daddy's voice became ominous. "Quick now. Mind me. This minute. And no squabbling together. You hear."

We went quickly, quietly.

Our playroom was in the basement, well above ground level, for our lot sloped steeply down from Greenwood Avenue. This drop allowed the basement a full two stories at the rear. Carpenters had worked for a week building a solid extra floor above the furnace and coal bin and storage area. Half of this strong platform was turned into a huge playroom. Its windows overlooked the side yard with its pines and oaks.

The other half was enclosed. This was George's domain—a bedroom with small bath attached. George, our one live-in servant since Daddy had brought him home from work one day. He had lived in the basement room since then, and seemed like part of the family to Blainey and me.

George's evenings were his own. Tonight he was already gone. Blainey led the way down several steps. We almost trod on Hooligan in the dark. We could hear him thump off down the stairs, headed for his sanctuary near the furnace in the depths of the basement. Now Blainey stopped, squatted there in the dimness halfway down, still balancing the Parcheesi board. I sank to the step beside her. We were past masters at eavesdropping. Here Daddy's voice, though muted, came to us quite clearly.

"What's the matter, honeybun?" he was asking Mother.

"Oh, Allen." She had lowered her voice too, but we sat very still, listening. "Blainey is such a handful, and she's only eight, well, nine in January. If I can't manage her now, what will it be like when she's older?"

"She is a lively one." Daddy chuckled. Blainey nudged me and grinned. "You wouldn't want a child with no spunk now, would you, hon? Besides, Margy is an easy one."

It was obvious he considered spunk a valued commodity. I wasn't at all sure about easy.

"Blainey brought a note home from school today." Mother sighed. "It said she's doing well with her studies, particularly with her reading. The reason for the note, though, she constantly speaks out in class without permission. 'A disturbing influence,' the teacher wrote."

"That doesn't sound too serious to me."

Blainey nudged me again, secure in Daddy's backing. But the silence from the other room was so long we shifted uncomfortably on our perch.

Finally, Daddy said, his words serious and the laughter gone entirely, "I'll give her a talking to."

"I've talked 'til I'm blue in the face."

"Then you should give her a good paddling."

"I just can't do that, Allen."

"I can." Daddy's voice hardened.

"Maybe just the talking to—"

"We'll see." But his words sounded grim.

Neither of us had ever been paddled. The thought of it, even for Blainey, filled me with terror. But she only rolled her eyes at me, more excited than fearful at the prospect of this drama.

"I became a mother too late in life." Mother's discouragement filtered down to us. "Thirty-nine when Blainey was born. Motherhood was meant for the young and hardy. Oh, Allen, I'm such a failure at it." She sounded close to tears.

"You're the best mother I know." We could hear Daddy kiss her.

This must have helped, for though her voice still trembled, there was a trace of laughter when she said, "Despite everything, I wouldn't take a million dollars for my two little chicks." Then she finished firmly, "Nor give two cents for any more."

When Daddy spoke again, it seemed to us he had changed the subject. "It's great having our own home, so much more comfortable, so much roomier than the Tenth Street flat. But I really don't like the separate bedroom business we started here. I miss sleeping with you, hon."

"We still sleep together sometimes," she began.

He interrupted, his voice impatient. "I want you beside me in the night."

Blainey looked at me and shrugged. The talk was no longer of us; it had lost our interest. She started to rise. Still, when Mother's voice came, soft, embarrassed, it held us.

"You know separate rooms makes it easier," she was

saying. "Two slip-ups, two little bundles, are quite enough, thank you. You know we decided no children, marrying so late in life." She gave a quick, nervous laugh. "But now we have two, despite precautions."

Finally Daddy's heavier reluctant chuckle chimed in. "You do have to admit, Mase, the whole thing was fun, those early days over on Tenth Street," he said. "There's nothing like a new bride and a new life to—"

"Oh, you men."

This fluttering, girlish, uncomfortable voice was not the solid, safe mother we knew. Blainey made a face, and still holding the Parcheesi board, stood, jerked her head at me to follow. But something in Daddy's tone came down to stop us again.

"You lived too long under the thumb of that puritanical old lady."

There was no laughter now. We had never heard him speak to Mother in just this way. Suddenly they both seemed strangers.

"My grandmother? She was the only one left to take me. You know that, Allen." Mother had turned defensive, half angry. "And you know, too, how young I was when my mother died, and my father less than a year later."

"I know, I know!" Daddy roughly tried to cut her short, failed.

In later years the exasperated chilly turn of Daddy's voice came to me, the sharp repeated words. With that distancing of time, I understood that this had been an old and unresolved argument between them. But to me, that night on the cellar stairs, there was the cer-

tainty this was the only real argument they had ever had. It did not occur to me then that much passed between the two of them of which we had no knowledge.

"I know, I know!" Daddy said, and some deep and hidden fear stirred within me. Blainey shifted uneasily, and I knew she was as disturbed as I.

"Left an orphan when I was younger than Blainey is now." Mother ignored Daddy's effort to stop a story told before. "It's true, Grandmother was a cold person. She did her best, though. It isn't easy to raise a child in your old age. At least she did bring me up to be a proper lady."

"Proper you are, Mase." Daddy's voice remained hard.

When Mother spoke again it was with her determined changing-the-subject tone.

"We did have fun those early times on Tenth Street, honey. And later, when Blainey and Margery were no longer babies, there were the young doctors to liven things."

"They did crowd us a bit, but their rent was a big help." Daddy went along on this new tack, sounding somehow relieved.

"Really dears, they were. I'm glad we decided to let out the extra two rooms at the flat. Weren't we lucky, Allen, that they applied that very first day of our ad in the *Constitution?*"

"Yes. We couldn't have found better roomers. And with my business just getting on its feet, that extra money did allow us to get ahead. We'd never have bought Cloudacres without it, or this place either."

"Cloudacres was lovely last summer," Mother said. "It's so good for the girls up there, comfortable and cool. I wish you didn't have to work at all in the summer months, Allen, so you could be with us."

"It's enough to know my three girls are having a good vacation. And there are the weekends for me." Daddy's voice was pleasant now, relaxed and easy and familiar to us.

"The Blue Ridge Mountains must be the most beautiful mountains in the world. It's worth the hundred-and-twenty-five-mile drive."

"The drive is half the fun," Daddy said, but his mind was still on the Tenth Street days. "Yes, letting out the spare rooms gave us a running start at things. Our first years were pretty lean, remember, hon."

"But the postwar building boom is what really swept your business along."

"Now, finally, we're on Easy Street, Mase."

There was only a comfortable pleasure in his voice. The strain between them seemed gone. I felt Blainey relax. The little furry beast of fear scurried to the far fringes of my mind.

"Taking in roomers did help," Mother said with pride. "The doctors were no trouble. So lively to have around during their last year of internship. Remember how they helped out when Blainey and Margy were sick?"

"I hear they're all in practice now and doing nicely."

"Yes, bless them. The girls were just crazy about them."

"And you?" We could hear the tease in Daddy's voice.

"Oh, Allen!" Again that disturbing girlish laugh.

"I wasn't too keen on having my three sweethearts crazy about those medical men."

"Why, I was old enough to be their mother!" Her laugh came, pleasantly outraged.

Then softly, tenderly, Daddy said, "Well, by jingo, you're still *my* dear girl."

This time the silence was very long, and we were afraid to move on the creaking cellar stairs.

Presently Mother's voice gasped, "That's enough of that, Allen. What if the girls popped in?"

"Hang the what ifs!"

"It *is* getting on, Allen. What time is it?"

Daddy sighed and said, "I guess we had better get a move on or we'll be late to the Theosophical meeting."

"Yes. Call the girls, and I'll start their bathwater."

We could hear the quick sound of her feet. Then the floor above complained under Daddy's tread. Blainey and I dashed below. In seconds his voice reached down.

"Come on, you two. It's time to get ready."

"I'll have to put the Parcheesi away," Blainey called back, her voice sweet, filled with docility.

"Okay, sugar. Make it speedy though. We're picking up Aunt Arlene tonight."

Immediately we flew up the stairs.

"Not Arlene!" Mother's agitated words came from the bathroom as we sprang into the hall.

"That was quick," Daddy spoke to us, with no sign that he had heard Mother's displeasure.

She poked her head from the doorway. The sound of running water almost swallowed her words. "When did Arlene get back?"

Arlene. Daddy's older sister. Unmarried. Arlene, with her Randolph-Macon Woman's College background, her modish clothes, her trips to Europe. She lorded it over Mother. Blainey once heard Aunt Arlene tell Daddy he certainly should have done better for himself than that Susanna Mason.

" 'Old-fashioned, overweight, countryfied, and older than you, Allen.' That's what she said about Mother, Magpie."

I knew Blainey had reproduced Arlene's conversation with fair accuracy. We both had a talent in verbatim reporting, a dividend from our eavesdropping activities.

Dismay filled me at Arlene's duplicity. "She's got her nerve! She's fatter than Mother. Anyway, Daddy says Mother is only pleasingly plump."

But Blainey went on, "Then Aunt Arlene said, 'How could you, Allen! Any of our lovely Atlanta girls were yours for the asking.' Daddy set her straight though. *He* said, 'I didn't fall in love with any Atlanta girl. Mase suits me fine, Arlene.' "

"I guess that told her, all right! Aunt Arlene's full of applesauce." And my anger was somewhat mollified.

Despite Arlene's antipathy to Mother, Blainey and I were irresistibly drawn to her. She never forgot birthdays or Christmases or Easters. Her gifts were lavish and foreign, for she did much traveling. When she was in town, she would take us with her to an expensive tearoom for lunch, just the three of us, then on a shopping spree. She treated us as though we were up-to-the-minute young flappers, buying us clothes much too sophisticated. We were bratty for days after—maybe because of guilt that we had betrayed Mother for Arlene's blandishments. Mother would frown, endure us, and see that we wrote thank-you notes, patiently spelling the words for me. Blainey always managed hers alone.

Thank-you notes. *A lady always writes a note of gratitude for favors done or gifts received.*

"When did Arlene get back?" Mother repeated. "Paris this time, wasn't it?"

"Day before yesterday. Yes, Paris," Daddy said. "I really couldn't say no when she asked that we pick her up, could I?"

"I suppose not."

"After all, it was Arlene who first introduced us to Theosophy, remember. Should I call her and tell her we can't come by?"

Mother relented, smiled. "No, of course not," she said softly, and came to put her head on Daddy's shoulder.

He cinched her to him with both arms, kissed her on the mouth.

"That's my girl," he said against her cheek.

She flushed, drew away. "We must hurry now. Come on, chicks." And she began to unbutton Blainey's dress. Blainey flinched from Mother's hands to do her own buttons, so Mother started on me. After the dresses were shucked, she said, "Run into the bathroom, you two. Take off your vests and bloomers, and hop into the water. I'll be there in a second to give you a scrub."

And she closed the door behind us to preserve our modesty. *A lady is always modest.* But Daddy had dried me yesterday. *Always* modest? How had Mother managed when she and Daddy shared a room? I wondered if that was why she now had one alone—to preserve her modesty.

Modesty or no, Blainey stripped off vest and bloomers before I was half started. Despite the height of the great tub with its clawed feet, she scrambled in, usurped the slanty end away from the faucet. She soaped the shining surface, perched on the rolled edge.

"Watch me, Magpie!" she cried, and on her bare bottom she slid into the water with a mighty splash.

Mother's voice came through the panel.

"Blainey! Don't slosh all the water out of the tub! Margy! Hurry now, little chick!" Then she was talking to Daddy again, but she cracked the door to see that we followed orders.

"Arlene isn't entirely responsible for bringing us to Theosophy, Allen," she was saying. "We were already questing, the two of us. Grandmother's Methodist religion no longer answered my needs, and I knew you were restless with all the handed-down, taken-for-granted ideas of—"

He interrupted, laughing. "Well, maybe if you can discard your grandmother's *religion*, there's some hope yet that you will—"

The bathroom door popped open, Mother slipped in saying over her shoulder, "We'll be ready in just a jiffy, Allen."

"What's questing?" Blainey said.

"Searching." But Mother frowned. *"Ladies don't eavesdrop on conversations."*

Blainey and I glanced at each other, stifled our giggles as Mother settled on the low stool she kept beside the tub. Then suddenly she smiled and kissed Blainey on the shoulder, me on top of my head, before starting on us with the washcloth.

"What would I do without you, my chicks?" she said. "You are worth all dangers and difficulties, worth any pain. . ." The words trailed away as though the thought had suddenly submerged and continued to follow its silent path inside her head. She set vigorously to work on Blainey's neck and ears.

Blainey held off the washcloth for a moment to ask, "What danger? What pain?"

Mother gave a quick laugh. "Nothing to worry your noggin about, honey." And she started on the ears again.

But I no longer concerned myself with Mother and Blainey. I had forgotten my earlier secret fear. Now there was only the thought of Aunt Arlene and tonight. What excitement would she bring us this time?

4

The Marvelous Electric Machine

Arlene rode in front with Daddy. Her hat was frivolous and from Paris. She had climbed into our Dorris and settled herself safely behind the windshield, protected from the night air of November.

"You don't mind, Mase?" she had asked after displacing Mother. She half turned to look at us. Not waiting for an answer to her question, she cooed at Blainey and me, "Hello, my doves. How I've missed you." Then back to Mother, "I wouldn't have asked for the front seat, but it's been forever since I've had a chance to talk with this brother of mine. You know how close Allen and I have always been, dear Mase. After all, he's the only brother I have since Marcel died."

Hospitality: One of the major tenets for ladies. *A hostess must see to her guests' every comfort; a hostess is kind and considerate; a hostess puts everyone at ease. . . .* There was so much more to the hospitality tenet that it was difficult to remember it all. And hospitality extended from one's home to one's automobile.

"Perfectly all right, Arlene," Mother said.

Her words and tone, exceedingly cheerful and pleasant, would have fooled most people. Blainey and I, who had crowded close together for Mother's shift to the backseat, glanced at each other, uncomfortable with the false note.

The Dorris started away from the curb. Now one of Arlene's hands found its way to Daddy's shoulder. The other rested atop her ridiculously stylish hat. Presently we were flying along. Daddy loved to drive. His grand passion was automobiles. He bought a new one each spring. Last year's had been an Overland. This year it was the Dorris.

Tonight he urged the Dorris along at a good clip.

"Isn't this a dandy auto, Arlene?" The pleasure of possession rode high in his voice.

"We're certainly burning up the track." Arlene sounded delighted with our speed.

"Twenty-five per." Pride straightened Daddy's spine.

"It's a real whizzbang, darling." Arlene laughed, a giddy little laugh.

The wind whipped through the back of the open auto with the speed of our passing. Mother clutched her coat at the throat, used her other hand to spread the Scottish plaid lap robe over Blainey and me. Her hat was securely anchored by a scarf over the top, brought down, tied under her chin.

Blainey and I held hands, delighted with this rush through the mysterious night. Blainey leaned close to talk in my ear over the racket of the engine and the wind.

"Daddy likes the Dorris better than he did the Overland," she said.

"Me, too," I told her, forgetting I had cried with Mother last spring at the departure of the Overland.

Daddy tootled the horn at a flivver that jounced along before us.

"Daredevil!" Arlene laughed her throaty laugh as Daddy zipped round the flivver. "Such a *sport*, darling."

But Mother pulled us to her in momentary fright. Mother held the automobile in low esteem. She lamented the passing of horse-drawn carriages, so elegant, so ladylike to manage, so civilized with no worry about tires or cranking or spark and throttle adjustment. But now, past the flivver, she chimed in with her own laugh.

"I discovered Allen was a sport when we first went out together. He came by for me on his motorcycle. So jaunty, with his checkered cap and coat!"

"Yes," Arlene said. "Allen has always caught the ladies' fancy. He could have had any girl in Atlanta, anyone he might have set his heart on. But he always preferred family and home. That is until he met you, Mase dear." Again the throaty amusement. "How did you do it?" And acid etched, every so slightly, the edge of her laugh. She adjusted Daddy's coat collar, gave his shoulder another little pat.

It was he who answered, "You should have seen Mase that day in Rich's. None of the Atlanta girls I knew could have held a candle to her. Frightened and tremulous—I didn't know then she was so recently from the protection of home and family—but saucy and self-possessed, too."

"After all," Arlene murmured, "she was hardly a child. Years do at least add a little self-possession."

Daddy ignored Arlene's words. "Mase was a little bit of a thing then, a reed in her black skirt and lacy shirtwaist, her face like a pink rose above." It was Daddy who was laughing now with the memory.

Arlene turned her head to Mother. "You were little then. The years add something more than self-possession. They do take a toll, don't they, dear?"

"I put on weight each time I was expecting. That's what took the toll. Quite usual though." Mother's voice was still cheerful, the false cheer of difficult hospitality. "But my girls are my real treasures. Besides, some women put on weight for no reason at all—"

Daddy, who seemed not to have heard either Arlene or Mother, went on, "Do you know, that first time I went by for her on my motorcycle, she sprang into the sidecar without a moment's hesitation."

He wagged his head, pleased with the memory, but then his attention went back to his driving as he eased the Dorris around a horse-drawn carriage, taking more care than he had in passing the flivver.

"Horses," he said, "they'll be a thing of the past soon." He sounded as though it would be good riddance.

I felt a pang, remembering the great, prancing, shiny

steeds of the parade. Since then, I'd dreamed of one of
my own.

Arlene twisted about to talk, again, to Mother.

"Mase, dear, you and Allen really must take a tour
of the Continent. It's a shame you've never had a taste
of it. I know Allen would simply adore it."

"We plan to go when the girls are older," Mother
said, "in about five years. They're too young to appreci-
ate it now. And Allen's business will be on firm footing
then. He'll be able to take time for a leisurely trip."

"Five years!" Arlene exclaimed. "That's forever. And
what if you have another baby? Nora already has three.
Who knows how many more will pop along."

"Your sister, Nora, said she doesn't mind how many
she has." Mother sounded disapproving, embarrassed.
She glanced at Blainey and me.

"Of course, maybe you don't have to worry about
that anymore."

"Now why would you say that, Arlene?"

"Oh, you know. Your age, Mase. Maybe you're
through with all that nuisance."

"The ladies in my family have a—a very long, ah,
productive life." Mother glanced at us again. Nevertheless she went on, "My paternal grandmother had her
last child when she was fifty-four," but her voice had
turned stiff and chilly, "so I have some time left to worry
about."

Arlene laughed, pleased with Mother's embarrassed
annoyance. "Well, these days there *are* precautions,"
she said, with an air that whatever the precautions might
be they were no concern of hers. I remembered that

earlier Mother had also mentioned precautions.

I leaned to Blainey, whispered, "What are precautions, Blain?"

"Precautions means being careful," Blainey said, looking wise.

"Being careful of what?"

"Anything at all, Magpie."

"What's Aunt Arlene being careful of?" I asked this more loudly and Mother turned to us.

But Blainey had time to say, "I don't think Aunt Arlene is the one being careful."

Mother reached and patted my knee. "Have you memorized the Golden Chain prayer, little chick?"

"Almost," I said.

"Blainey, help Margy with it. Then she'll be able to say it right along with the rest of the children next Sunday."

"Do I have to?" Blainey groaned.

"Remember, Margy's new to the group this fall, and you've had two years practice saying the prayer. You should be happy to help your little sister."

"Do as your mother says." It was Daddy who ordered this time, so we worked on the Theosophical verse.

> *I'm a link in the golden chain of love*
> *That stretches around the world.*
> *I will keep my link bright and strong.*
> *I will help and protect*
> *All who are weaker than myself. . . .*

And on to the end, thus missing the rest about Aunt Nora having a lot of babies, Mother not having any more if she could help it, and Aunt Arlene not really worried about the question one way or the other. Despite our interest, we caught only snatches of the conversation, for Mother's glances told us she was keeping track of our Golden Chain efforts.

Presently, though, she forgot about us. The subject of babies had been dropped. The talk of travel on the Continent, taken up once more by Aunt Arlene, promised possible adventure. Unnoticed, we stopped to listen.

"Dear Mase," Arlene was saying. It was always especially interesting when Arlene started off with a "dear." "Dear Mase, you have no idea the excitement of exchanging views with other intellectuals in a Paris *salon.*" She pronounced *salon* as nasally as Blainey had sung the "Marseillaise." "Or the thrill of gadding here and there in all sorts of quaint conveyances. Those exotic European autos, the carriages, the phaetons, the railway cars; and even occasionally second class to rub shoulders with the hoi polloi. Ah, Paree, Paree. Of course, Great Britain—London especially, but Oxford, Stratford, Brighton, too—Great Britain is still my favorite.

"But those dear friends of mine, the Parisian literati. We spent a great deal of time together at the opera, the ballet, evenings talking of books. Even I learned much from them about the avant-garde European writers. And they asked me about the new American fellow. Ah, what is his name? Fitzgerald? Yes, Fitzgerald. I had to admit I knew little of him. After all, the classics are my forte."

"F. Scott Fitzgerald," Mother offered.

Arlene gave a quick, amazed little glance over her

shoulder. "That's the one." She snatched a breath to go on about Paris.

"Have you read Mr. Fitzgerald's *This Side of Paradise?*" Mother asked.

Arlene, irritated at having the flow of her talk broken, said, "What, Mase? What was the book?"

"*This Side of Paradise.* Everyone I know has read it. It came out early this year. Quite a shocker. Good though. Mr. Fitzgerald has an interesting style. Different. His material is a bit racy. But I'm looking forward to his short-story collection, *Flappers and Philosophers.*"

"There's so little time for reading in a life as busy as mine," Arlene said. Then she slipped back into her own interrupted talk. "Yes, what a gay time we had in Paree this season! The styles! How do you like my new chapeau?" She adjusted her hat. "We must really do something about *your* hats, dear Mase. Hopelessly out of date."

"I'm rather fond of this hat," Mother said, and as Daddy drew the Dorris to a stop before the Lodge Building, she undid the scarf that had tethered it to her head. The wide brim rose into place, the curl of feather next to the crown resumed its proper turn.

Daddy cut the motor, set the brake, sprang from the driver's side to rush around and open the doors for Arlene and for us. On the sidewalk, Mother took a small soft brush from her purse, smoothed our hair, while Arlene captured Daddy's left arm. She had almost made off with him, when he reached, scooped Mother to his side with his free arm.

"Take Margy's hand, Blainey," she said, and linked

together, we all trooped into the Theosophical Society Lodge.

Blainey and I liked the cookies, the punch, and the attention that always started the evening. Tonight, as usual, there were complimentary remarks to Mother. "Such little ladies." "During the lectures, I've noticed they always listen to every word." And "Surely, perfect little sixth-race children."

But the compliments were small reward for our coming agony of boredom. There were always the lectures in the Meeting Room. We did not listen to every word. We did sit still with our eyes glued on the speaker. *Young ladies sit silent and attentive during lectures.*

There were seldom other children at the night meetings. Since George's evenings were his own and we were too old for a live-in nursemaid anymore, Mother brought us along. She would not hear of a part-time nurse hired for an evening every now and then.

"I won't leave my chicks with a stranger," she would say so decisively that Daddy usually remained silent. He did make it clear, from time to time, that he had no such compunctions about leaving his children at home. For Mother's loyalty to us, Blainey and I gave her our best behavior on Lodge nights.

"What's a sixth-race child?" Blainey asked Mother before we found seats for the lecture.

"Sixth race. In Theosophy it means a high level reached after a soul has lived many lives and progressed far along the way. Theosophists believe in reincarnation, that we live many lives, and that the soul learns important lessons in each life. Those on the first level have a long way to go. But the sixth level means that a particular soul has grown old and wise. You see, it takes many, many lives to make up each level."

"What's Mother talking about, Blain?" I whispered. She shrugged. "Search me." But she persisted with Mother. "Are Margy and I really sixth-race children?"

Mother's eyes twinkled. "I rather doubt it," she said.

Daddy chuckled, looked down at Blainey. "I don't think a sixth-race child would talk out in school and disturb the whole class," he told her.

"Oh, Allen," Mother said softly, frowning.

But at that moment she was distracted by friends who wanted to chat with her, and she turned aside as Aunt Arlene led us down the aisle. Arlene found four empty seats near the front.

When we paused, Blainey pulled at Daddy's hand so she could look him squarely in the eye. "What if a sixth-race child had something very special to say in school? Something everyone else *ought* to hear?"

For a moment he tried to scowl, but then his laugh broke through, he swept her to him, his arm about her shoulder. Aunt Arlene urged them both into the row of seats. She ignored Daddy's effort at gallantry in trying to seat her first.

"Go on in, Allen, you and Blainey. I'll hold Margy on my lap. We might as well sit down. Mase can't resist stopping to chatter. We'll leave the aisle seat for her, and that will give you and me a chance to catch up on talk."

So Daddy sidled in, drew Blainey into the seat beside him, his arm still about her. Arlene slid into the place

next to Blainey. When Mother found us just as the meeting began, Arlene had already perched me on her own
knee. Arlene smiled, refused to give up her hold as
Mother reached to retrieve me. So Mother sat there
alone, somehow detached from the rest of us.

Tonight the incomprehensible lecture was about the
reasons behind Theosophy . . . a practical philoso-
phy . . . all religions brought together revealing the
truth in each . . . harmonizes religion and science, an
understanding of both . . . laws of nature that rule
physical, psychic, psychological . . . occult knowledge
of visible, invisible . . . teaches the brotherhood of all
mankind . . .

The words etched themselves on my mind, but their
meaning escaped me. The agony of not wiggling on
Arlene's lap crept up my spine. My eyes glazed with
this terrible effort. A light sweat dewed my forehead.
My legs gave one frantic flop. Mother glanced at me.
Arlene drew me a little tighter against her. My sweating
increased, but now my legs remained as still as though
they had died.

When the lecturer said, "brotherhood of all mankind,"
I turned my thoughts to the prayer Blainey had taught
me. I forgot the lecturer and the brotherhood. It was
easier to understand that I was a link in the golden
chain of love.

The delicate cloud of Aunt Arlene's Paris perfume
surrounded me. Earnestly, silently I vowed I would try
to keep my link bright and strong, and to help and protect all who were weaker than myself, as our prayer

instructed. Drowsily I wondered who these weaker ones could be, where they could be found. The reward for my noble resolves was, finally, blessed sleep against Arlene's well-padded body.

The Dorris lurched. I awoke with the wind cold on my face. Mother's warm bulk supported me. Vaguely I was aware that Blainey was on her other side, head pillowed on Mother's knee, sound asleep. Arlene's voice wedged itself under the edge of my drowsiness.

"You and Allen should really get away from it all, Mase. You *need* it to keep from growing dull."

"We go to Cloudacres every summer," Mother said defensively.

"That's just it. *Every* summer. Dull."

"Last fall I took the girls to visit my sister, Fannie. Fannie, who lives in Virginia, you'll remember."

"Oh, yes. On the farm." She emphasized farm with a deprecatory little laugh.

Daddy's voice cut in. "Mase and the girls had a fine time, Arlene. You're being very pushy with your opinion." Lightly, a brotherly joke.

I could see their two silhouettes in the glow of an occasional streetlight. Arlene reached now and touched his neck. This time her laugh came, soft and easy. Then, idly, she asked over her shoulder. "How was your sister? Last fall, was it?"

"We came back just before school started last fall." Mother sighed, wrapped in the memory of our Virginia trip. "Fannie was such a pretty girl when we were growing up. Not clever, but pretty and amiable and really nice. We were very close. I loved seeing her again."

Mildly Arlene said, "Had she changed much?"

"How could she not have changed! She's had ten children, and two more stillborn. Yes, certainly changed."

"Added years change us all," Daddy put in as though to console her.

"Yes, of course. Twelve years ago when I left Lynchburg, Fannie had only five children. Her eyes still had their sparkle. You wouldn't believe how blue they were when she was little, and innocent as a lamb's."

"I suppose after the first five babies, the second batch eased along with scarcely a ripple." Daddy seemed half amused, half sympathetic.

"None of the ten were easy. She had serious complications with the last, and the first baby, twenty-three years ago, almost killed her. That one took three days to get born. I stayed by her the whole time. I had never seen anyone suffer so!"

Comfortable against Mother's side, I stayed perfectly still. What had Aunt Fannie's suffering to do with babies? How could a baby, tiny, helpless, almost kill a woman as big and slow-moving as Aunt Fannie?

"Farm women must be strong as oxen," Arlene was saying. "Ten children! Ridiculous!"

"Fannie was such a slip of a girl when she married Walter. She took after our mother, feminine, delicate in appearance. More stamina though. Mother simply faded away a bit more after each child. When the sixth came she died. Fannie has only turned heavy, and as sodden as a half-wrung dishrag."

"They should have stopped after five," Arlene said.

"You don't know Walter. Walter's an impossible man to stop. Oh, he's good in his way, but very coarse, too."

"Not a gentleman, like Allen, you mean?" Arlene asked.

"Not a gentleman," Mother agreed. "He claims a farm needs lots of hands, and right from the beginning he expected Fannie to furnish them. The first baby came nine months to the day from the wedding night. Everybody in Lynchburg was counting months. Walter laughed and said—said—" Mother's words trailed away as though she were sorry she had started this story of Walter.

Daddy caught up the dropped sentence. "The way I heard it, Walter said he'd always been known throughout Campbell County as the best shot in Virginia."

Amusement touched his voice, and a little envy. Mother stiffened against my side. Even Arlene turned silent.

Presently, Daddy drew to the curb in front of Arlene's swank apartment building. As earlier, he sprang out, hurried around to open the auto door for her.

On the curb, Arlene said, "Oh, my, I almost forgot to tell you, Allen. *Maman* will take the girls for a ride in her electric car tomorrow."

"*Maman* it is now?" Daddy smiled.

But Mother said, "Good heavens, Mother Standfield has never taken them out in the electric car before."

Daddy, still amused, asked, "What's the occasion?"

"No occasion, brother mine. Only she's very lonely, you know." Arlene didn't even look in Mother's direction now. Her full attention was on Daddy. Lightly she smoothed his lapel. "And she told me yesterday, she feels she's had very little influence on your children. She feels they *need* it." She gave Mother a brief glance.

The thought of a ride in Grandmother's electric car filled me with uneasiness. It was true—we had never been invited for a ride before. Grandmother, herself, was so proper, so formal. We seldom saw her. Children, she said, wearied her terribly.

"She hasn't been well, Allen," Arlene continued. "She mentioned that you seldom visit her anymore, which really, in a way, is quite beastly of—"

"I was there last Tuesday." Daddy's laugh was gone. "I stopped off on my way home from the office." He sounded uncomfortable, guilty.

"You know how she adores you, dear," Arlene persisted. "She needs you especially since Marcel died. You're the only Standfield man left. You must know how much that means to *Maman.* Yes, you're the last of the Standfields since there are only your two girls in the direct line. It's a pity that Margy wasn't a boy. I know how much you wanted a boy the day she was born."

Arlene touched Daddy's shoulder again, watched his face as she said softly, "It was tragic about Marcel, too. Our own Daddy was so gratified to have you *and* Marcel, so sure that his line of the Standfields would be carried on. Well, it's good he didn't live to know . . ." Arlene's voice slid away.

"Poor Marcel," Mother murmured, saving Daddy a reply.

"Why was Marcel poor?" I asked.

"How long have you been awake, sugar?" Mother said, startled.

"Why was Marcel poor?" I repeated.

"Because he died so young." She rearranged the lap robe over me. "He died the year you were born."

"He drank himself to death," Daddy said.

"Allen, please. The girls—" Mother glanced at Blainey and me. But Blainey's day at school, the evening's lecture without the softness of Arlene to sleep against, had worn her out. She remained sound asleep.

"He did, you know." Daddy's neck and shoulders took on a stubborn set. It was obvious he meant to have his say. "Marcel claimed drink let him escape once in a while. It let him escape all right, and now the only thing left of him—a thin volume of poetry. Odd poetry. Very original. He really did have a talent for writing. Not the drive for it, though."

"Nevertheless, he was very good with *Maman*," said Arlene. "The youngest of us four, but even after you left to marry Mase, he was loving enough to stay on at home with *Maman*."

"Trapped. He was trapped," Daddy said.

Arlene gave him a little kiss on the cheek. "But that's beside the point. The point is that *Maman* wants to take the girls for a little spin. It will give her pleasure, just a short drive, she said."

Daddy took Arlene's arm to escort her to her apartment door. "The girls will love to have a ride in their grandmother's electric car." He sounded stiff and distant. "What time will she pick them up?"

"Oh, you'll have to bring them here to my apartment. Greenwood Avenue is too far for *Maman* to drive."

"I'm due at the office in the morning."

"Take the morning off, dear. It's a pity I don't drive, or I'd come and get my two loves." She threw a smile in our direction. "You'll bring them here tomorrow? Eleven o'clock?"

Arlene's voice came to us lightly from the small balustraded porch, where she had turned to face Daddy. She gave him another quick kiss on the cheek. Then, balanced and delicate in movement for such a big woman, she slipped inside the door. It clicked shut with a definite snap before Daddy could offer any objection. Daddy sprang from the porch. In seconds he had climbed into the front seat. Angrily he whirled the Dorris away from the curb. Mother, still in back, sheltered us from the November wind with the lap robe and her arms.

Usually, it was Blainey who was on the qui vive and I who missed everything. This time it was she who missed the night ride, the overheard grown-up talk; and a small flare of triumph blazed up in my heart. But through the triumph, Arlene's words returned to haunt me. *It's a pity that Margy wasn't a boy. I know how much you wanted a boy the day she was born. . . .*

Presently, Daddy's voice came, disgruntled, resigned. "I guess I'll have to take the morning off to trot the girls over to Arlene's."

He seemed to be talking to himself again. Mother took a breath. She started to say something to him. Instead, she tucked the robe closer about us and remained silent.

⁂

The drive in the electric car turned out to be a strange and marvelous and amazingly soundless excursion. The car looked like a small glassed-in parlor on wheels, as straight and erect and proper as Grandmother herself. And as silent. Its fore and aft looked identical. Fastened to the metal upright inside the door was a slender crystal vase. It contained a fine column of water and one fresh red rosebud. Grandmother drove with a firm hand, and an imperious certainty that the street belonged only to her.

The little horseless carriage moved along, quiet and stately. It had none of the foolishness of clutch and gears and spark lever and crank that the Dorris did. It had a steering bar instead of wheel. Grandmother thrust the bar this way or that with neat, decisive movements. We flew along at fifteen miles an hour. This seemed more magical than the Dorris's twenty-five in Daddy's hands.

Blainey sat beside Grandmother on the gray plush seat, I in the rear, where I had a clear view of Grandmother's ramrod back, but, much to my relief, none of the responsibility of conversation. Above the stiff spine, the white collar arose from her dove-gray velvet jacket. The lace of it was braced up her slender neck with stays. This controlled, delicate sheath was as snowy as the mound of gossamer and shining hair piled on top of her regal head.

The drive lasted fifteen minutes. Mother had warned us, "Do not speak unless spoken to."

My worry over conversation proved unfounded. No word was uttered on either side until the drive was ended and we had glided up before Arlene's apartment building. Then Grandmother turned to fully face Blainey. Though she did not look at me, one of her hands reached back and fastened a steely grip on my arm.

"Before I was married, my name was Washington. My maiden name, *Washington.* You girls are to remember that." Her words were spaced, separate, important, clear. "Ann Washington, before I married your grandfather, Mr. Standfield. *My* family has a direct lineage back to one of George Washington's brothers. Therefore, and never forget this, through your *father's mother's* side of your family you are both aristocrats. George Washington is your seventh great-uncle. *Seventh.* "

Silence reigned while we absorbed this information. To the fact that we must be little ladies at all times, and the chance that we were sixth-race children, now was added the blight of aristocracy.

"Our great-great-great-great-great-great-great-uncle?" Blainey ticked off the greats on her fingers.

"Precisely." Grandmother beckoned to Daddy, who had come down to retrieve us. "You may remove them, Allen," she said.

Removed, together we said, "Thank you very much for the drive, Grandmother."

Blainey dropped an uncertain curtsy, I a secondary bob. We had been removed not only from the car, but from Grandmother Standfield's consciousness. She did not give us another glance. Instead, she leaned slightly toward Daddy. He kissed her lined, delicately rouged cheek. A moment later the silent car and the erect old lady glided away.

5

Christmas
and Terrors
and Changes

Christmas vacation was sunny and cold. We saw nothing more of Grandmother; and Aunt Arlene was off on a winter cruise of the Caribbean. But Aunt Nora brought her children to visit one afternoon. Bethany and Jeanine and Little Dan.

Aunt Nora wasn't much of a stickler for ladylikeness, so Bethany and Jeanine were noisy and rough, but they were good-natured. Little Dan was another matter. He was four, and spoiled because everyone was delighted he was a boy. Especially Aunt Nora, who settled her girth in the most comfortable chair and, as usual, rested on her laurels.

Still, though Little Dan was a boy, he was not truly a *Standfield* boy, and I remembered that Aunt Arlene had spoken of Daddy's disappointment that I had been born a girl. Now, to add to the burden of aristocracy and tenets and sixth-raceness, the responsibility was also mine for ending the line of Standfields.

The day of our cousins' visit, Little Dan, in a fit of anger, threw my Kewpie doll at Bethany. It crashed against the toy chest and broke into fine mealy pieces. Only a portion of bright dimpled smile remained intact. Jeanine and Bethany laughed.

Blainey whispered to me, "What a beastly little boy. Never mind, Magpie. Here, you can have my Kewpie."

When Mother and Aunt Nora came down to the playroom to see the cause of the crash and my crying, Aunt Nora's voice had a proud lift as she said, "Well, boys will be boys!"

Later that evening after an infraction of the tenets, Blainey shrugged and said to Mother, "Well, girls will be girls."

Mother said, "Where did you get that expression? *Girls* should be little ladies."

"Aunt Nora said boys will be boys when Little Dan broke my doll," I said in defense of Blainey.

"Oh." Mother laughed a little. "That's another matter. Boys can't always control themselves, but girls must."

This ruling from Mother, the soul of fairness, seemed frightfully unjust. Blainey, hands hiked on hips, feet planted solidly, outrage underlining her words, demanded, "*Why* shouldn't girls be girls if boys can be boys?"

"Because"—Mother fixed us both with a serious gaze—"little girls will be grown ladies someday. And it is *ladies* who must show control in many grown-up situations. When certain bounds are overstepped, it is ladies who are at fault, it is ladies who suffer the consequences."

"How can ladies control anything when ladies are always supposed to be sweet and try to please?"

"Blainey, are you being impudent?" Mother's face grew stern.

"I just want to *know.*" And the distressed gravity of Blainey's voice canceled any suspicion of impudence.

Mother softened, patted Blainey's shoulder. "It is part of the art of being a lady."

"And what—" Blainey hesitated, frowning, working to recall the word. "What situations must a lady control?"

Mother flushed at the question. "When you're grown up, your intuition will tell you." And she turned away as though the discussion were ended.

But Blainey wasn't finished. "*Who* oversteps *what* bounds?" she asked. "And *why* do ladies suffer consequences?"

Mother spoke over her shoulder. "You both will learn about these things in the future, when you are older."

Her mysterious tone did not hide from us that she had blushed even more deeply.

Blainey fired her final shot. "Well, I'll be older pretty soon!" But Mother continued on her way.

As for me, older and the future seemed safely distant.

In addition to Aunt Nora and her children, the house was busy with other drop-in callers during the holidays. The afternoons were set aside for such visiting. There was always fruitcake and hot coffee served on our Haviland china; and pralines in crystal candy dishes. Most of these callers were lady friends of Mother's. Some were from the Theosophical Society. Some were Atlanta Women's Club friends, among these latter Mrs. Hewitt, who was served tea instead of coffee. And, of course, Marian Pickett. Finally there was Aunt Ellie.

Aunt Ellie—not really our aunt; nor was her husband, Uncle Frank, really an uncle to us. But Frank and Ellie Benton were friends from the earliest times of Daddy and Mother's summers in the mountains of north Georgia. Friends even before Blainey was born. Thus the aunt and uncle. The Bentons' summer estate, Pinewood, was just down the road from our mountain place. We had owned Cloudacres for only a couple of years. Before that, we had rented it each summer. But the Bentons had owned Pinewood forever. Cloudacres was more modest in every way than Pinewood.

Ellie and Frank were Theosophists, but their friendship with us was deeper than philosophical affinity. Blainey and I stuck close whenever Aunt Ellie came calling. She loved us and we loved her. Mother allowed Blainey and me in the sitting room when Ellie was there, the four of us together, talking like four ladies, sometimes laughing like four children.

For most company, though, we were banished to the playroom. Sometimes, bored, Blainey would go to play down the block with Marilyn Louise Carstairs, Marilyn Louise who had no use for younger sisters except to tease them.

My only consolation then was to retreat to the warm

kitchen and George. George wasn't much of a talker. He only answered direct questions, as a rule. Sometimes with me, though, he would go on a talking jag of several sentences.

George had come to our house almost straight off the prison chain gang. In connection with the building-supply business, Daddy spent part of each week in the field checking supply deliveries and building progress. One day when a roofing crew was busy on a six-story industrial building, he saw one of the men faint and almost fall those six floors to the cement. That was George, one week out of prison and on his first job. And sick. Daddy brought him home.

George. Nineteen, small, thin. More scared of life than I. He had more reason. He was very black. Colored, Mother made us say, which was considered more polite.

"George was sent up for carrying a concealed weapon," we overheard Daddy tell Mother. "A straight-edged razor."

"Why would he carry a wicked thing like a razor?" she asked, worried.

"The colored neighborhoods are poorly policed. Even peaceful men carry weapons there."

"But a razor—"

"Yes, cheap, easy to get. And a man would always hope he could convince the police he'd just bought it to shave with." Daddy gave a rueful little laugh.

"How was George caught with a razor?" Mother's voice turned more fearful. "Did he use it on someone?"

"Now, Mase," Daddy soothed. "He was stopped for

an on-the-street search; the razor was found in his pocket. That was all. You know that any time they're out of their own districts after dark they're likely to be stopped and searched."

Even I knew that *they* meant all the coloreds. Quite different from *us*.

"Yes, I know. It doesn't seem quite fair," Mother said. "But then with the danger of race riots and such . . ." She let the words trail vaguely away.

Blainey rolled her eyes at me. We had heard talk of race riots before. They were scary. We stayed silent and continued to listen as Daddy went on.

"If you're going to talk about fairness, it wasn't fair to send George off to prison on a charge like that. Only a sixteen-year-old kid at the time. He'd never done anything to anyone, never been in trouble before."

"Not just prison, but the chain gang. Awful." And there was a shudder in Mother's voice.

"He fainted on the roofing job because he was sick. A few months more of the chain gang would have killed him. It's a blessing he escaped."

"Escaped!" Mother cried, truly alarmed. "How?"

"Don't get excited, hon." Daddy spoke calmly. "George may not be sturdy enough to stand the punishment of a chain gang, but he's smart and nervy. He just walked off when the guards weren't looking, walked off, leg chains and all, hid in the back of a car, got out at night here in Atlanta, made it to his uncle's house. An uncle named Franley. Franley managed to cut the leg chains off and give George some clothes. George got a fetch-and-carry job on one of our construction crews."

"Poor George, such troubles, so young. And all of it so unjust." Mother's voice had softened and her fears were lost in concern for George. Then the worry crept back. "Aren't you taking a terrible chance, hiding him from the authorities?"

Daddy laughed. "I'm not *hiding* him. Besides, it's not likely they'll catch up with him in a big city like Atlanta. If they did, it might be a little awkward for me. But they haven't found him so far. Anyway, I'm willing to take the chance."

"Only awkward for us, but a tragedy for George," Mother said, now as ready as Daddy to take a chance. In her own way Mother was a sport, too.

"George told me all this after he'd been with us about six months. Said he didn't want to get us in trouble after we gave him a job and room and bath of his own."

"You'd think he'd be afraid to tell anyone."

"I guess by then he had decided he could trust me," Daddy said.

As to the riots, sometimes there *were* race riots. This threat crept darkly beneath the surface of white society. Blainey and I heard grown-ups talk of it, their voices subdued, their faces grave, as though they feared some alien rage would spill over into our safe neighborhoods, some rage in which they had no part.

Mother taught George to cook and to clean. His room was comfortable and quiet, with windows that looked out onto the piny woods and stream at the rear of our lot. He was always silent, but pleasant, and we thought him safe and happy. Safe he was, but later we learned that at nineteen safety is not enough. Not nearly enough.

There was ample food in the serving dishes from our table for George. He ate after we did, in the kitchen. Since we were Theosophists we were also vegetarians. It never occurred to us that he might miss meat with his meals. It never occurred to us either that George might be lonely.

The last three summers he had gone with us to Cloudacres. It made things much easier for Mother to have him along. Blainey and I loved George; quietly, George loved us back. He probably would have loved any child. We never dared to ask, but we did wonder, Blainey and I, just how he had managed to escape from the chain gang by simply walking off. We thought it tremendously brave.

George looked forward each summer to Cloudacres as much as we did. He seemed less jumpy there, and didn't turn ashy if you walked into the room unexpectedly.

When I sidled into the kitchen a few day before Christmas, sour that Blainey had deserted me for her friend down the block, George asked softly, "What's the matter, Miss Margy? You-all looks like somebody licked the 'lasses off your bread."

"There's nothing to *do*. Blainey's gone down to that dumb Marilyn Louise's."

"Well, just sit yourself at the table there and talk to George. You can keep George comp'ny any old time."

I settled, sighed. The smells were enticing and seemed to bring Christmas nearer.

"What are you making?" I finally asked.

"Apple pies. Your momma done showed me. And cookies." He snatched a pan from the oven. "And just about burned 'em! They gets done quicker'n scat."

He glanced a smile at me, then sank to serious silence, flipping hot cookies onto a platter, globbing bits of dough on the emptied cookie pan. He thrust it back in the oven. There was a splutter of juice from the disturbed pies, and the sweet aroma of burnt sugar and spice.

Presently he said, "Here. This'll pick up your spirit some." And he slid a glass of milk and a saucer with three warm cookies onto the table before me. When I smiled, he smiled.

"That's a whole heap better." Lightly he touched my head. "They's lotsa little chil'un would trade places with you in a minute, Miss Margy." And he snatched another batch of cookies from disaster in the hot oven. "Yessiree, lotsa little chil'un—"

How would it feel to be traded out of my safe place with Daddy and Mother and Blainey? And yes, with George. Fright leaped up in my heart. How would it be to lose the friends who came calling on us, singly or in pairs, or gathered all together from time to time to fill our house with chatter and laughter and cheerful warmth? How would one bear it, to be traded out of summers at Cloudacres, out of this safe home on Greenwood Avenue, Atlanta, Georgia?

Presently, my fright subsided and the warm kitchen, smelling of Christmas spices, seemed an unusually secure, safe haven. Who cared that Blainey had deserted me for Marilyn Louise Carstairs?

※

Christmas Eve was there before I knew it. Each year on the twenty-fourth, Blainey and I went caroling with other Golden Chain children at dusk. We always sang for the joy of it, but at each stop the hat was passed. Any donations went to the Unfortunates.

Blainey and I had known the songs forever. "Silent Night," "O Little Town of Bethlehem," "It Came upon a Midnight Clear," and all the rest. This Christmas Eve, Daddy and three other parents were to escort the carolers from house to house through the chilly dark. I felt safe with him there, and with Blainey, rosy nosed, bright eyed, beside me. She held my mittened hand, smiling down at me now and then from between her rolled wool knit cap and her muffler-wrapped chin. She sang, sweeping me along with her voice, strong and clear and true.

It was always the lot of one of the youngest carolers to sing a solo. It did not worry me that I had been chosen for tonight. There was Daddy in the background and Blainey for support.

Aunt Ellie, at the Christmas planning session in November, had said, "Margy will be our soloist this year. All the other children will hum along like little pipe organs. We'll do the solo at some house that's partying.

'Away in a Manger' is always the high point of the evening, very persuasive for generous donations, you'll see."

Maybe not as grand as singing to Marshal Foch in French. Nevertheless, singing "Away in a Manger" alone on Christmas Eve had its own importance. "Away in a Manger"—the Christmas song Mother had sung to Blainey and me since before we could remember. It sprang easily from our hearts, unforgettable.

So there we were, on Christmas Eve, the Golden Chain carolers, filling the night with song. At most houses people appeared at the door, smiling, thanking, making a modest donation. Sometimes other children hung, grinning, from windows. Not until near the end of our caroling did the time arrive for "Away in a Manger."

This next-to-the-last house stood grander than the rest. Every window blazed with lights. Laughter and talk, music and the clink of glass and silver and china, lanced into the night. We burst forth with "Hark! the Herald Angels Sing." Midway through, windows were suddenly flung open. The door swung wide. Laughter and talk rushed out, drowned us. In seconds the revelers quieted each other with hushes and sh-h-hs and be-quiet-will-yous.

Our "Glo-ry-y to the new born King!" rang triumphantly into the quick silence. Immediately, at Aunt Ellie's signal, the Golden Chain hummers began "Away in a Manger." We all buzzed along together the first time through, I with all my heart, aware only of the quiet all around us and of the familiar melody. When it was time for me to change humming to words, the party people no longer existed for me. Blainey's hum strengthened a little to give support. It was some other child's voice that came from me, clear and easy. I was lost in the comfortable dark, engaged by the plight of a baby with no crib for a bed, yet how peaceful to lay down one's sweet head and sleep in the hay.

The burst of approval startled me. In the next instant carolers and escorts were swept inside for sweets and cider and a babble of talk. By the time we left, the hat, passed for the sake of the Unfortunates, sagged heavy with coins and bills.

On the sidewalk Aunt Ellie said, "You see! Margy was the hit of the evening!"

Daddy smiled at me and at Blainey, leaned to say, "I'm proud of my girls."

Suddenly, though the act of singing itself had been pure and free of pride, unholy glory was mine there in the frigid night. Personal glory—a new and heady taste. But like Mrs. Hewitt's pride on Armistice Day when she had demoted General Pershing, then been brought low by Mother's *Sic Semper Tyrannis*, yes, like Mrs. Hewitt's pride, mine cameth before a fall.

Mother and Daddy's own party had gathered by the time we reached home. The house was warm, filled with the scent of pine boughs, the cheer of voices. Mrs. Hewitt's voice ruled one corner of the room; Mr. Hewitt stood, silent, beside her. Marian Pickett, on the sofa, leaned softly against her husband, deferred to his words. It did not show that she had canceled his vote with her own last November. With that thought, again my

Suffragette sprang to mind—*Get ready for some changes, little girl!* Was my glory tonight part of these changes?

Aunt Ellie shed her caroling wraps, then rushed to Uncle Frank's side. They were older than Mother and Daddy, but now they embraced as though their short separation tonight had been a long one, and they eager and young. I wondered if they needed each other so much because they had no children of their own to love.

Our sitting room was in a hubbub of talk and laughter. George circulated with Mother, seeing that all guests had punch or coffee or small sandwiches or cakes. His hands shook from the tension.

It occurs to me now, looking back, that George never talked of what he did on his time off. That night would he rather have been with his own family instead of serving ours? Did he have any people of his own, or only Uncle Franley? If he wanted to be somewhere else on that Christmas Eve it did not show on his face. His smile was permanent, his eyes were lowered. He did not even glance my way.

It had been agreed days ahead of time that Blainey and I could be part of the gathering unless we seemed fatigued or upset by our stint at caroling, by the late hour, or by the difficulty of maintaining ladylikeness at an adult party. Blainey was perfect. There was no crack in her armor of decorum. Nor was there in mine until the high point of the evening.

The high point turned out to be the new Victrola. Daddy, in great triumph, rolled this magnificent surprise from the hall closet and into the sitting room. A grand console model. Stacked on top, a half dozen Victor

Red Seal records, a good selection of Mother's operatic and instrumental favorites. Everyone exclaimed over the size of the console, admired the mahogany of its lid and sides. Everyone insisted that all six of the Red Seal records be played. Daddy was mightily pleased.

He laughed like a boy. "My Christmas gift to Mase," he said. "A bit early, but you can't hide a console for very long."

Carefully, he wound the crank in the machine's left side. He eased a Red Seal into place, flipped the on switch, held the needle arm delicately poised above the turning disc. He let the suspense grow. Blainey came by her showmanship naturally. At last Daddy set the needle exactly in place. Everyone settled to silence while the magic of Caruso filled the room.

By the end of the third record, my ladylikeness was a definite torture. The fourth record was too much for me.

" 'A Medley of Favorite Songs: John McCormack, vocal,' " Daddy read from the Red Label and set the needle in place again.

Now he settled on the arm of Mother's chair, he rubbed one hand across her shoulders, she tilted a little into his half embrace. As the medley began, he leaned his head back against the wall, closed his eyes to listen.

John McCormack's vibrant tenor filled the room. "Kathleen Mavourneen," "In the Gloaming," "When Irish Eyes Are Smiling." It was in the middle of the next song that the day's excitement and strain caught up with me. "A Long, Long Trail A-winding"—Mother and Daddy's favorite. It had comforted them while he was off to training camp during the Great War. Off to camp, but finally, after much worry on Mother's part, not off to war. His trick knee, the result of an old basketball injury, kept him stateside, and in uniform for only a short stint. As to "A Long, Long Trail," how many times had Mother told us, dimpling, that she and Daddy claimed it as their own personal love song?

Suddenly Daddy's quiet face and closed eyes looked weary, old, not at all the Daddy I knew. Mother still tilted in his direction, but his arm had slipped from about her. As I watched, his familiar face faded, disappeared. The still one in its place was that of a stranger.

Terror leaped into my heart. Had Marcel looked this way when he died? My world whirled in a blur of fatigue. A jumble of disconnected scenes and sounds filled my muddled head . . . *Get ready for some changes, little girl* . . . changes . . . changes . . . the ugly crowd shouting down the changes, wounding my Suffragette . . . Mother aghast at Marian Pickett's change to boldness . . . changes . . . Aunt Arlene and Grandmother Standfield setting the Standfields apart from Mother . . . Daddy hating separate rooms, Mother liking them . . . Mother loving horse-drawn carriages, Daddy loving autos . . . Marcel, Marcel unknown to me because he drank himself to death . . . Arlene's voice, *a pity that Margy wasn't a boy* . . . ladylikeness and sixthraceness and seventh-great-uncle George Washington spiraled together . . . and me ending any hope of other Standfields . . . boys will be boys . . . girls must not be girls . . . the success of a Christmas solo . . . changes . . . George's voice, *They's lotsa little chil'un would trade places with you* . . .

The glory of my successful solo was swept away. Yes, pride certainly did goeth before, for now, with no warning, I burst into tears, a baby in this gathering of grownups.

Daddy's eyes flew open. He had not died after all. Mother gathered me up. Blainey, distressed by this display on my part, began demurely to pass cookies among the guests as Mother hustled me off to bed.

She sat beside me for a while.

"Daddy told me you sang so sweetly tonight," she said. "I wish I could have heard you."

Without waiting for a reply to filter through my sobs, she began to hum "Away in a Manger." She seemed in no hurry to return to her party. Presently she was singing the words softly, again and again, until after a bit the old song sounded the way it always had over all my years. She rubbed my back until I yawned and sleep rose around me.

Tomorrow there would be the wonder of Santa's visit, and the mystery of the decorated tree and presents where before there had been only the ordinariness of the sitting room. And there would be Daddy and Mother and Blainey and me. Our safe circle.

6

Black Bloomers, Dear Rears, and Such

It snowed just after New Year's Day that winter, which was unusual for Atlanta. Daddy and Mother woke Blainey and me after midnight to see the full moon on the fresh fall. Even beneath the dark pines it glittered. We stood there at the window, entranced, the four of us, Mother and Daddy with their arms entwined. As I leaned against Blainey, I could feel their warmth behind us. After a bit, Mother made hot chocolate. I was asleep before it was ready, but Blainey, only a week short of nine, didn't miss a thing.

Despite the cold winter, spring came early. At the beginning of April, Blainey and I found the first violets beneath dead oak leaves and winter's castings from the pines. Later we remembered how early, how lovely that spring had been.

Blainey and I were still hunting for violets down our hill when Daddy brought home his great annual spring surprise. We were so busy with our search that we didn't hear him drive up. The woods smelled of humus, moist and primeval. The morning gloomed dark one moment under misting showers, the next it turned brilliant, iridescent with sun lances. Peering from beneath our hooded rain capes, we laughed at the flashing glory, then bent again to the slick layered leaves, easing them up to grub beneath for violets.

"Oh, this one is huge!" Blainey's voice filled with satisfaction as she picked the flower to carry to Mother.

I was jealous of her and of the find. And of the bright mahogany curl of her hair. It seemed unfair that mine was straight and pale. Blainey had the edge in almost everything. There was her stout spirit. And how she did most things so well, so much better than I. There was the fact that until my birthday in July, she was three instead of two years my senior. Nevertheless, I was crazy about her, even now as she flaunted the prize of violets. This double pull of jealousy and love aroused my unruly inner demon.

Blainey looked up at me from where she squatted in the matted leaves. The sun struck across her eyes, highlighting the green, muting the brown.

"If we put our violets together, we've already enough for Mother's Doulton vase." She thrust her fistful up at me. "You give them to her, they match your eyes and hers."

She was really being nice now, for Mother's and my eyes were blue-gray, not this beautiful intense violet. The demon straddled the fence. Smiling, I took the flowers, then gave Blainey a push. Because of the hill she sat back hard in the wet leaves. She kicked one foot out and caught my ankle. The sharp pain made me want to cry. Instead I sang out, " 'I see London, I see France, I see someone's underpants,' and they're muddy as all get-out!"

But the day was too beautiful for a fight. She sprang up, laughing. "I don't care. It won't show much." And it wouldn't on the black sateen bloomers we wore under our skirts for outdoor play.

The sound of Galli-Curci's voice came warmly down to us from the open window of the sitting room. The crystal notes of "The Bell Song" hung in the sweet cool air like the raindrops on the glossy pines. Mother was playing one of her Victor Red Seals on the Christmas Victrola console. The new machine ran down just like the old if it wasn't kept wound. Then even Caruso seemed overcome with dreadful nausea, his voice dragging lower and lower until we rolled screaming with laughter, as Mother rushed in, laughing too, to wind it up again.

On this day, Galli-Curci did her beautiful best and finished as Blainey brushed the mud from her bloomers. Mother changed the record. There came Rosa Ponselle's voice and the flashing fire of Carmen. Presently I was wriggling my behind to the "Habanera."

Blainey, delighted at this wickedness, said, "You're crazy, Magpie!"

Her approval filled me with joy, and I loved her fully again when she called me Magpie.

In the midst of my "Habanera," there came the sound of an auto door from up on the street. In a moment, the Victrola stopped, and Ponselle was cut off in mid-aria. Seconds later, Mother's head appeared at the window. Her face was pink, her eyes bright. Daddy's voice came from the room behind her. The words were unclear, but his excitement reached down and brought us to attention.

"Come up, little chicks," Mother called. "Daddy has a surprise for us."

This surprise marked the start to that disturbing summer; we had no way of knowing it also marked the beginning of the end of an era.

All Blainey and I did was to fall against each other, laughing, as she said, "I wonder what make he bought this time. One nobody ever heard of, I bet."

"Or maybe a Model T," I said.

"Not a chance," said Blainey. "Daddy and Mother started out with a flivver, but he wouldn't be caught dead with one now. Remember when he brought home the Overland two years ago, and last year the Dorris? *Nobody* owned a Dorris. He loved that."

"Nobody'd even *heard* of a Dorris." Then as I remembered how fond we had become of it, a new idea occurred to me. "Maybe Daddy kept it when he bought the new one this time. Mother could learn to drive if she had the Dorris for her very own auto."

"Oh, Magpie, Mother's afraid to drive."

It was true. The thought of learning to drive terrified Mother, and though she had made up her mind to follow Marian Pickett's bold example and vote in the next election, she made it clear that there were still some things better left in the hands of men. Unladylike, she said of women drivers.

Now, though, the thought of the Dorris, our elegant but probably abandoned metallic friend, distressed me. When Blainey heard my sniffle, she put her hands on her hips and glared.

"Now you aren't going to cry again, are you, Magpie?"

With an effort I kept the tremble from my voice. "You're wacky, Blain!" I said. "Who'd cry over an old auto?"

"You and Mother."

Then Daddy's voice came down to us. "Hurry up you two. Mind your mother."

As usual, though, it was Daddy we minded, especially when he spoke in that sharp tone of command. So Blainey and I raced up the hill together.

This year's Great Annual Surprise turned out to be nothing as prosaic as a Ford, nor as exotic as the Dorris. It was a Hupmobile, a real beauty, blue, shiny, high—very high—and long and open.

"What a beautiful color it is!" Mother exclaimed. "Such a relief from black."

"Hupmobile blue it's called. A real innovation," Daddy said.

"The Dorris was much more elegant though." Mother's enthusiasm faded a little.

Daddy ignored this. He patted the Hupmobile's high fender. "This time a touring car," he said grandly. "We'll travel in style when we drive up to Cloudacres in June."

My sorrow over the Dorris departed. *Touring.*

We circled the Hupp, Blainey and I, climbed in and out, peered into every cranny. Under the backseat we discovered canvas panels with insets of isinglass.

"Storm curtains," Daddy said, and showed us how they snapped into place to close us in a dim interior. *Touring* and *storm curtains.* My excitement rose, my mind swept up in dizzy spirals of fancied adventure.

Blainey said, "With a pillow under my bottom, I'd be big enough to drive the Hupmobile." She looked boldly up into Daddy's face, flashed him a smile. "You can work the pedals," she told him.

Mother frowned. "Say derriere, honey."

"But it's a Hupmobile," I said.

Blainey giggled. "Magpie, you're a silly. Derriere is French for bottom. It's more ladylike."

Ignorance embarrassed me, especially my own, so I glared at her and said, "Why is a French bottom any more ladylike than any other kind of bottom?" Daddy's eyes glinted. Mother shifted uneasily. "Than any other kind of dear rear," I amended softly, contrite.

Quickly Daddy said, "On our way up to Cloudacres this summer, Blainey, once we're out in the country, you can sit on my lap and steer. How will that suit you?"

Though his words had been serious enough, suddenly he was laughing, shaking his head. Presently Mother laughed too, and for a second he put his arm around

her. This was the first time I had seen them close since
that midnight early in January when they had wakened
us to see the moonlight on fresh snow. Though Blainey
and I had not overheard any quarrels like the one we
had eavesdropped on from the cellar stairs months ago,
there was still a vague sense of fracture. How much
do children sense when adults think all is hidden from
them?

Now it did not matter to me that Daddy was chuckling
over my question. His arm about Mother drew our family tight again and kept the little beast of fear in its
lair.

The Hupmobile was already attracting some attention. Mrs. Carstairs, down the block, glanced our way,
then quickly she bent over a rosebush and continued
to clip her bouquet of early Hadleys. But Marilyn Louise
had begun to walk toward us. I still hated Marilyn
Louise. She was stuck-up and uppity, always tossing
her long hair. I hated the sight of her prancing down
the street, coming to take Blainey away from me.

"Oh-oh," said Blainey, "here comes Marilyn Louise."
And she pretended not to see her.

"I thought you and Marilyn Louise were good
friends," Mother said.

Blainey didn't look at Mother. Instead she shrugged.
"Oh, she's all right, I guess."

"Has something happened to make you not like her
anymore?" Mother's face pinked as she bent her plumpness to gaze directly into Blainey's eyes.

Blainey lowered her voice, glanced about. "Her
mother and daddy got a divorce last month."

I whispered. "What's a divorce?"

Only Blainey seemed to notice my question. "They aren't a family anymore, Magpie. Their daddy left them and isn't coming back. Ever."

Mother straightened, still watching Blainey. "I know. A real tragedy. That's no reason for you not to play with Marilyn Louise, little chick. She needs a friend more than ever now."

"Everybody talks about her at school." Blainey sounded defiant. "I don't even *know* anybody else who's"—again she dropped her voice to a whisper—"divorced."

"Ladies are loyal to their friends," said Mother. "And not unkind to anyone."

Blainey turned reluctantly and started off toward the Carstairs house. Presently she waved at her friend and began to skip to meet her.

I looked at Marilyn Louise, tossing her hair, and wondered if her daddy had left her because she was so uppity.

7

Our Merry Hupmobile

June eleventh, Saturday. School over for the year, the
first grade behind me, fourth grade awaiting Blainey
in the fall. The Hupmobile stood, ready packed, waiting
at the curb. At the breakfast table Daddy scanned yesterday's Atlanta *Constitution*.

"Warren Gamaliel Harding," he muttered to himself.
"Three months in office and nothing to show for it. I
said in the beginning, the country might just as well
have no president at all as Harding. That bunch of ninnies around him—"

Mother was silent, and the only thing that caught
my mind was Gamaliel. It had a familiar sound. Presently I said, " 'One table-spoonful to be taken at bed-

time. But Flopsy, Mopsy, and Cotton-tail had bread and milk and blackberries for supper.'"

Daddy glanced at me. "What?" he said, frowning.

Blainey laughed. "She's talking about President Harding's middle name. Gamaliel. Except it's camomile in *Peter Rabbit*. Camomile tea, Magpie, silly."

"You think you're so smart," I said.

Daddy returned to his paper. I sank into a sulk, picked at the spoonful of egg Mother had put on my plate. We were eating breakfast in the dark before dawn. George had scrambled the eggs. They steamed on their platter. He came in and slid a plate of freshly baked biscuits onto the table at Mother's elbow. He glanced quickly into my face and away, but not before I saw the smile in his dark eyes. A friendly smile, comforting. In a moment he was back with a bowl of hot grits. Then he was gone again, silent as a shadow.

As we ate breakfast in the gray dawn, Greenwood Avenue there beyond the dining-room window looked mysterious and empty. For no reason at all, panic seized me. Even the Hupmobile seemed suddenly foreign and threatening. Since April we had ridden around Atlanta in it, out to the Chattahoochee River on the west and to Stone Mountain over on the east. But now the Hupp sat stiff and forbidding, a complete stranger to me. The backseat was packed level with sheets and pillows, blankets and towels, and clothing. Accordion racks had been attached to the running boards. These were jammed with books and toys, with sundry supplies and food.

Everything was cheaper in Atlanta than from the general store in Tiger.

Tiger. Except for a few scattered houses, the general store *was* Tiger. In front of the store stood one glass-sided pump where you could watch the gas churn and bubble after it fed your auto. Each summer, only perishables were bought in Tiger when Daddy came up on weekends. Weekdays he stayed in Atlanta to tend his building-supply business. But without fail, every Friday he drove the hundred and twenty-five miles to Cloud-acres.

Mother and Blainey and I, and Hooligan, would sit up late listening for the low-geared sound of the auto climbing the steep grade up from Tiger. Sometimes George would come from the little cabin he slept in over on the fringe of our mountain acres. Before any of the rest of us could hear Daddy's auto, Hooligan would dash wildly about the house, his gravelly voice loud and joyous.

Maybe it was that he remembered the night he had become part of our family, a Friday night with Daddy on his way to be with us. A regular gully washer of a Georgia mountain storm had turned the red-clay road treacherous. It was only luck that the headlights had picked up the kitten in the road.

When Daddy came in the door with the rain and wind slashing at his heels, the first thing we heard was a hoarse mew. Daddy slammed the door against the storm, then opened his overcoat at the chest. Out came a soaked striped head, scrawny neck, pink nose, huge green eyes. The head shook on its thin stem.

Mother dried the ratty little thing, and Blainey and I could hardly fall asleep with excitement. Mother stayed up all night to nurse the kitten, half dead from the cold and wet. Mother would nurse anything in need, man, woman, child, animal; white, black, or any shade in between. With her help, Hooligan survived the night. Since then, he had never had a sick day. He became bold and tough and a terror in town. But we loved him and named him Hooligan, after Happy Hooligan in the Sunday funnies.

So, at Cloudacres, when Hooligan got excited on Friday nights, so did Mother and I. We dashed about too, and forgot our dignity as surely as he. But it was Blainey, alone out into the dark mountain night, who always swung the big gate wide for Daddy. If business allowed, he would sometimes stay a week or two. But the weekends were always certain, and Mother was always flushed and elated all day Friday. That night, Blainey and I would fall asleep in our room at the end of the hall with their muted conversation humming through the dark. Then I felt as though a safe wall encircled us, shutting out those nameless terrors of childhood's black hours.

Mother and I cried when he left each Sunday. George would turn serious with the coming responsibility of being the only man about the place. Daddy would ask us all to give him a smile. It was only Blainey who did, and she would stand in the road and wave until he was out of sight. But on Monday, Blainey was subdued. And until he came again there was a breach in my safe wall. Mother planned something special for

Mondays to coax back our vacation joy, and began saving up things for Daddy's next visit, things that she said only the head of the household could do about the place.

On that June morning, I peered out the window at the Hupmobile. Hooligan, who loved travel, was already perched, compact and tall, on the packed bedding, his eyes protruding like green grapes. It was then that foreboding seized me. I ran to the sleeping porch at the back of the house and hid behind Blainey's bed. Outdoor sleeping went with the vegetarian effort, though Mother and Daddy slept inside all year, in their separate bedrooms. It was finally Blainey who found me, huddled out of sight.

"Of all the ninnies," she said. "We're ready to go right now."

"I'm not going."

"Of course you are."

"I'm not!"

"Why?" Blainey fished for my arm.

"I'm scared."

"What of, for pity's sake?" She fastened a firm grip on me.

There was no way to explain that the little beast of fear had crept from its lair, fastened its claws in my heart. Tears were easier than words.

"Oh, Magpie!" Blainey pulled me out of my safe place. "Mother said you were good as gold when you were real little. But you've turned into a terrible crybaby."

I twisted and wiped my face along the bedspread, but Blainey kept her hold. There was no way to explain these tears.

"It's easy for you. You aren't ever scared." I kicked at her. "You're Daddy's little trooper." But she was too fast and my kick missed.

At the front door, I braced with my free hand against the frame, wrenched my captured hand from her. Suddenly, to my own amazement, the answer to my unreasonable terror burst forth.

"They didn't laugh together when they were packing." With both hands I glaumed onto the doorframe. "They didn't even hardly talk to each other."

"What?" Blainey, puzzled, stopped struggling with me for a minute. "Who're you talking about?"

"Mother and Daddy, they didn't laugh or talk or anything."

"Margery, you're really wacky." Blainey recaptured my left hand, pried my right one off the doorframe, one finger at a time. "They were too busy to talk. It takes a lot of getting ready for a whole summer."

Then, dragging me out the door, across the porch, she started a rapid persuasive chatter.

"Remember the huckleberries at Cloudacres, Magpie. And the blackberries. We'll see America Woodall again. And there's Aunt Ellie and Uncle Frank. We'll walk down through the woods to the spring for picnics, and hike over to the Gap. The azaleas will be out. And the rhododendrons. I bet you'll even be able to pump up in the swing and touch the high branch this year."

She didn't stop for breath as she nudged and pushed and bumped me down the steps.

"Hey, Magpie, remember the willow whistles Tessie and Pauly John Woodall always make for us? And the

broken-down flatbed wagon they pulled us in last summer? We can ride old Bobby again after he's finished
in our kudzu. And there's Tag-Along. You remember—
the hound puppy we had last summer. The one we had
to leave with the Woodalls. He'll be big now . . ." And
she maneuvered me across the lawn and sidewalk.

But by the time we stood beside the auto, and despite
Blainey's firm chin and bold tawny eyes, I realized she,
too, was aware of some rift between Mother and Daddy.
Suddenly it came to me, Blainey was as worried as I
about this secret change that had slowly crept into our
family.

Except for that evening when we had crouched on
the cellar stairs, we had never heard Daddy and Mother
quarrel. Before then there had been only talk and frequent laughter. But these reassuring sounds had dwindled. Mother seemed happy, caring for Blainey and me,
busy with her friends, and with the running of the
house. Yet if we came upon her unawares, her face was
often serious, her gray eyes puzzled, confused. She
would brighten immediately at sight of us though,
bounce up with some lively suggestion.

"Let's walk over to Piedmont Park," or "Let's play
a game of Parcheesi, the three of us," or "We've finished
the last lot of books. Let's take them back to the library
and get some new ones. I'll read to you tonight at bed-
time."

And off we'd troop, laughing together, worries submerged. But on this early morning in June they surfaced,
and we remembered other summers filled with chatter
and scurry.

Still, by the time we were finally in the Hupmobile, and Daddy had climbed in behind the steering wheel, our fears began to seem foolish. His overcoat was buttoned against the morning chill, his driving cap was in place, checkered and jaunty. Just the same as in all those other good summers. He started the motor with the newfangled self-starter. It caught at once and gave a satisfying roar. Daddy, his hands clever and quick on the levers, retarded the spark, adjusted the mixture. Magically the engine quieted, settled to its job.

"Sure beats cranking," he said, sitting very straight, gratification with himself and his Hupp neatly wrapped in the three words.

Blainey and I looked at each other and grinned. We clutched hands, thrilled at the prospect of adventure, bolstered by our confidence in Daddy at the wheel. He made us feel very safe.

Mother steadied herself against the dash with one gloved hand, the other arranged the scarf that held the creamy soft wide-brimmed straw hat in place and kept the chestnut swirls of her piled coif from the wind. She hadn't succumbed to the new bobbed hairstyles. Nor had she changed to the chic cloche hats, shrugging off Arlene's insistence on a new, more stylish chapeau. Maybe she felt herself too old for such frivolity or thought it unladylike.

Today, she was braced against the mild terror of the hundred and twenty-five miles before us in the Hupmobile, which she didn't trust any more than I had earlier in the gray dawn. She drew the scarf more tightly. It would be a long and breezy drive.

Blainey and I, in blue chambray coveralls and tennis
shoes, gloved and sweatered, bounced up and down with
excitement. My fears were forgotten entirely. Startled,
Hooligan spit, looked foolish, then ignored us. We settled, suddenly very still, our legs stretched straight
before us on the blanket-padded paraphernalia of summer.

Daddy put the Hupmobile in gear. We rolled forward.
Now Hooligan crawled to his usual position. His front
claws dug into the thick wool shoulder of Daddy's overcoat. His striped body, sleek and pampered from its winter indoors, turned primitive and predatory. He leaned
forward at an angle, braced against the blast of air as
we picked up speed. Eyes squinted, nose aquiver, whiskers streaked flat along his masculine jowls, he was as
bold as a dog against the elements of the world.

Mother turned her head. She smiled, reached, patted
my ankle. She winked at me. All at once I was happy.
She didn't think less of me because I had hidden on
the sleeping porch. I made a silent kiss at her. She
winked again. So I had been foolish—it didn't really
matter. Daddy began to sing, " 'Come away with me,
Lucille, in my merry Oldsmobile.' " Except he said Hupmobile. Blainey joined in, her voice strong and clear.
Between lines Daddy managed to say blithely, "That's
my little trooper!"

Before we turned the corner at the end of the block,
I glanced back at our house. George was standing there
alone. In my own earlier misery I had forgotten about
George. Even with the distance, you could see he was
watching the Hupp. Frantically I waved, but we turned

the corner so there was no way to know if he waved
back.

"We forgot George!" I wailed.

The earlier frightening conviction sprang to life. My
world was changing and tears would not stop it.

Mother's voice was composed. "George is staying in
town this summer to keep house for Daddy and to cook
for him."

"I don't see why. Daddy's with us almost as much
as in town." It was a flat statement from Blainey.

"It's a little different this year. Your father's business
will keep him in Atlanta. And later in the summer he's
going to England to visit your Aunt Arlene." Mother's
voice still seemed unruffled. The words *your father*
caught in my mind. They made him seem half stranger.
"He'll come and see us a time or two, of course." Then
there was doubt in her next question. "Won't you, Allen?"

"I'll be up for sure on Margy's birthday. We'll have
the biggest birthday party ever."

He made the words swell with excitement. The fear
scurried away at this glorious prospect. I had never had
a birthday party of my own, so now I knelt on the
luggage to be nearer to Daddy. His good scent came
to me as he went on.

"You can invite all the mountaineer youngsters,
Margy, hon. They've probably never seen a real birthday
cake with candles. Let's see, seven, seven candles this
year. We'll have cases of soda pop and all the trimmings.
A really grand shindig. We'll do it up in style, sugar.
Maybe I'll even bring your aunt and your cousins."

"Not Arlene!" Mother said. Then more sharply when Daddy didn't answer. "Are you bringing Arlene, too?"

"Of course not." Daddy's voice chilled. "Only Nora and her children. Arlene's already sailed for England. Three weeks ago. She'll be there for the entire summer, and may even stay to teach next fall."

"That should enlighten the British." Mother's tone was sarcastic, dry.

Blainey giggled. Daddy looked straight ahead at the road. Except for the vibrations of the motor, silence settled in our touring car.

My thoughts went back to the birthday party, my spirits rose again, and I almost forgot George, alone for the summer in Atlanta's heat. Blainey's birthday in January made parties easy in town. Summer meant we had left all our town friends behind, so I had had no party before. Now, in my imagination, I was just getting down to the details of the pending grand shindig when Blainey broke the silence.

"We won't have an auto to run errands down to Tiger. You'll *have* to come up on weekends, Daddy."

Her voice was oddly insistent, tense.

"I'll stay over a few days this week and teach your mother to drive. She can keep the Hupp all summer. I'll go back on the train."

To part with his beautiful Hupmobile surely would be a terrible wrench for him, but he went on blithely.

"In town I'll use one of the light trucks from work. I'm already teaching George to drive. He's good at it. Very quick. He'll get a big kick out of chauffeuring

me around. He can even help out with some of the
business driving."

When Mother glanced over at Daddy, I could see her
lips tighten. Despite the fact that some of the women
she knew drove, she was plainly terrified at the thought
of managing the Hupp by herself. Daddy didn't take
his eyes from the road, but he must have sensed her
distress.

"It'll be safe for you to practice in the country, Mase.
You have a good head on your shoulders." His use of
her nickname sounded affectionate, and he gave her a
quick smile. "You'll be a fine driver."

"I hope so," Mother murmured. A year ago she would
have refused. Now she said with strained gaiety,
"Women are learning to do all sorts of things since getting the vote. But I'm not too sure I like all this independence." Then she finished with her own maxim to
protest these speeding times. "It was not the style in
my grandfather's day!"

She turned and smiled at Blainey and me, gave a wink
and a rueful little twist of her head, half admiring, half
disapproving of this giddy 1920's decade.

But my own thoughts were busy with the promised
party. I did not let myself think of how far away it
was—the end of July, almost two months. George returned to my mind, his solitary form on our veranda,
his head turned in the direction of the vanishing Hupp.
How he would hate missing summer at Cloudacres.
Learning to drive wouldn't make up for that.

It seemed impossible we could give the party without

his help. He had been with us for so long I could not clearly remember what life had been like before we had George. Frantically I swallowed at the lump in my throat, sniffled the tears back into my nose.

"Let's play beaver," Blainey said.

And somehow I managed to forget about George and the birthday party and Mother's terror at learning to drive. We were outside the city limits now. The farther north we rolled, the more open the country became.

Presently, from my side of the auto, I saw a farmer working his fields. I knew I had won the first round of our game, for his chin sported a wonderfully thick beard—a beaver. He looked up as the beautiful blue Hupp rolled past in all its regal height. He waved. The beard parted, showing a flash of teeth.

"*Beaver!*" I shouted at Blainey.

8

A Regular
Barney Oldfield

As Blainey had promised, the azaleas were in bloom in the woods around Cloudacres; and rhododendron and dogwood. Along the rail fences the pale Cherokee roses were blowing in the sunny air.

There were huckleberries and blackberries, still unripe but promising much. And in the yard, before our wide-verandaed house, the kudzu vine was threatening us with a return to the jungle. Mother insisted you could see it grow. But Mr. Govan, who lived partway down the mountain and three miles away on his little scrabble farm, sometimes lent us his old horse, Bobby. Bobby would come to eat the rampant kudzu, filling his lean belly and saving us at the same time.

The very next day after we arrived at Cloudacres

Daddy insisted Mother must learn to drive the Hupp. Blainey and I went to stand beside the road and watch. Daddy started the motor, then climbed out to let Mother slide over into the driver's seat.

"You girls stay clear," she warned, voice sharp, eyes very bright. She settled herself firmly on the high seat. Hands atremble, she straightened her hat, grasped the steering wheel. Daddy sprang around the Hupp as though he were afraid it would leave without him. He leaped into the passenger seat.

Blainey, who longed to drive, laughed at Mother's fright, called out, "Don't worry about us!"

In a moment, slowly, then with startled leaps, the Hupp moved off down the road. Daddy had given many instructions earlier. Now he sat almost as stiff and straight as Mother. From time to time he would reach and do something with the levers or turn the wheel. The auto zigzagged off along the level road toward the wide fork before the Bentons' estate. We could see the Hupp silhouetted against Pinewood's rolling lawns and dark trees. Daddy reached to cramp the wheels for the turn, straighten them again.

He waved at Blainey and me as the Hupp came back and passed without slowing. Mother did not even glance our way. Rigid at the steering wheel, straw hat knocked crooked again, she stared at the road with the same concentrated gaze she used on us when we got out of hand. By sheer will, she forced auto and road into loose agreement as to direction. The Hupp disappeared, the plume of red dust slowly settled. The little tree frogs piped in the silence. It must have been the growing of the kudzu that stirred and rustled, for the air was very still. It pressed gently around us, a warm light cocoon. I jumped at the sound of Blainey's laugh.

"Well, Mother's a regular Barney Oldfield." There was merry raillery in her words.

"Who's Barney Oldfield?" I asked.

"Everybody knows he's just about the greatest race car driver in the world!"

"You're such a smarty. Besides, you're mean, Blain, making fun of Mother. It's scary to learn to drive."

"It didn't scare me when Daddy let me drive coming up here."

"You just sat on Daddy's lap and did the steering. He worked the gears and brakes and gas. Mother has to do it all."

"Steering's the hardest part."

"She didn't run off the road anyway!" I defended.

"Not yet."

"Daddy won't let anything go wrong." But the emptiness of the road worried me.

"Yes." Blainey sobered. "He'll see they're safe." Presently she sighed. "Daddy will take the train back to Atlanta next Sunday. Then we'll have to manage without him."

The dark import of her somber words sifted down through my mind as slowly, as quietly as had the red dust on the road. *Summer without Daddy.*

We waited a long time, but the Hupp did not reappear. Finally I said, "Something's happened to them," and began to cry. "Daddy's mean, making Mother drive when she hates it so."

Blainey hiked her hands to her hips, glared at me. "Daddy's just trying to help her. She'll like it when she learns how." Then she softened, put an arm around my shoulder. "There's no place to turn until they're almost to Hayes Field, Magpie. You know, where the road starts down to Tiger. They can use the old Jefferson house driveway to turn around. They'll be back before you know it. Let's go swing."

As he had in all the other summers, Daddy had put up the swing in the big pine, this time even before insisting on Mother's driving lesson. He climbed and shinnied to a high limb, tied the ropes there, then descended and set the sturdy notched pineboard seat in place. He stepped up on it, jumped a few times with an eye on the knots far above. Next he pumped up, his dark hair ruffling in the breeze, his slim body athletic, able. He even forgot to favor his trick knee, the knee he had injured playing basketball at the Y. We laughed, loving him, for he looked as carefree as a boy, flying on the swing, testing it so we would be safe.

In a dozen great thrusts he had the swing high enough so at the back of the arc with the ropes stretched taut, parallel to the ground, his rear brushed a branch that stood at the same height as the swing limb, a good twenty feet above the needle-padded ground. Blainey shouted with glee and my heart leaped into my throat. I longed to rise to that dizzy height. Blainey had managed it for three years. All the Woodall kids could do it except Billy Jim and Katie May. And they were only five and three. My hands turned icy as I promised myself, *this summer.*

Now Blainey said, "Let's pump up together." And hand in hand we ran for the swing.

We stood on the board seat, facing each other, and pumped in turn. Despite my recent brave promise to myself, when the rope gave a loopy jerk at the height of one sweep, I said, "Let's sit down, Blain."

Today she did not give an extra pump to tease, but settled at once on the wooden seat. Quickly I sat too, straddled her across her lap, face to face with her. We were still swinging when the Hupp flew down the road, wheeled in at the gate with a bump and a thump.

Daddy drove now, with Mother beside him. She had one hand on top of her hat, and they were laughing. Blainey dragged her feet, stopped the swing, stood up, sliding me down onto the needles. It was so lovely to have us all safe that I didn't yell when Blainey dumped me. Mother and Daddy—laughing together!

"What do you think of the renters down at the Jefferson place?" Mother was asking Daddy as they climbed out.

"Cowan. That was the name. Seemed nice enough," he said, but his voice became guarded.

"That was hospitable of them," Mother said, "inviting us in for coffee." Her face pinked a little as she went on, "Mr. Cowan is quite the *galant.*"

She made the last word sound foreign. Mother liked words as much as Daddy liked clothes and cars. She was easily Aunt Arlene's equal there, Randolph-Macon Woman's College notwithstanding.

"Yes." Daddy's smile was gone. "That's part of the creed—womanhood on a pedestal, chastity, all that, you know."

Mother winced at the word chastity, and I wondered what it meant.

"Which is all fine," Daddy continued, "if they don't use a narrow kind of morality to cover up some darker side."

The green flecks had faded from his eyes. They looked as hard as hazelnuts now. Blainey watched, waiting for a turn to speak. None came.

"They? What do you mean, they?" Mother glanced quickly at Daddy. Her cheeks were still flushed. She took off her hat, pushed the piled hair into shape.

"Mr. Cowan's picture was in the paper last week. Second page of Monday's *Constitution*. I noticed it particularly since the Klan tends to put so much store on secrecy. Some newspaper photographer, a brave one, must have snapped it. There were several burly fellows in the background who looked like they were running up to have a go at whoever was behind the camera. The shot was a good clear one of Cowan, though."

Mother frowned, searching her memory. Blainey started, "Do the Cowans have any—"

Absently, Mother said, "Don't interrupt, chicken little."

"Cowan. Ethan Cowan," Daddy said. "Had his name right under the picture. Same name as on the Jefferson mailbox now. He was calling for a Grand Konclave, the paper said, of the Ku Klux Klan, to be held out near Stone Mountain in August, I think it was."

Mother nodded, but she was no longer flushed with pleasure over Mr. Cowan's *galant* ways. Instead she looked worried. "You think it's the same Cowans?"

"Pretty certain of it. Grand Dragon of the Georgia Klan."

Into the following silence, Blainey inserted her question. "Do the Cowans have any children?"

Mother's face cleared. She smiled down at Blainey. "Yes, hon, two girls, eleven and nine, and one boy. We didn't see him, but they said he's six. And there's a Shetland pony."

Would the girls play with Blainey and leave me out? Were they uppity like Marilyn Louise Carstairs? A Shetland pony. Would it be at all like the Welsh Mountain pony in "Greylight"? The one Mother had read about to us last summer, the story continued from issue to issue in *Saint Nicholas* magazine. Suddenly I didn't care whether the girls proved uppity or not. A beautiful sleek little white pony had become enmeshed in my dream of someday owning a horse.

※

Later that day I found Blainey bent over the dictionary. Blainey, adept at spelling, had become an expert in word searches.

"What are you looking up?" I asked.

"Something Daddy said." She ran a finger down the words.

"Chastity?" I asked, remembering Mother's wince.

"Uh-huh." Her finger stopped.

"What does it say?"

She read, " 'State or quality of being chaste.' "

"Like something running after you?"

"It's spelled different. I'll look up 'chaste.' "

"What does that say?" I prompted.

" 'Virtuous.' "

"What does that mean?"

"I think it means being good." She turned pages again.

"What—" I began.

" 'Virtuous' means 'chaste, pure.' " Blainey gave a little snort of dissatisfaction. But she bent more closely,
reading further. "Here's something else it means. 'Potent.' " And she turned to the P's.

Potent: Having the power of procreation.

More pages.

Procreate: To beget.

And on.

Beget: To procreate, as a sire.

Finally—

Sire: The male parent of a beast, especially a horse;
a stallion.

That struck a chord with me. Somehow unfulfilled
but relieved, my mind returned to the Cowans' Shetland
pony. I wondered if it was a stallion.

9

The Bony Bags
of Clay

Mother did learn to drive the Hupp—after a fashion—
but she never brought herself to let Blainey and me
ride with her on any stretch of road she considered dangerous. And certainly not on the steep grade up and
down from Tiger. Then we had to get out and walk.
We became very good walkers that summer.

We were alternately hilarious or disgruntled at her
caution. It did not occur to us then what a valiant spirit
Mother had. Her jaunty wink, her ready laugh, her tender touch with us, hid the loneliness and hurt of that
summer without Daddy, made a joke of our walking
the steep grade while she was certain she faced injury
or death alone in the big unwieldy Hupp. Yes, for
Mother a time of trial and challenge. And the first of

these challenges was conquering the gears and levers and pedals of the awful auto. Daddy stayed with us for that week to teach her.

He also saw that everything at Cloudacres was in good shape. The pump at the spring, a quarter of a mile down from the house, needed checking and oiling. Without the pump we would have no water. He went over all the roof shingles and replaced those split by last winter's storms. He mended a broken tread on the veranda steps, and checked the flue of the wood cook stove. All the kerosene lamps were filled, and plenty of wood was stowed in the woodboxes and an ample supply in the garage—lightwood, split wood, and small logs.

He made certain that America Woodall would live in with us for the summer to help Mother with the cooking and housework. And there was a relative of hers, young Beau Tulley, the only man we'd have about the place to do outside chores. He would come and stay at the cabin, unoccupied now with George in the city. Handsome Beau. Nineteen years old. I fell in love with him that summer.

The June days were long. Blainey and I managed to forget, most of that week, that Daddy would be leaving soon. Mother's face was pinched. Daddy, quieter than usual, uninterested in hikes or picnics as in other summers, had become the soul of consideration as to her wishes.

"Is there anything at all you'd like done before I leave on Sunday?" He asked this on Friday morning.

Slowly she shook her head.

Daddy gave me a wink, said almost gaily, "I'll be back, anyway, toward the end of July."

My birthday in July! He had not forgotten.

But more immediately, there was to be a gathering on Saturday down at the Bentons' place. Parties at Pinewood were an occasion. Frank and Ellie did it in fine style, for they were wealthy. "Old money," Mother once said, "so they wear it well."

The Bentons as opposed to the Woodalls gave me my first real understanding that there were rich people and poor people and that we fell somewhere in between.

When we heard about the Bentons' party, Blainey simmered with excitement. We had both been invited.

"Imagine, Magpie," Blainey said, "*invited* just like grown-ups."

And it was true, for Aunt Ellie had written out a separate invitation to the two of us.

Blainey rummaged through the mountain clothes. Finally, she fished out the only party dress that Mother had packed for her—a straight white organdy with a ruffle at the bottom and ribbon straps over the shoulders embellished with embroidered hairline stems. She held the dress up to herself, preened before the mirror. Like Daddy, Blainey was a dresser. Even at nine she had style. She had always been Aunt Arlene's delight on those infrequent shopping sprees. As for the shindig at the Bentons', I wanted to go in my coveralls and tennis shoes.

"Magpie, don't be silly." Blainey laughed. "Uncle Frank and Aunt Ellie have invited most of the Theo-

sophical Society up from Atlanta. All the bedrooms at
Pinewood will be filled. Aunt Ellie borrowed America
Woodall from Mother again. That's why we haven't
even seen America yet. She's been cleaning for days,
setting out fresh linen, cooking. Oh, everything! And
that's besides the two regular servants."

"I hate dressing up," I said.

"You *can't* go in your coveralls. Here." And Blainey
fished out my organdy dress and threw it to me. "Smooth
it on the bed. Like this."

Her clever hands were quick with her own creased
garment. She finished hers and helped with mine. Next
she set out our Mary Janes, the straps barely creased,
their patent leather glossy, the new scarcely worn off
black soles and flat hard leather heels. I was pained at
the thought of giving up the fleet springiness of my
tennis shoes, even for that one evening.

⫚

We could see the lights of Pinewood as we drove out
of the gate at Cloudacres. A half dozen autos had passed
down the road during the day, each filled with Theosophists. Some of them waved to us, friends from the regular meetings in Atlanta.

As our Hupp rolled up the long curving drive at Pinewood and stopped beneath the porte cochere, we saw
that every room, upstairs and down, was alight. With
no electricity in these parts, it was all done with kerosene
lamps, the glow muted, mysterious in the black mountain night. But inside, the talk was as animated, as lively

as though Pinewood were a city mansion adazzle with cut-crystal chandeliers.

"Let's go see America," Blainey whispered to me.

We flew to the kitchen. At sight of us, America Wood-all broke into a smile, revealing where two upper teeth were missing. She smelled of flour and vanilla and onion when she gathered us to her. We had never seen her gaunt frame decked out in so grand a fashion. Self-consciously she smoothed her pale-brown hair into place, hair streaked with white.

"Miz Benton bought these special for me. Ain't they the prettiest though?" America beamed and ran both hands down her blue uniform and white linen apron. "I was afeard the shoes might pinch my corns. I got feet tetchy as thunderation."

Tonight she wore honest-to-goodness shoes, not the usual old gray-felt slippers, or in warm weather noth-ing at all, on her knobby feet. The shoes made her limp a little. Despite this, her eyes, alight with plea-sure at the sight of us, were lively, and blue as a jay's wing.

"How's my two little city girls?" she asked in her rough voice. "When'll we get our readin' started? Lord, them tales your momma reads from *The Satidy Evenin' Post*. They do pleasure me, and that's God's truth!" She rolled her eyes, squeezed us once more.

"We've already got two issues ahead," Blainey said. "One copy we brought from town, and yesterday one was put in the mailbox here." America's face showed pained disappointment. Blainey hurried on, "Oh,

Mother hasn't started reading yet. She's waiting for you."

"Bless her heart." America laughed aloud, pleased as a child. "I just been endurin' the time since you 'uns left, end of last August."

Every summer Mother read to the three of us. Usually from the *Post*, which came folded and thrust into our mailbox at the gate once a week; or from *Saint Nicholas*, the children's monthly magazine. We doted on the *Post* serial. It didn't matter to me that parts were beyond my comprehension. The words were grand, the action exciting. The *Post* had good writers. Mother tucked us into bed each evening when Daddy wasn't there. Then she settled in her wicker rocker on one side of the table that held the kerosene lamp, with America on the other side.

Mother read. The rocker made its dry reedy crackle. America mended or stitched bright cotton scraps together for the quilts that would keep her family warm through the cold winters in their dark, drafty, dirt-floored little cabin. Sometimes Blainey and I would recognize scraps from our own dresses, for Mother saved all the pieces to give to America each summer. As Mother read, America would stop her stitching from time to time, lost in the wonders that came from the printed page to fill the shadowy corners beyond the circle of lamplight with magic. She couldn't read a word, herself. She couldn't even write her name.

"What's the serial this time?" America asked us there in the Bentons' kitchen.

" 'The Covered Wagon,' " Blainey said. "All about

pioneers going west and Indians and fights among the men—"

"Well!" America breathed. "I declare!" But then she was busy again at the stove, and we and the story were forgotten.

Back in the living room a new couple had arrived.

"Mr. and Mrs. Cowan," Uncle Frank had just started the introductions as we edged in, "from down the road . . . new here this summer . . . getting acquainted. . . ."

Ethan Cowan. *The Grand Dragon.*

But for me Ethan Cowan proved a Grand Disappointment—only a plain man, beefy, apparently jovial, obviously pleased to have been included in this gathering. Somehow, to me, he seemed out of place. Maybe it was his shoes. They were blunt toed, cracked a little across the top. There was a split in one that had been mended with strong twine. A workman's shoes. Probably no one noticed that but me. Shoes and trousers and skirts and underchins and nostrils made up much of my view. Mr. Cowan's nostrils were wide and hairy, while Uncle Frank's were narrow, discreetly hiding their interiors.

Mr. Cowan's color deepened as he said his *galant* words to the ladies, bowing slightly from his sturdy hips. Most of the men smiled, and the ladies pinked, including Mother, though she gently withdrew from those who stood greeting the Cowans. Daddy looked distant and cool. Then he caught my eye, winked and smiled, so I didn't feel lost in the roomful of trousers and skirts.

Blainey was in her element. She sashayed around the

parlor, demure but noticeable. When Mr. Cowan had
finished with his homage to the ladies, his eye lit on
Blainey.

"Now there's a real little Georgia peach. I'll bet she's
the apple of her daddy's eye. I have two young ladies
at home myself, two sweet little Dixie belles. Makes a
man proud to be a Southern gentleman."

But I forgot about Mr. Cowan when I stepped on
the hem of Mrs. Cowan's long lacy skirt. Her hard hand
thrust me away and she stabbed me with a quick, fierce
look. She recovered immediately.

"What a dear child," she said in my direction, but
then she was smiling at all the faces above me.

She was almost a beauty, cool, and pink and white;
and her ladylikeness plainly showed a moment later
when her handkerchief fell to the floor. She exclaimed
prettily as one of the men scooped it up, returned it
with a flourish. She dimpled. Still, there was something
hard about the set of her mouth, even as she murmured,
"Oh, just whatever would we do without you handsome
gentlemen?"

Presently I saw her eyes shoot cold fire at Mr. Cowan
when he beckoned to Blainey. The venomous look was
again quickly masked by lowered lids and those artfully
curled and darkened lashes which had fluttered so
charmingly at the hanky retriever.

"Come here, you pretty little lady." Mr. Cowan still
beckoned to Blainey.

He eased himself into a chair. His hand went under
her bottom as he hoisted her into his lap. Blainey looked
suddenly uncomfortable, confused. She told me later

that Mr. Cowan had pinched her tender parts as he had lifted her.

But at that moment, there in the Bentons' drawing room, I felt hemmed in by legs, stifled by the talk drifting back and forth above my head. Quietly I crept out and settled in the empty, dimly lit, screened side veranda. The night was warm. Aunt Ellie came out after a bit. She sank into a chair and sighed, then she saw me, smiled, and came over to sit beside me on the couch.

"It's nice and peaceful out here," she said softly.

"Yes," I whispered.

Aunt Ellie bent to hear me, patted my knee, kissed the top of my head. When she spoke, it was in a whisper too. It was really too bad that she and Uncle Frank had no children of their own. They should have.

"Sometimes people talk too much and don't think enough," she said.

I nodded and we smiled there together. Finally she arose. "Would you like to listen to some records, dear?" she asked.

"Yes," I answered quickly. "Could you play the one about the bony bags of clay? I heard it last summer."

She laughed and I blushed there in the half darkness. Maybe little girls weren't supposed to like such a ghoulish record. I loved it, picturing all sorts of gristly bits of bone poking from the noisome wet clay as it bulged in its rotting bags.

"You like Harry Lauder?" Aunt Ellie asked.

"Oh, yes." It was a relief that she didn't seem at all shocked.

" 'Roamin' in the Gloamin' ' is one of his best records," she said, but then she was laughing again. "You do his Scottish talk very well, indeed. So you like the words to this?"

She set the record in place. As she wound the Victrola she sang softly and distinctly,

> *"Roamin' in the gloamin'*
> *On the bonnie banks of Clyde,*
> *Roamin' in the gloamin'*
> *With my lassie by my side—"*

The needle made a faint hiss as it searched for the groove.

"In Scotland, 'bonnie' means 'pretty,'" Aunt Ellie went on. "The pretty banks of the River Clyde, that's what Harry Lauder is singing about, though it's very difficult to understand with his Scottish dialect."

The needle settled in place and Aunt Ellie drifted back to her guests as Harry Lauder's voice burred from the machine. I pulled a chair to its mahogany side, climbed up, carefully set the needle arm back on its rest, and clicked off the turntable. The bonnie banks of the River Clyde seemed deadly dull. I tried to recapture the feel of the bony bags of clay beneath my feet as, in fancy, I roamed through the rising dark.

Instead, the babble of voices flowed into my sanctuary from the other room. Someone was talking about the Theosophical Society and Annie Besant in India, where the Society had its roots. Ever since Mother had read us "Rikki-Tikki-Tavi" from *The Jungle Books* and *The Secret Garden*, India had fascinated me with its deadly cobras, its intriguing, difficult little girls whose parents had died of cholera, and its strange animals and mongooses. Or was it mongeese? Uncertainty filled me. After all, I had been wrong about the bony bags of clay. The voices snagged my mind.

"—there's our colony in California. My, wouldn't you just love to visit there—"

"—Krotona? Yes, Krotona—"

"—near Hollywood, isn't it?—"

"—in the hills above Hollywood—"

"—have you heard of the young man from India? Annie Besant discovered him there at Adyar—"

"—Krishnamurti?—"

"—yes, that's his name. Krishnamurti. They say he's just the most inspirin'—"

But I stopped listening. I kneeled on the couch and watched the moon come up over Rabun Gap. Presently, there was Blainey, escaped from the Grand Dragon, come to watch the moonrise with me.

"Mother's promised we can visit the Cowan girls tomorrow," she told me. "Mr. Cowan invited us."

"They have a Shetland pony," I said. Blainey was welcome to the girls if I could be friends with the pony.

But when Blainey went on, her voice had turned somber.

"Tomorrow is Sunday. Daddy's leaving then." She sighed. "This week went awfully fast. It's so far from Cloudacres to Atlanta. And England, that's forever away."

We were silent for some time, watching the moon free itself from the spiky pines of the far ridge. Its white light failed to dispel the dark shadow of a summer with-

out Daddy. Restlessly my mind began to toy with a
word or two filtered from that flood of talk that had
come from the other room.

Krotona. How mysterious that sounded. *Hollywood.*
Hollywood, California. Even I knew where that was.
Clear across the country, at the edge of the Pacific Ocean.
A land of make-believe. As unreal as India or Baghdad
or Neverland. The realm of Charlie Chaplin and Wil-
liam S. Hart and Rin-Tin-Tin and Jackie Coogan and
Theda Bara and Douglas Fairbanks and Mary Pickford
and all the rest. But most especially, that world belonged
to Charlie Chaplin. We loved him. Who else could make
you laugh and cry at the same time?

Krotona. Hollywood. They were a long way from Atlanta. Even farther from Cloudacres and Pinewood and
the Bentons' party and all the things I knew. Suddenly,
uneasiness seized me. Krotona. Hollywood. They had
nothing at all to do with me.

"Do you suppose the Cowan girls will let me ride
their pony?" I asked Blainey.

"Mr. Cowan will let us ride. He likes ladies."

"We're little girls."

"He called me little lady." She frowned then. "I'm
not too sure about the Cowans. I was in the library,
looking for a book to read. The Cowans came in for a
few minutes and I heard her say something to him about
all the people sounding like—like Bolsheviks with their
Theosophy and all."

"What's a Bolshevik?" I asked.

"Search me." Blainey shrugged. "Then Mrs. Cowan
said she wondered if it was her beholden duty to write

a letter to Attorney General Palmer. Whoever *he* is. Some muckdemuck in the army, I guess, or in the government."

"What about?"

"About the Theosophists maybe being Bolsheviks, I guess. She said she was sure she had heard somewhere that Annie Besant was a Socialist. And Annie Besant has a lot to do with running the Theosophical Society."

"Why would that general care about Socialists and Bolsheviks and all that stuff?"

"Who knows? Mr. Cowan said at least nobody here seemed to be Catholics or Jews."

"Why did he say that?"

"Oh, Magpie, you ask too many questions!" And Blainey, obviously through with the subject, sank into silence watching the moon again.

Presently I asked, "Do you know of a place called Krotona?"

"No." She sprang up. "Let's go see if we can help America in the kitchen."

I leaped after her and forgot about Jews and Catholics and Socialists and Krotona and Hollywood. Briefly, though, despite my penchant for questions, I realized one could learn too much, for there was a real flash of regret over Harry Lauder and the bonnie banks of Clyde.

"Bony bags of clay," I whispered to myself.

10

First Love

When Blainey and I awoke Sunday morning, Daddy was gone. One of the Bentons' guests had offered him a lift into Atlanta. They had started before dawn.

This was a great relief to Mother. We had planned to take Daddy to the train station. Now she was saved the horror of driving the Hupp alone back up the steep grade below Hayes Field. The station stood a little distance outside Tiger itself, a mustard-colored little shed, solitary beside the steel rails of the Tallulah Falls Railroad Line. Unless flagged down, the train did not even slow, but racketed past on its way to Tallulah Falls. On a quiet night we could hear the lonesome wail of its whistle clear up at Cloudacres.

I was glad to have escaped the ordeal of waiting on

the narrow platform for the locomotive and its swaying cars. The engine's overpowering roar, the earsplitting screech of brakes all down the line, flattened and erased me. But Blainey was in a black mood. She had had no chance to say good-bye to Daddy. Taking a book under one arm, she trudged off down toward the spring. When I started to tag after, Mother's hand stopped me.

"Leave your sister alone, Margery," she said. "Blainey will be better company after a while."

I scowled up at her. "Daddy left without kissing us good-bye." For some reason I felt angry at Mother over this.

She cupped my chin in her hand. "He did kiss you both, in your sleep, chicken little."

"What if he forgets about my birthday?"

"He's already promised he'll be here at the end of July for your party. You know Daddy never forgets a promise."

She sat down and pulled me to her. The smell of her violet sec toilet water and the feel of her cushiony thigh below the firm edge of corset dispelled part of my crossness. She smoothed my pale straight bangs, touched one finger across my nose where the freckles had blossomed profusely in the summer sun.

"He didn't have the heart to wake you so early this morning. Remember how late we stayed at Pinewood last night? Coming back, just the short way here, you fell asleep in the auto. Daddy carried you in and put you to bed."

Sadness hung on the edge of her smile, but I scarcely noticed it then.

"Was it him put my nightie on me?" I asked, liking the thought, wishing I had wakened to the touch of his hands.

"Was it *he*. Yes. Ever so gently, not to disturb you." But here eyes showed that only half her mind was on me. Then she straightened a bit, firmed her voice. "It's good we'll be on our own for a few weeks. We really must learn to depend on ourselves more. Times are changing for us."

"Changing for *us*?" I asked warily.

Last night's uneasy feeling returned. I remembered the strange talk that had filtered out to me from the party, talk of Hollywood and Krotona. A foreign and exciting and frightening name—Krotona. Changes. And I remembered, too, the feeling that had made me cry on Christmas Eve, months ago.

"Changing for *us*?" I repeated.

"Yes." She looked directly at me now and smiled. "Times are changing for us women. When I was a girl, the most important thing was to be a well-bred young lady, and to marry a gentleman to care for you. A man strong and brave enough to protect you from this rough world. But one tender and loving and considerate."

"Like Daddy," I said. "Not coarse like Uncle Walter."

Mother frowned. "What a thing to say about your Uncle Walter."

She had forgotten her conversation with Arlene about Aunt Fannie and her ten children, about Walter's coarse unstoppability. For a moment my mind was snagged again by the unsolved puzzle of Aunt Fannie and her strange difficulty with babies.

Mother's voice went on, still talking aloud but mostly to herself. "When I was a girl, independence in a lady was frowned upon. But now we have the vote and bob our hair and shorten our skirts and drive autos and do all sorts of outlandish things."

Suddenly there was my Armistice Day Suffragette, crowding Fannie and Walter and babies from my mind; my Suffragette marching across the fringe of my memory, throwing me a kiss, waving to me as Mother continued.

"Why, I remember hobble skirts, little chick, long to the shoe tops and so narrow at the ankle it was almost impossible to get on a streetcar. Oh, very feminine, very pretty, they were, with high-necked lace-bedecked voile shirtwaists to top them off. No real lady would have thought of showing her lower extremities like some of the young ones do nowadays. Believe me, it was not the style in my grandfather's day."

But there was a wistful sound to her words as though all these changes unsettled and fascinated her at the same time.

"Well, anyway, *I'm* not a woman," I said with some relief. "I'm just a little girl."

"You're a little woman," Mother insisted. "A little *lady*," she corrected.

"I'd rather be a little woman."

It was obvious to me that little ladies missed most of the fun.

But Mother had half forgotten me again. She was telling herself, "Of course, *I* was an independent woman before I met your father. I earned my own living, rented my own room at Mae Martin's Rooming House for Ladies, over just off Piedmont Road. I made a very good life for myself. A woman can remain a lady even if she has to work."

Mother proudly drew herself up, stiffened a little in her already stiff corset, but her thigh remained as vulnerably soft as ever against my side.

"At Rich's Department Store," I told her.

"What?" she asked, dragging her mind back from another time.

"You worked at Rich's Department Store," I repeated.

"Yes." She nodded, once more speaking directly to me. "In Ladies' Notions. Handkerchiefs and scarfs and sachets. Needlework supplies. That sort of thing. Very respectable."

"I know," I said, suddenly as impatient as Daddy once had been at this repeated tale.

Blainey and I usually doted on these stories of the past. Mother was a gold mine of remembered things. She could even recite great sections, memorized in school, from McGuffey's readers. She had a remarkable memory and a southerner's gift for spinning a yarn. But today, with Daddy gone and Blainey sunk in the blues, I was restless, in no mood to hear the old stories.

Mother sighed. "Then I met your father, we fell in love, and my working days were over."

There was that same unsettling dual sound; this time, of triumph and defeat. Presently though, she shifted, squared her shoulders. When she spoke it was with new resolution.

"Yes, we really should learn to depend on ourselves

more. Whether we like it or not, times are changing."

"Whether your grandfather would like it or not," I said, but she didn't hear me.

Her gray eyes still looked into mine. They had turned somber, her lips had thinned. I reached and my finger traced a wrinkle from beside her blunt, rounded nose to the corner of her mouth. I had never noticed it before, perhaps because its crease was usually lost in a laugh or a smile. At that moment she seemed as old as the grandmothers of other children. And I remembered one night, waking in the Greenwood Avenue house to Daddy's and her voices. They were deep in some continuing conversation, unaware I was no longer asleep on the sitting room couch. I had dozed off there earlier, trying to wait up for Blainey, out late visiting a school friend.

"—too old for a baby when Margery came along—" Mother was saying. Almost the same words Blainey and I had overheard from the cellar stairs.

"Why, hon," Daddy laughed softly, "you still seem only a girl to me."

"I was no girl when we married, Allen. I was thirty-eight," she had reminded him. "And that was ten years ago. Besides, I'm five years older than you. Remember what a fuss your mother and sisters made over that."

"Calendar age doesn't make any difference."

"They still resent me."

From beneath my lashes, I had glimpsed him taking her hand. They sat in silence, but she had not looked at him. Finally she said, "If I was younger I wouldn't have had such trouble when Margy was born. It frightened me later when Dr. Baird told me he thought, for a while, he'd lose me and the baby, too. You know what a terrible and difficult time—"

"Yes. I remember." He released her hand. A strained and guilty tone had arisen in his voice. Suddenly, that night, I hadn't wanted to hear any more. I closed my eyes tightly, took a deep breath, stirred as though a dream upset my sleep.

"Sh-h-h," Mother whispered, but after a short silence she continued to Daddy, "You told me that day—"

"—I'd never put you through anything like that again," Daddy had finished for her in his deeper voice, a voice that never seemed able to sink to a whisper. But a slight tremor had crept into it.

When I had peeked again, he was on his feet. Mother, eyes averted, said nothing. Finally, he went on, standing there, looking down at her, his words squeezed out, compressed, making him a stranger to me.

"I haven't forgotten," he said. "It's just that I miss the way it used to be, hon."

I stirred again. This time it had put a stop to their talk. Daddy had come, gently picked me up, carried me to the sleeping porch. I still feigned sleep as he tucked me carefully beneath the covers. His hands shook a little. After he was gone, for some reason I didn't understand, I had cried into my pillow. But when Blainey finally came, I had sunk so far into real sleep that it sucked me away before I could say anything to her.

Afterward I had forgotten Mother's and Daddy's nighttime conversation. It was only now, as I traced the line on Mother's somber face, that I remembered she was too old for a baby when I was born.

She was finishing to me, "So you see, today you must depend on yourself for entertainment, and not on your sister. People do need time alone every once in a while."

"Like Blainey today," I said.

It came to me how welcome the solitude of Aunt Ellie's porch had been last night, and I forgave Blainey for going off without me.

"Yes, like Blainey," Mother said.

The thought seized me of the swing in the empty yard. Today I might conquer it. Today alone. I pushed away from the comfortable curve of Mother's arm.

"I like to be by myself sometimes, too, you know."

"Well, run along then, sugar." Mother, forgetting her own dark thoughts, laughed her comradely laugh. I was halfway out the door when her voice stopped me for a moment. "The Cowans invited us to come for a visit this afternoon. Would you like that?"

"Oh, yes!" I said, remembering the pony.

"Blainey will be back after a bit, and maybe a walk over to the Cowans' will pick up our spirits."

She did not offer to drive the Hupp, but for a tick of time she frowned as though something bothered her about a visit to the Cowans' house. Then she smiled at me and waved me on my way.

Out in the yard, a breeze stirred the fine-grained grape leaves on the arbor, rustled the coarse kudzu. The swing's heavy board held the ropes motionless, those hemp ropes that reached far into the dark pine shadows above. It hung, quiet, an animal's quiet, waiting for me and my promise to conquer it this summer.

Would Daddy call me his little trooper if, when he

returned for my birthday, I had won out against the swing? Gathering my courage, I resolved to touch that farthest branch with my bottom by the last week in July. "With my dear rear," I said aloud in deference to Mother's sensibilities.

I hoisted myself onto the seat. My feet missed the ground by quite a bit. Shakily I arose, balanced on the board, tightened my grip on the bulky ropes, and began to pump. Yes, good to be alone. No one to see the jerky effort. It took weight to bend the tough hemp strands, weight I lacked. At last I managed the initial sway. After that it went more easily. The pendulum sweep gradually widened. Foot-thrust-arm-pull, forward and up; relax, ride the back sweep. And over again. Thrust and pull and forward and up; sweep back, pause, and plunge; thrust and pull and forward and up; sweep back, pause, and plunge. All this I had done before.

Almost imperceptibly the arc increased. High, higher I flew, until, at last, the air on the back sweep made me laugh. Hair whipped forward, blanking sight. Coveralls fluttered against shanks. Wind pressed on spine and bottom like some great invisible hand. My stomach tickled. My private parts tingled. I chortled aloud. And pumped with every fiber of my being. Again. Again. Again. Each time soaring farther. Each time horizon wider. Each time ground more distant.

At last, certainty—this time or next there would be the touch of that lofty horizontal branch. My rear quivered, awaiting the brush of it. Fear? Forgotten! Oh, joyous triumph.

Once more. Surely this last great thrust, and victory

would be mine. Arms, legs, body strained at the ropes.
Tremendous back sweep . . . no touch of branch . . .
moment of pause . . . swing motion stopped . . . a frozen second . . .

Poised there with the world small below, I relaxed
for only an instant, leaned my weight against the ropes.
In that final second it happened. The tight ropes sagged
in my hands. No other warning. Suddenly the board's
pressure under my soles vanished. I, a soaring bird, wing
shorn in midflight. An endless second of free fall.

I stiffened. With a wicked snap the ropes yanked taut
again. My trusty tennis shoes lost their perch. My hands
skidded down the rough hemp. Somehow they kept their
hold. Legs flailed. Feet searched. But the board escaped
them. It thumped against my bottom. The swing
swooped down. I hung on like grim death.

At the bottom of the arc, my feet hit the ground with
a terrible thud. My fingers ripped from their hold. My
body slid and tumbled, end over end, in the dirt. At
last I lay still on pine needles. Shaken, stunned, skinned,
scared, I sat up. The world continued to spin. A fist
of pain clutched in my stomach. It kept me from yelling.

A strong hand lifted me to my feet. A man's voice
said, "You surely got a peck a spunk, flyin' lark high
thataway. I was afeard you'd never come down, Missy.
You be all right?"

"Yes," I gasped, wondering if it were true, abashed
that anyone had seen me. "The rope looped. It shook
me loose." Tears burned behind my lids.

"It sure enough did. Like I said, you was as spunky
as all get-out, not lettin' go."

There was something about him that reminded me of America.

"Are you a Woodall?" My words sounded a little strangled. But I managed not to cry for the moment, pleased he thought I had a peck of spunk.

"I'm Beau Tulley. Come to help your momma for the summer. My own momma is a second cousin twice removed of America Woodall."

Beau Tulley. Dark-haired, handsome Beau. Serious of voice, laughing of eye, he stood looking down at me.

"I been a-watchin' you, sailin' back'ards and for'ards, pretty as a swallow bird. You got a awful wallop though, when the swing ducktailed on you, and you just about ready to touch the sky, too."

It was easy now to see he was a Woodall relative. His eyes, like America's, were blue as a jay's wing, but a crackling, sharp-edged blue because his were a good sight younger than hers.

He was brushing the dirt from my coveralls, and went right on talking as he turned me around, checking for breaks or blood. He gently shook each of my arms, my legs, stooping close enough for me to catch the smell of fresh work sweat, of wood smoke, and of his naphtha-washed shirt. Satisfied I was all in one piece, he straightened again.

"You be a peart little old thing"—his eyes danced, admiring, mischievous at the same time—"hangin' on to them ropes tight as Satan to a sinner."

My heart bounded up and I fell in love for the first time in my life, fell in love with the masculine face that smiled down at me. A young face, lean and rich in color from sun and wind, firm jawed, firm lipped, as handsome as any prince from a storybook. Beyond that, he would be the man around the place to keep us safe through the summer with Daddy too busy in town, with Daddy sailing off to England for a visit with Aunt Arlene.

Free-floating love attaches itself to someone; it was easy to let my heart go to Beau as he finished, "—and spunky as a little old bluetick pup."

Spunky and peart. These seemed even better than trooper. I smiled back at Beau Tulley and took his hand to lead him in to Mother.

11

The Grand Dragon's Family

It was a mistake that afternoon for us to call on the Cowans. A week later when Blainey received an invitation to a tea party there, Mother wrote a polite note of refusal, polite but plainly revealing without unladylike bluntness that any other invitation would receive the same response.

The whole thing came back to me weeks later, that terrible night at the end of August when we returned to Atlanta with George driving the Hupp for us, that night when the Klan fires lit up Stone Mountain as though the devil himself had painted it with flickering light. The night Mr. Cowan's voice came from behind the white hood and for the first time I had an inkling of what the Klan and its Grand Dragon were about.

Strangely, that afternoon when we visited the Cowans, it was the Shetland pony that caused the real trouble. We hadn't bothered with the Hupp, but walked
over since it was only a couple of miles. The dappled
shade along the way was pleasant. Blainey and I, foraging on either side of the track, forgot our loneliness at
Daddy's departure.

Finally, tiring of side excursions, we hiked sedately
along with Mother, arriving in good spirits at the old
two-story Jefferson house. The last part of the way,
Mother had started us off singing rounds, Blainey and
I together against her stronger voice.

We finished "Row, Row, Row Your Boat" as we
turned in at the gate. The covered porch, stretching
the width of the house, was pleasant and shady. Mother
knocked on the door. I noticed Mr. Cowan's shoes of
last night. They sat on the railing in the sun. Someone
had covered the sewn split with black polish. The hard
twine had refused the color. It still showed gray against
the black leather.

It seemed a long time before the door opened a crack.
One of Mrs. Cowan's beautiful eyes peered out. Under
its sharp, cool inspection we passed muster, the door
swung wider. She smiled at us.

"How neighborly of you to come visiting," she said.

A tightness at the corners of her mouth, a thinning
of the upper lip, were the only signs that not all casual
visitors were welcomed here.

"Come right along in," she said smoothly to Mother.
"We'll have a nice chat and a cup of tea while the girls
get acquainted. Mr. Cowan is fixing a rail in the pony's

pasture. The nasty little beast kicked it loose yesterday."

Through my inner avid desire to see the pony, a brief uneasiness arose at the word "nasty." But mostly, at the moment, we were curious, Blainey and I, about the inside of the old Jefferson house. We remained demurely silent, but our eyes were busy. Despite those cracked shoes on the porch, it was plain the Cowans didn't lack for money.

The bright slipcovers of the furniture matched the window drapes. Indian-design throw rugs hid most of the wide pine boards of the floor. There were numerous small tables with veneer tops of imitation inlaid wood, and several wicker stands with lush cascading ferns. A large dining table and chairs with bentwood backs filled the end of the room near the kitchen. The house itself had stood empty for several years. It would have cost a pretty penny for the Cowans to bring all of this up from Atlanta. Grand Dragoning must pay well.

"Oh, don't you bother with tea," Mother was saying. "We just dropped by for a friendly call. The girls were dying to meet your children, and Mr. Cowan was good enough to invite them to stop in today."

"Yes," said Mrs. Cowan, still smiling. "Perhaps tea a little later."

"How do you like it here in the mountains?" Mother was asking as we trooped in and settled on the flowered cretonne. Her voice had that surfacy sound that adults use before they're really friends—very polite, a little higher than usual, faintly, oddly false. "Are the children enjoying themselves? It must be great fun for them with the pony."

Mother posed her fingers with ladylike delicacy on a lace antimacassar. The questions were meant to keep the words moving back and forth. Surely there was some social rule governing this. Only children let silences happen. Silences, like spilled milk or muddy feet or nosebleeds or chicken pox, must be a blight of the young. Though occasionally there was a grown-up, like Aunt Ellie, who understood how really nice a silence could be.

My heart warmed at the thought of Ellie and of our closeness together last night on the porch. I felt suddenly secure and happy knowing she and Uncle Frank would be our good neighbors through the summer. The same as last year. The same as it would be next. And America Woodall, and all the little Woodalls. And now there was Beau Tulley. I almost wished I had stayed at Cloudacres to watch him work.

Sitting there in the Cowans' cheerful parlor with the aimless talk flowing over me, I forgot about my Suffragette's promise of change. Instead my mind fastened on all the permanent and comfortable things in my life— the long summer before us, walks in the woods and picnics down at the creek; picking apples in Hayes Field; the Woodall kids to play with; Hooligan enjoying his freedom, and in the evening arching his back against our legs, his gravelly demands for food, his head butting into our hands for petting. And tonight Mother would start reading "The Covered Wagon" to America and Blainey and me. The Cowans were impermanent, not included on this list of old and everlasting blessings.

I thought only for a moment of Daddy's absence. Besides, at the end of summer we'd all be together again. In September there would be the second grade for me with all the fears of the first grade left behind. Yes, in the fall I'd be an old hand at the Greenwood Avenue School. An easy September—friends from last year and teachers who knew me.

But then, my errant thoughts summoned up the picture of George. George standing before the house on Greenwood, watching us leave for a mountain summer without him. And now from across the months my Suffragette did wave and call her promise. Unreasonable fear swept me, as chilling and dark as the leading edge of a winter storm. I wished George had not stayed in Atlanta to care for Daddy. I wished Daddy was going to be with us as in other years so he'd have no need for George in town.

Well, never mind, the end of summer would come. . . . I remembered the Shetland pony. How soon could I excuse myself to go and find it?

We heard muffled giggles, the soft but repeated opening and closing of the kitchen door. Now after a flurry of audible whispers, the giggles burst forth into stifled laughter, and the door banged harder than before—the Cowan girls, being blatantly rude.

Blainey drew herself up with haughty dignity, ignoring the foolish girls. But I didn't care about them anyway; only the Shetland pony claimed my interest. Why had Mrs. Cowan called it a nasty little beast? Why did she own a pony if she hated it so much? I itched to slip away to find him. The leggy size of Mr. Govan's Bobby had always awed me, and the massive cows that sometimes wandered loose to graze the roadside grasses were terrifying.

But this Shetland would be even smaller than the Welsh mountain pony, Greylight, of the *Saint Nicholas* story. I pictured myself on such a sturdy little mount flying swiftly, nobly, safely through the dells and byways, over the crest of the Blue Ridge range, as far as Tallulah Falls, or even north to Rabun Gap and Rabun Bald.

Finally, unable to ignore her daughters any longer, Mrs. Cowan snapped, "*Girls.* Come in here this minute, you hear, and stop acting like two young heathens!"

I slid from my chair and asked, "Could I see the pony?" But the Cowan girls came bursting in, choking back their giggles, and no one heard me.

The younger, Cora Jane, was as tall as Blainey, and the other, Una Lynn, was even bigger than Marilyn Louise Carstairs in town.

"Take your little guests out and show them around," Mrs. Cowan said, smiling her tight smile. "You may each pick an apple from the tree by the garage."

But there had been times when Blainey and I had picked as many apples as we wanted from Hayes Field, and the thought of apples held no charm for me today. Outside, I repeated softly, "Could I see the pony, please?"

Cora Jane and Una Lynn burst into laughter. "You don't really want to see him," Cora Jane said, quickly sobering, and she shot a sidelong glance at her sister.

"Sure she does." Una Lynn turned to me, pointed toward a path that led off to the right. "Go on along there. You'll see a shed with a fenced yard. He's shut up in the yard. Daddy's over on the far side of the big pasture mending the place where Lucifer tried to kick out yesterday."

"Daddy really laid into him for that. He whipped him until Lucifer squealed." Cora Jane looked strangely woebegone for a moment. "And I cried."

But Una Lynn only laughed again. "You cry easy!" she said. A flicker of sympathy arose in my breast for Cora Jane. "Besides, like Daddy says, niggers and horses do better with a good whipping every once in a while."

My stomach felt suddenly sick, and Blainey stiffened, but Una Lynn did not notice. Instead she pointed the way for me again. "Go along that path there, you'll see him."

"Lucifer. That's a funny name for a pony." Blainey's tawny eyes studied the girls.

"A funny name? Not really," said Una Lynn. "It suits him." And she and her sister were off into another gale of giggles. They laughed more than any other girls I had ever met, but somehow it wasn't catching. I watched solemnly until they stopped for breath.

"Would Lucifer mind if I patted him?" I asked.

"Coax him over with a bunch of grass. He loves green grass. Then you can reach through the rails and stroke his side. He's very silky. Rub him real good," said Una Lynn, but there was something in her looks that made me vaguely uneasy.

When Cora Jane started to say something she got such a jab from her sister's elbow, she cowered away and started to cry. Una Lynn, unperturbed, asked Blainey with a thumb thrust in my direction, "What's the matter with *her*? She's sure a sobersides."

As I turned and trotted off down the path, Blainey was saying, "She laughs when something's funny. She just doesn't see what the joke is." I might have felt betrayed, but Blainey added firmly, "And, really, neither do I."

"You will," said Una Lynn snickering, but then she seemed bored with the thought of Lucifer. "Let's go pick apples. We can take as many as we want. Mother won't know the difference. Besides, they're still green."

"Then we can't eat them anyway," said Blainey, and I waited, thinking she might follow after me to see the pony.

"Who cares? It's fun to yank 'em off the tree. We can throw 'em at a fence post and see who's the best shot."

"If they stay on the tree they'll be ripe later."

"So what? They'll probably still be green when *we* leave the middle of August. My father has to be back in Atlanta for business then. There's going to be a Grand Konclave out at Stone Mountain the end of August." There was pride in her voice at this last announcement. "My father is head of the whole Georgia Klan."

"You're not supposed to talk about that." It was Cora Jane.

"Nobody'll know unless you tell 'em, blabbermouth."

What kind of business did the Grand Dragon have in the city? And why shouldn't Cora Jane talk about it? With the hope that the bigger girl would explain further about the Konclave, I stayed where I was, partway down the path that ran beside the fence. There the tall grass hid me from view.

But their talk had held Blainey and she did not join me. "You two and your mother could stay on up here. And your brother," she said. "You have a brother, don't you?"

"Yes. Henry's his name. He's six and puny." Una Lynn's voice was flat, as though Henry didn't count for much.

"Well, anyway, you could stay here until school starts, even if your father does go down to Atlanta," Blainey went on. "Ours has to be in Atlanta all summer this year, but Mother and Magpie and I will stay at Cloud-acres alone."

"Magpie?" Una Lynn said.

"My sister."

Una Lynn snorted her mirthless laughter. "What a dumb name! Magpie! Magpie!" She made the name I loved from Blainey sound ugly and foolish.

"Aren't you scared, staying alone?" It was Cora Jane, recovered from her tears—the nicer one, I had decided, for she had sorrowed over her beaten pony.

"Not a bit," Blainey said airily.

"*My* father wouldn't think of leaving *us* alone," Una Lynn's voice rose in angry superiority. "What if some crazy nigger came prowling around, and you had no man here to protect you?"

It seemed to me Una Lynn needed about as much protection as a buzz saw.

"Our daddy knows we're very capable." Blainey's tone was cold and haughty. I knew she was giving Una

Lynn her *look*, the one that always withered and silenced me. "Besides," she continued, "I've never heard of any crazy people around here, colored *or* white. We're probably safer at Cloudacres than in the city."

But Una Lynn would not be stifled. "A lady should always have a man's protection. *My* father says those young black bucks are just looking for a chance to catch a white woman alone. He says that's all they ever think about—how to catch one of us alone. And when they do, they turn into savages and do awful, terrible things, like—"

But they had been moving off, on their way to the green-apple tree. Una Lynn's voice diminished so I couldn't hear as she went on, detailing, I suppose, the awful terrible things. I thought of George and decided the Cowan girls probably made up beastly stories to be important. My mind turned fully to the thought of Lucifer as I ran along the path.

12

Lucifer

The hammering that we had heard earlier was going on unabated. The thick curtain of grass that screened me did nothing to muffle the sound. Farther along, the path came out into the open. There, away across the pasture, was Mr. Cowan still struggling with the broken rails. But near at hand stood the shed inside its small fenced yard.

Lucifer heard me, for he raised his head from the trough with its meager sheaf of dry hay. A golden wisp hung from his mouth. He gave a tentative chew. His ears came forward. He tossed his small fine head; the forelock fell shaggily over his brown eyes, eyes that showed wild rims of white around the edges.

"Good boy, Lucifer," I said quietly. "Don't be scared."

Plain to see, across his firm shiny rump and over the bowed ribs of his barrel, were the stripes of Mr. Cowan's whip, the stripes that had made him squeal. Suddenly, I hated the thickset man there across the pasture. Lucifer shimmered through my angry tears. I longed to console him. Then Una Lynn's words came back to me—*He loves green grass.* Not a sprig of green remained inside the enclosure, and for a double handspan outside the fence the ground was also bare. Even as I watched, Lucifer thrust his muzzle through, his lips winnowed for the nearest but unreachable blade.

I rushed back to where the grasses grew thick and tall beside the path, began to snatch handfuls. Lucifer was smart. He knew exactly what I was doing. He gave a sharp, commanding whicker. Through the curtain of waving green, I saw Mr. Cowan jerk and straighten.

"Shut up, you ugly little devil!" he shouted, angry with his work and the cause of it.

Lucifer laid back his ears, made a quick hard kick at the air with both neat hind hooves. But Mr. Cowan had returned to his hammering, unaware of Lucifer's riposte or of my presence.

To forestall another whicker, I rushed over with what I had already picked, thrust it through the rails. Eagerly, Lucifer's lips fanned forward and like soft unfingered hands gathered in the sweet stalks. In his greed, his teeth grazed my fingers. I snatched my hand away, dropping the grass. With a wary white-rimmed eye on me, Lucifer scavenged for the fallen blades. I could hear those teeth, so large and yellow for such an undersized beast, chomp hollowly on the stems.

I rushed back to wrench away more grass, flew to the corral again to forestall that aggressive whicker. But then I hesitated. What if Lucifer, in his avid efforts, bit me? A terrifying thought. I still ached from my earlier fall, and though Beau Tulley had admired my spunk, the swing episode had used up my quota of daring for this day.

It came to me, if Lucifer had to stretch for the grass his teeth couldn't reach me. I held the stalks far from the rails. Eagerly he thrust his muzzle through, strained forward with his neck, but nervously I jerked away. Angered, he butted at the stringers with vicious strength until it seemed that Mr. Cowan would surely hear us.

"Oh, Lucifer," I cried in a whisper, "no, oh no—"

I scrambled up the ladder of rails until I balanced with my knees braced against the top. Holding the grass well above the pony's nose, I trembled for us both—I in danger of being chomped, Lucifer in jeopardy of Mr. Cowan's ire and whip. The pony stretched his neck, lipped the blades down into the grinding machine of molars.

With great relief, I smiled. But at that moment, Lucifer decided he had been cheated of the great mouthful he expected for his efforts. With a hop of his front hooves, he reared up, agile as a dog, grabbed the rest of the grass. Only reflex saved my hand. I yanked away, almost fell backward, lunged forward to regain balance. The top rail caught my knees, levered my feet from their perch. I flipped into the small corral with Lucifer. In terror I scrambled up. But Lucifer, ignoring me, only continued to search the ground for fallen grass.

Now with no fence between us, he looked overpowering, huge. Still, he was not even half the size of old Bobby, and in his foraging he had turned away from me. Instead of the head with its white-rimmed eyes and fearsome teeth, there close enough to touch was the round sleek side. Una Lynn had said to rub him real good. My uneasiness at the look she had given me was forgotten.

Now, tentatively, I reached. My fingers barely touched the brown hide. It quivered for a tick of time. But Lucifer had not even looked around. Boldly, I put the flat of my hand against him. He was silky as Una Lynn had promised. And warm and faintly moist under my palm. For a moment my stomach tickled with the same elation that had buoyed me when I had flown so high in the swing.

Then there had been no warning before the disastrous loop of the rope. Now there was no hint of danger. My hand slid along the lovely sleek living body. I had forgotten the ridged whip cuts until I felt them scrape under my palm.

A rattlesnake could not have struck more swiftly. One moment I had my hand on Lucifer's side. The next he whirled, fastened his teeth on my upper arm. A single quick bite, instant release, then again he whirled. The pain from those yellow chomping teeth sent me lunging away. It was the only thing that saved me from his wicked heels, for I fell over my own feet, lay flat on my back as Lucifer's lightning hooves lashed once, twice, three times above me. Then he went bucking away in the small enclosure.

Later I could not remember how I cleared the fence as Lucifer completed his sunfishing circle. It must have been done in complete silence, for Mr. Cowan had not even stopped his hammering when I stood once more on the grass-curtained path.

Which was more wounded? My arm or my feelings? I had trusted Lucifer. But he had lived up to his name. It suits him, Una Lynn had said. Devilishly he had bitten me when I had offered only grass and love. Beyond tears, I fled up the hidden path, out and across the Cowans' yard. I crept into the parlor, quiet, subdued, eyes downcast.

Mother and Mrs. Cowan were drinking tea after all. They did not interrupt their conversation. But Mother reached, put her arm around my back. My own arm grew more painful by the minute, throbbing and hot. Afraid she would bump it, I drew away from her hand. She glanced at me, then back to Mrs. Cowan with no break in the smoothly flowing talk. Her fingers brushed my forehead, her palm slid to my cheek, a touch familiar to me, feeling for fever. So she had noticed how subdued I was.

Despite my own misery, a small movement at the back of the room caught my eye. A boy stood there in the dimness of the doorway. Certainly Henry, puny Henry. He seemed very small for six. His large shadowed eyes looked fearfully out at me. There appeared to be nothing in him of his aggressive father; and how unlikely a brother to the rude, raucous girls. Only those beautiful eyes, staring from the shadows, showed a link with any one of the Cowans. They were as large, blue, dark lashed as his mother's. Still, the resemblance ended there, for hers were cool and calculating, while his were as timorous as a rabbit's.

Even while I watched, he faded from sight, erased by the sudden sound of girls' laughter rushing in at us, and moments later the girls themselves. Even Blainey seemed caught up in some huge joke, but she subsided quickly while Una Lynn and Cora Jane kept laughing as though at private secrets of surpassing hilarity. In spite of the increasing pain of my arm and feelings, I could see that Blainey had had enough of the two Cowan girls. Immediately she crossed and settled on the other side of Mother.

"Hello, chicken little," Mother said, and finally she removed her attention from Mrs. Cowan. My side vision caught the two girls as they shot looks in my direction. The big one nudged her sister, who seemed to have become apprehensive.

"We must be on our way home," Mother was saying. "Beau is probably through with mending our fence and the trellises. He won't know what to do next. Yes, we'd better be going along."

"Good," Blainey muttered, while Una Lynn and Cora Jane whispered together.

But Mother ignored this, arose, turned to me, asked, "Did you see the pony, hon?"

Now the Cowan girls fell suddenly silent, waiting. When the only answer Mother had to her question was a bob of my head, she realized a fever was not my difficulty. She sat down again, drew me to her. As she brushed my arm, I winced away from her once more.

Without a word she gently pushed up my sleeve. Even I was shocked at the sight. Lucifer hadn't broken the skin, but there on my upper arm were his deeply imbedded tooth marks, a clear horseshoe curve of them below my shoulder cap. Already the surrounding bruised flesh was darkening though the pits left by his teeth remained dead white.

Mother's voice was very quiet. "Did you do anything to the pony to make him bite you?"

"I fed him some grass," I whispered. "When I smoothed his side I touched the place where he was whipped. I didn't mean to."

But the words brought home the enormity of Lucifer's betrayal and the guilt of my own callous complicity. Against my will, tears squeezed from beneath my lids, my nose began to run, saliva thickened in my mouth. It became hard to breathe, for my chest was puffed up like a balloon with held-back crying.

Maybe if Mr. Cowan had not come at that moment, I would, somehow, have conquered this breakdown and we could have left, dignity intact. Instead, the front screen banged open and in stomped Mr. Cowan, speaking before he saw there was company.

"If that damn pony kicks a hole in the fence again, I'll get out my shotgun—"

But at sight of Mother and Blainey and me, his face cleared, the jovial smile of last evening returned. "Well, a roomful of lovely ladies. What an engagin' sight this is after a most aggravatin' morning—"

"Lucifer bit Magpie," Una Lynn announced.

The use of Blainey's name for me was more of an

affront than her hidden smirk of triumph. Cora Jane
started to cry.

Suddenly Mr. Cowan realized he had walked in on
more than a social conversation. His quick eye fastened
on my upper arm where Mother held it tenderly with
the sleeve lifted away.

"Why that ugly devil!" Mr. Cowan grated, instantly
a furious man with vengeance in his heart. "Don't you
worry, little lady"—he softened his voice for me, reached
and patted my head. "I'll take the whip to him real
good. This time he won't likely forget it. I'll break that
ornery spirit of his or kill him trying!" He turned to
make off toward the front door, talking to me over his
shoulder. "Don't you feel bad, sugar. I'll make him sorry
he ever set his big nasty teeth in your sweet little arm."

The awful words opened the dam of my tears. How
unbearable for the whip to fall across the already tor-
tured sides of Lucifer. I remembered the brave, sassy
lash of his heels in answer to Mr. Cowan's earlier
shouted threat. I knew Lucifer would die rather than
have his spirit broken. Now Cora Jane's quiet sobs were
lost in my own desperate wail.

In amazement Mr. Cowan wheeled about. It was obvious he had thought my pain and fright would be as-
suaged by the prospect of new agony for Lucifer.

"You want to watch me whip him, honey—" he began,
and at my increasing volume of sound puzzlement
creased his ruddy face.

But staunch, blessed Blainey spoke for me.

"She's not crying because Lucifer bit her. She's crying
because you're going to whip him."

"What?" Mr. Cowan's quandary increased.

"It was Una Lynn's fault more than the pony's," Blainey said.

When Una Lynn pointed at her and cried, "Liar! Liar!" Blainey only stared coldly back and continued, "She told my sister to go on down and pat Lucifer if she wanted to, and to rub his side real good." Now she turned to me. "Is that why he bit you, Magpie? Did you rub his side?"

Then she came and put her arm around my shoulder, lending me strength to face up to the terrible Cowans. With an effort, I stifled the gulps and sobs, nodded a vigorous assent.

"She probably rubbed him by mistake where you had whipped Lucifer before."

Her tawny accusing eyes did not waver before Mr. Cowan's incredulous stare. But his hand went to the shoulder of big Una Lynn.

"Why, I don't think my little girl would do a mean thing like that. Now would you, sugar?" he asked her.

Before Una Lynn could answer, Cora Jane burst out, "She did! As sure as God's in heaven, she did, Poppa. She wanted to see you whip Lucifer again. It's her should have the whipping!"

Now with great dignity Mother arose.

"We must really be going along. Margery's arm will be all right. It's just pinched. The skin isn't even broken. You mustn't worry about it. Not for a minute, you hear? And you certainly must not whip the little pony." Her voice remained polite, but she added as though each word held special significance, "That would be most unfair and cruel. We would be heartbroken to hear that you had punished Lucifer."

She pushed Blainey and me before her. At the door she turned, gave a cool smile in the direction of her hostess. "Thank you kindly for the delicious cup of tea, Mrs. Cowan. Good afternoon to you all."

In moments we were down the drive, out the gate. We paused for Mother to settle her wide-brimmed straw hat on her head, tie the streamers beneath her chin. As I stared back at the house, there was a movement of curtain at the upper window.

Henry Cowan peered down at me. I remembered Mr. Cowan's threat to break the spirit of Lucifer, I recalled Mrs. Cowan's hard hand and fierce gaze last night when I trod on her gown. Now Henry's big timorous eyes looking through the window, across the yard into mine, made me wonder if the Grand Dragon or his wife had anything to do with their expression.

13

The Enticement of Beau

By evening I was running a fever, and though my arm was no worse and the pits left by Lucifer's teeth had almost leveled out, I tossed in my sleep and cried aloud. In my dreams, a fire-breathing dragon pursued a beautiful, little wild pony with me astride its back. Though the pony ran as fast as the wind, the dragon roared down on us like a freight train, rumbling and filling the air with smoke and flame and showers of sparks. The pony fought valiantly to escape the slash of cruel razor claws, but he was no match for the dragon. In the melee, I was thrown free to watch in frozen terror. I screamed in my sleep as the pony was torn to ribbons and the dragon turned on me.

Finally Mother woke me. It was some time before

she could stop my crying. Then she said, "Come and get in bed with me, sugar. Nothing can scare you there."

It was true. The feel of her soft warm ample presence in the bed beside me was even more reassuring than having Daddy in the house with us.

But it was Aunt Ellie who really effected my cure. She stopped by next morning, came into the bedroom where I sat propped in bed, listlessly coloring pictures.

"What's the matter, little love?" she asked softly.

It was a relief to tell her of yesterday, to put my terrible anxiety into words.

"What if Mr. Cowan whips Lucifer to break his spirit?" My chin began to tremble.

Ellie smoothed the hair from my forehead; the light smell of flowers came to me as she bent and kissed my cheek.

"The Cowans really should not own a pony. I understand they only bought it for the summer to entertain the girls." She straightened, smiled down at me. "Uncle Frank and I will drive down that way, and I'll see what can be done to save Lucifer. Don't you worry anymore, Margery, my love." She bent again, gave me a firm little pat, and left.

My bedroom windows overlooked cleared land with open forest beyond. Daddy had started a small vegetable patch in the clearing. Fresh summer vegetables were a special blessing for our vegetarian fare. Today the garden proved to be a blessing in another way, for presently Beau appeared, hoe in hand. The sight of him promised to liven this weary morning. He began to weed up and down the rows.

His beautiful back showed beneath the tight stretch of the faded blue work shirt. The muscles of his forearms turned smoothly inside their tan flawless skin. His biceps, snugly banded by the rolled-up sleeves, swelled, relaxed, swelled as he swung the hoe. Seeing him there dulled my worry over Lucifer.

Beau proved to be a treasure to Mother that summer. He was good at the work, but even better at talk. When Mother settled into a bit of conversation with Beau on the veranda or in the yard where he worked, she would become animated, flush a little, her eyes would brighten and the sadness there would disappear. Sometimes Blainey took Beau over for a while, as pleased as Mother at his attention.

But I knew he belonged to me. After all, it was he who had found me wounded and lifted me up the day of the swing disaster. He had told me I was as spunky as a bluetick pup, and admired how bravely I flew lark high. We had held hands and I had taken him to Mother. His crystal-clear eyes still kept a certain look for me, of that I was positive. Without Daddy he was our man, but most especially mine.

Now as he stooped to uproot a stubborn weed, the patched denim of his breeches outlined the neat proportions of his hard rear and thighs. He stood, wiped the crook of his arm across his brow, leaned on the hoe, gazed off across flats and uplands and piny ridges to the smoky far hills. Even from my bed I could see that incredible blue of his eyes. Presently he went back to work again. Beneath the hot June sun the cotton shirt darkened along the line of his spine and in a circle beneath each arm.

Fever made me drowsy. Added to the pleasure of watching Beau, there was the comfort of Mother's and America's voices drifting down the hall. My eyelids drooped. I must have dozed.

Beau's laugh inserted itself into my sleep. A masculine sound, yet soft, intimate. For a moment I dreamed it came from beside my bed. A delicious pleasure filled me. I reached to take his big hands in mine, remembering how they felt the day of the swing. Then fully awake, I saw Beau still in the vegetable patch beyond my window. Now his hoe lay idle on the ground.

Again his laugh, low, careless. An altogether entrancing sound. But it was not for me. Nor were his fine hands in mine. Instead, for this moment, they rested easily on a pair of feminine shoulders. I saw them give a gentle shake to those shoulders, the girl's tousled yellow hair swung fetchingly in response. Beau's hands dropped away as her light laughter joined with his. They stood in animated talk, their voices murmuring together. I strained to catch the inaudible words.

Once Beau's hand reached to slide down the wind-blown long hair. His palm passed over the last strand, down to the limber swaying waist, briefly on to the rounded curve below. He gave it a light pat. I wondered if she was as thinly clad as the little mountain girls. She reached to trap his hand with hers, to hold it there on her bottom. He was adroit. His hand moved quickly to brush something from her forehead, then he stepped back a step, still talking his soft talk, untrapped.

America tiptoed into the room. She peered into my face. Her eyes, almost as blue as Beau's, lit with her smile.

"Well, you be awake now. Would a mite to eat pleasure our sweet chile? Good eatin' keeps up the stren'th."

Suddenly the reason for my being in bed came to mind. Lucifer! Worry sprang alive again and stole my appetite. A quick burst of merriment from outside turned America's gaze to the window. She stooped her gaunt frame a bit, squinted nearsightedly.

"Well, look at that. What's that little no-'count Noni doin' clear over here? She's a far piece from home."

"She came to talk to Beau." Jealousy turned my voice sour. "Who's Noni?"

"Noni Shattock. Old man Shattock's place is up on the tableland. He's head of the Shattock clan. Noni is fourth of his second son's passel o' chillun."

"How did she know where to find Beau?"

America chuckled. "How does a homin' pigeon find its roost?"

"Is Beau her sweetheart?"

"Not so's you'd notice. Beau's got his sights set a notch higher'n Noni."

"He likes her a lot, though."

"Likin' and sweetheartin' ain't necessarily two peas in a pod. Beau likes a little moonshine likker now and again, too, but he don't let it play king with him. Beau's not one to wear the bells."

"Wear the bells?" I asked.

Frequently America was difficult to make out. Mother

said sometimes it was because her words harked back to the original mountaineers, settlers from old England.

"Beau ain't nobody's fool," she said, and interposed her body between me and the window, eclipsing Beau and Noni. She leaned toward me, looking down with affectionate eyes.

"Now what about some vittles to bring stren'th back to our little girl?"

"No thank you, America." I slid down in bed, pulled the sheet higher. "I'm awfully sleepy."

"Maybe sleep's best," America agreed.

She straightened my pillow, turned it, smoothed the sheet across my shoulders. Her rough hand rested briefly on my crown. Then she was gone.

My breath felt hot, my eyes burned, my head ached. The thought of Lucifer pestered me again. And even Noni Shattock wasn't worth rising up for.

It was Ellie's and Mother's voices that awoke me.

"—no trouble at all," Aunt Ellie was saying. She laughed an airy trill. "The Mr. Cowans of this world respond to ladylike wiles, especially when we give a secret, slight showing of our claws."

None of the sadness came through in Mother's voice now. Instead she sounded very pleased with Ellie. "Do tell me how you managed it."

"I said to him, I simply could not live without owning that beautiful little pony, and I was sure everyone hereabouts would think him a perfect beast if I let it be known he wouldn't sell me Lucifer, especially since we all knew their family would have to dispose of the pony when they go back to town."

"Ellie, you minx!"

"That last was just a stab in the dark, but it worked, Mase. His pride didn't want to be brought down. And he wanted to play the gentleman with me if it killed him."

The two of them went off into a gale of laughter. Mother and Ellie laughed a lot together. Their friendship was made of closeness and understanding.

"Oh, Ellie, you're really a caution!" Mother said.

"Yes," Ellie agreed, "I guess I am! But I feel responsible for Margy's troubles. After all, if we hadn't invited the Cowans to our party—"

"Now, now," Mother soothed, but then, puzzled, she asked, "How in the world *did* the Cowans ever wangle that invitation?"

"Frank says I have more heart than sense, sometimes." Ellie's voice turned rueful. "Mrs. Cowan was at the Tiger store when I was shopping there. She dropped a package. Frank picked it up for her. Somehow we wound up chatting. She said how lonely it was up here in the mountains. And *I* asked her to the party."

There was exasperation with herself in Ellie's voice. Then she and Mother were laughing together again. Presently, though, she went on somberly.

"There seemed nothing I could do for the little boy when I was there this morning. Poor sickly little fellow."

"I didn't see him yesterday," Mother said. "Is something wrong with him?"

"He slipped in from a back room and sidled up to

me while I was talking with his mother. She said he's six, but the little thing looks and acts more like a puny four-year-old."

"Poor chick."

"Mrs. Cowan gave a great, gusty sigh as though even the sight of Henry was a heavy burden to her."

"Such an unpleasant woman," Mother murmured.

"She is that. Really cruel when she told me right in front of the boy that they think he's very backward. Dim in his wits she said."

"Mrs. Cowan has a very chilly eye."

"She told me, 'Ethan tried to strengthen him, to make a little man of him.' It made me shudder when she said that."

"Such a difficult family for a sensitive child."

Mother sounded as upset as Ellie.

"Little Henry Cowan seemed more frightened than dimwitted to me."

"A gentle spirit in a harsh household?"

"I'm afraid so." Then Ellie went on, puzzled, "A strange thing though—as we drove away, I glanced back. Mr. Cowan had appeared from somewhere. He picked Henry up, lifted him quite tenderly. And Henry laid his head on his father's shoulder. Mrs. Cowan was no longer in sight. Well, I suppose there is some good in even the worst men." But Ellie's voice lightened as she finished, "One can't cure all the world's ills. At least the pony is safe."

"Where is he now?" Mother asked.

"In a fenced field in the southeast corner of our acres. Pauly John brought him over for me. That boy is so

good with animals. He's promised to curry and feed
and water the pony every day. And even to take care
of him when we leave in the fall. There's a snug little
barn at Pinewood that can house Lucifer during the
cold months."

"Lucifer! Don't you just love that name!"

"Very apt. He does have a devilish temper, you know."

"Not improved by the Cowans, I'm sure."

"The Cowans would turn an angel ugly! Still, the
pony is saved, Pauly John will earn some extra spending
money, and when dear Margery wakes she'll be happy.
You'll see, Mase, her fever will leave and even her arm
will be cured."

You could hear in the way that Ellie laughed how
pleased she was with herself and with the way the ar-
rangements benefited all. Ellie would have liked the
whole world happy.

Ellie Benton—the good fairy of my story books. It
is too bad her magic could not perform all the miracles
we needed.

She was right, though. By nightfall my fever was gone,
and even my arm had improved. I had almost forgotten
Noni's enticement of Beau, though the memory of that
sprang up life-sized the second night of August.

A week later when we found Mrs. Cowan's note in
the mailbox asking Blainey to a tea party, Mother wrote
the reply at once, firmly, very politely refusing the invitation. Beau delivered it for her. The Cowans could not
miss the fact they had been snubbed.

14

The Grand Shindig

July twenty-eighth, and Daddy arrived just after mid-night. Blainey and I had been in bed for hours. She was asleep, but I had been restless, turning and tossing. The hall clock had just struck twelve when the sound of voices brought me wide awake. First Daddy's. My heart leaped up with joy and a terrible relief. Thirty-five kids had been invited for tomorrow's party—the grand shindig Daddy had promised me in June. Tomor-row's party? No. Today! Thirty-five mountain kids—Woodalls, Shattocks, Tulleys, Martins, Creaseys.

All week I had been in a panic of excitement, tension, terror. Suppose Daddy, in this summer that was differ-ent from all the other summers, had forgotten? What if everyone came for this birthday party of mine and there were no cases of soda pop, no cakes except the one Mother and America had baked and iced late in the day? No popcorn or crepe-paper baskets with small candies and favors, no ice cream? No paper roll-ups to unfurl with a blast of breath against other kids' faces and necks? No crepe-paper-covered tubes with their little tabs at either end to jerk for a pistol-cap explosion, and their bounty of one paper party hat and one tiny toy?

A party would not be a party without the miniature candles in their hard sugar holders thrust into the cakes. Seven candles on this twenty-eighth day of July 1921. Yes, it would be terrible if the miracle of the great wooden freezer were not performed—the freezer with its silvery metal container packed round with crushed ice and rock salt, the freezer that required everyone's effort, each in turn working the handle to rotate dasher and interior container on their geared and opposite courses until the freezing mass of pure cream and sugar and fresh peaches became so thick it took Daddy's strength to force it the last revolutions. There would be Beau, this time, to spell him, Beau, as excited at the idea of the party and all that exotic food as was Katie May, the smallest of the Woodalls.

But mostly, it would not be any sort of a party without Daddy himself to hold me tight and give me my birthday kiss.

Oh, ye of little faith! Here was Daddy's voice, just after midnight, snatching me wide awake! He had not forgotten! Daddy, here!

"We had trouble with the motor just before we turned

off the highway at Cornelia. And a flat about a mile
outside of Clayton. I was afraid you and the girls would
worry, Mase," he was saying. "But here we are finally,
safe and sound."

Aunt Nora's voice broke in, heavy as mush and com-
plaining. "Such an ordeal. I thought we'd never make
it."

Daddy again. "Now, it wasn't that bad, Sis."

"Oh, you know Allen and autos, Mase. He'd think
they were marvelous even if they fell in a million pieces
beside the road."

Mother laughed. It was difficult to tell if she was really
amused.

Daddy laughed too, and said, "A great exaggeration.
Besides, it's your auto, and if Big Dan kept it in repair
we wouldn't have had so much trouble."

Aunt Nora ignored this, went on, "The children became as cross as bears, especially Little Dan. Finally
they all fell asleep."

"What a blessing," Mother said.

"They're still asleep. Where can we put them?"

"Bethany and Jeanine can use one of the two beds
in our girls' room. Three-quarter width, but big enough
for two children. I'll shift Margery over with Blainey,
and your two can sleep together."

Nora, who prided herself on not hiding her feelings
with smiles or good manners, said, "They'll probably
kick each other out of bed, crowded up that way."

It was Aunt Nora who first made me leery of anyone who starts a sentence with "I believe in being
honest . . ." or "I just say what I think. . . ." Yes, Aunt

Nora taught us that seldom does a kindness follow.

Still, she could be easygoing and jolly when things suited her, and now she managed to pass off the grumpiness. "I already warned Beth and Jeanine they'd have to rough it up here at Cloudacres. After all, it isn't the city."

Now, fully awake, I scrambled from bed, bounced out of the room, flew down the hall and into Daddy's arms. He swept me up and there was no doubt in my mind that he was delighted to see me. Delighted and something else, for he laughed and kissed me, but his eyes turned moist as though he might cry.

He nuzzled my neck. "You smell warm and sweet in your cotton p.j.'s," he said, then held me a little from him to look into my eyes. "You see, sugar, here I am right on *the* day."

He fished for the watch in his vest pocket with some difficulty, for I had wrapped my legs about his middle, my arms about his neck. He snapped open the gold case.

"Yes, twenty minutes past midnight, and what are you doing awake at this hour, my little Margy?" He sang out the last three words and took a dancing turn with me. "Where's your big sister?"

"Asleep," I said with satisfaction, and tucked my head under his chin.

But by the time he had put his watch away, Blainey was there, awakened by all the commotion. Still holding me, he swept her up with the other arm. He sagged slightly under the double burden.

"You and Little Dan can have the guest room, Nora,"

Mother was saying. "Dan couldn't come up this time?"
She asked now about Nora's husband.

"Big Dan didn't want to come for just a couple of
days. Not worth the trouble, he said. He likes his com-
forts, you know. But Allen will drop the girls and me
and Little Dan off at the early train day after tomorrow."

"So soon?" Mother sounded politely regretful. One
of the hospitality tenets.

"You know Big Dan, he doesn't like us to be gone
from him for too long." Nora gave her mushy, mellow
laugh.

"Yes, you're such a good cook, and Dan does love
his food," Mother murmured.

"Food's not all he loves." Nora gave another laugh,
one so knowing that Mother flushed and I wondered
what the secret meaning was behind the words. But
Nora gave no clue, for she was back to the subject of
autos again. "If I knew how to drive, Allen wouldn't
have to take our auto back to Atlanta for us. I could
do it on my own. You and I should take lessons, Mase.
Everyone's learning." But her sigh was one of self-
content as she finished, "Still, I probably never will.
Driving lessons, too much trouble."

"Allen taught me to drive the week he brought us
up this year," Mother said with some pride. "I've been
practising on the Hupp. I'm getting rather good at it,
too." Which was extravagant bragging for Mother. *Ladies should not be boastful.* She did not mention the difficulty with the steep grade down to Tiger.

"Good for you." But Nora's voice had turned sour.

"I'll bring your auto back to Atlanta, no trouble, Sis,"

Daddy broke in. "The motor sounds bad though. I hope it doesn't play out completely. It does need work. Dan really should—"

"Oh, you and your *should*, Allen. Don't be such a stickler about how things should be." And Aunt Nora's abrupt tone canceled any thought of difficulty.

When Daddy tucked us in, I could hear in Blainey's happy sigh the safe contentment we both felt at having him back. I didn't let myself wonder how long he would stay. At least I had him for this one glorious birthday.

As sleep folded around me, the thought came that with Beau's coaching I had learned how to keep the swing from looping. Maybe tomorrow after the party I could have Daddy to myself and show him how high I could fly. Maybe with Daddy watching I would even sweep high enough to touch the high branch.

✳

Daddy hadn't forgotten a thing. He had even brought two huge cakes of ice, wrapped in gunny sacks, stowed in a washtub. Wedged between them was a great canister of pure cream. Safely separated from the wet ice was a box of rock salt. Mother had bought a bushel of ripe peaches from the Woodalls' place yesterday. So there would be fresh peach ice cream!

I knew Daddy had special ordered the two store-bought cakes, one with yellow roses and rosettes and fluting, the other with pink. They both had *Happy Birthday Margery* in icing script across the top. Aunt Nora had made one of her famous fudge cakes, the cake pale yellow, the icing honest-to-goodness homemade fudge, half an inch thick between the four layers, and another half inch swirled over sides and piled on top. Aunt Nora really was a terrific cook. Maybe that explained her great girth. And Big Dan's. She scoffed at our vegetarianism. Daddy had even brought a gift from Aunt Arlene, mailed all the way from England, a marvelously huge book with pages stiff as cardboard and giant-sized print.

Three more galvanized tubs—the same kind we used for a bathtub here in the mountains—stood at the shady end of the porch. They were chocked with ice and six kinds of bottled soda pop. Even the Delaware punch in heavy tricorn bottles would be frosty by party time. And this day promised to be sunny and hot.

America Woodall arrived in midmorning. Since Aunt Nora and Little Dan had used the spare room, America had slept at her own cabin. Her son, Jake, drove up in the Woodall wagon with America beside him. All the little Woodalls, including his own children, were loaded in the back. The party was scheduled to begin at noon. America and the children piled out of the wagon. From the end of the porch, Blainey and I and our two girl cousins could see Jake eying the house.

"He's purely green, wishing he could trade places with his momma or one a them shirt-tail young 'uns of his." It was Beau edging down the porch to watch the arrival. "Or even wishin' he could be me for this one day." He laughed with some pleasure. "You don't know, little missy, but news a your party been spread far and wide. It's the talk a summer hereabouts. They'll still be recollectin' about it next spring."

"Jake can come, too," I offered.

"Not on your life, Miss Margery." Beau laid a hand on my shoulder. It felt friendly and warm and altogether pleasant. A satisfying thought slid across the corner of my mind—Noni Shattock hadn't been back since that day in the vegetable patch. "You'd have nary a mite a elbow room at your own whingding if you asked ever' hill man and woman who'd like to come. No, this is a young 'uns' come-all."

"There's plenty of food," Blainey said.

"Whee-o-o." Beau winked a lively eye at her. "Ain't there just! You mind what I say, though, Miss Margery"—and he turned again to me, gave my shoulder a pat, before taking his hand away—"stick to young 'uns. Even then you may have a scrap or two, though they'll be mindin' of their manners, you can bet your gold tooth on that."

Jake had waited long enough for America to settle the ten Woodall children beside the road. We could hear her voice call back to them as she opened the gate.

"You young 'uns stay clean. Y'hear me? I'll give you the sign when it's party time. If them highfalutin Shattocks show up early, don't you go scrappin' with 'em."

I wondered if Noni would help get the little Shattocks here. I hoped not.

"Don't you disremember your comp'ny manners today," America was still instructing, "y'hear me?"

A chorus of "Yes'm" came floating to us on the warm July air. Jake was turning the wagon and it had rattled from sight by the time America came up the walk, past the swing tree. She edged along the narrow way between kudzu and petunias, then turned to roll out a last order.

"You, Tessie. You be the momma. You shirt-tail kids mind her, y'hear me good now."

Beau had gone out to meet her. We heard him say, "You got them chil'un here a mite early, didn't you?"

"Their momma and me wondered which would keep 'em lookin' peartest. Walkin' over at twelve, or ridin' and waitin' now. We decided ridin' and waitin'. You know how dirt just jumps up offn the ground at 'em." With the flat of her hand she smacked him good-naturedly on the backside. "If what we do with them young 'uns be any business of yourn, Beau Tulley." But she planted a kiss on his handsome cheek. He swung an arm around her and hugged until she pushed him away, laughing.

Fifteen minutes later, when Daddy noticed the ten Woodalls watching the house with monumental patience from there across the road, he took me by the hand.

"It's your party, hon. Would you like it to start now?" he asked.

"Oh, *yes*, right this very minute!" I cried, distracted with waiting. After all, I'd been waiting for six weeks.

"It's only an hour early. Come on, you can invite Tessie and her brood in. I'll bet they're as eager as you."

Tessie was being a good momma. She had lined the little ones up on a log, with Pauly John to guard one end and she, herself, the other. They were playing How Many Sounds Can You Hear?

Daddy smiled at her. "Hello, Tessie," he said. "You've got everything under control here, I see."

"Mornin' to you, Mr. Standfield." Tessie managed to look Daddy in the eye for a moment. She flushed and smiled and looked down at her dress. America had told us she and Tessie had, together, sewn it, just for the party. The cloth was from a feed sack, bleached to fade the printing—the words hardly showed at all—dyed reddish pink with beet juice.

"You must be a great help to your mother. I'm sure she treasures you," Daddy said.

"I do the most I can. They're all pretty good young 'uns, anyways. And Pauly John backs me up if they get outa hand."

Daddy now included Pauly John, at the other end of the line, in his smile. This next-to-the-oldest Woodall gave us a grin, in no way as abashed as his sister.

But I burst out, "It's time for the party. Everybody come on!" And thereby destroyed Tessie's and Pauly John's holds on their charges. In vain those two shouted orders and reminders of manners and, at last, threats, but the stampede was on.

"Let them go," Daddy consoled Tessie, whose chin trembled and whose eyes filled with tears at this humiliation. But Pauly John, seeing the battle was lost, delightedly took out after the others.

As it turned out, the little Woodalls did uphold the family honor. Despite that initial rush, they became subdued in the presence of city people. Nevertheless, they shook hands and bobbed and smiled and said their soft, polite we're-pleasured-to-be-heres.

Our cousins, Bethany and Jeanine, in their fine party dresses, stood regal and aloof for the first ten minutes. But by the time the Shattocks and the Creaseys and the Tulleys and the Martins all arrived, we had mixed together, and clothes, whether voile and lace and ribbons or clean washed calico or dyed feed sack or patched, faded denim, were forgotten. Even little Dan shrieked with glee as the rituals were observed—pinning the tail on the donkey, blind man's buff, Simon says, statue. There were prizes for winners and losers and all those in between.

Daddy stood on his head, he did handstands and impossible juggling tricks. Oh, he was very good at these. Blainey applauded him more loudly than anyone. Her eyes shone. Her chestnut curls sprang lively about her moist forehead. Mother laughed; her face pinked. Aunt Nora made uneasy sounds. And I was sure there had never been a party like mine.

Beau displayed the power of his hands and arms for all of us to see by bending an iron spike into a giant fishhook. Pauly John and the other bigger boys followed this by performing feats of strength. The youngest children did impromptu dances—skips and jumps and whirls and a kind of stomping clog to handclapping. I noticed on that day, even the smallest of the girls had on her underdrawers. Daddy played the harmonica and the rest of us clapped to help with the dancing rhythm.

The middle ones recited poems or monologues or Bible verses. Six of the older girls, despite Beau's warning that Shattocks and Creaseys and Martins and Tulleys and Woodalls could not cooperate, sang "Shall We Gather at the River," learned on Sunday. Sunday, the time of peace between them all, at the church school near Tiger. On that day of my party, their sweet blended voices rose lark pure into the golden afternoon air.

And finally there were the candles and cakes. Mother and America had lit seven candles on each of the four cakes. Suddenly I was abashed, as all the gathered voices sang out the ritual song, *Happy birthday to you, Happy birthday dear* . . . And on this day it was *dear Margery.* Oh, the glory and the agony of it! For a moment I wanted to run and hide. But hands pushed me forward.

Some instinct led me to Mother and America's cake, more plain than the store-bought ones, not quite as luscious as Aunt Nora's fudge creation. Mother and America discreetly nudged each other, smiled. Their secret pleasure banished my stage fright and I blew mightily. In an instant my cake stood extinguished with seven candles smoking. A shout went up and the other cakes were put out with great huffs and puffs from Shattocks, Creaseys, Martins, Tulleys, Woodalls, cousins, and Blainey. I had no breath left from my own blowout and laughing.

The strongest boys and Beau finished the last turns of the freezer handle. There was a scramble to lick the dasher when it came out of the cylinder wedged with the pale creamy peach ice cream. But Daddy scraped it until there was nothing left to fight about.

My nightmare had not become reality. There was enough food to have fed the whole Confederate Army. Later, Mother wondered and worried how many children were sick that night. Yet, secretly, I knew it was worth it, no matter how many. No matter if I were sick myself. But none of us at Cloudacres was sick. Not Bethany or Jeanine or Little Dan. Not myself. Not even Blainey who, though she managed all crises and tensions with brave aplomb, sometimes threw up after everything was over.

We fell asleep so early that evening, I forgot all about Daddy and the swing and showing him what a little trooper I had become now that I was seven. It wasn't until later that I remembered I had not wished on my candles. A wish unused at the proper moment must be forever lost, for when I tried to reclaim that one at the beginning of autumn it did not come true.

15

Oh, Ye Little Pigs
of Summer

Three days after the party, on the morning Daddy had
planned to leave, his premonition about Aunt Nora's
auto did come true. Big Dan should have seen to it long
ago. The crank would not turn the motor over. Daddy
tinkered with the machine's mysterious innards for a
long time. Finally, it was obvious, nothing could be done
but leave Dan's auto at Cloudacres.

Rather stiffly Daddy announced, "I'll talk with Dan
in town. He'll have to get a mechanic up here to fix it
and drive the thing back to Atlanta. Or sell it here for
junk."

"I thought *you* could fix anything," Blainey said. The
thought of Daddy's leaving, the prospect of August without him, had turned her sour.

Daddy didn't look at her. Instead he glanced at Mother, then quickly away.

"Some things can't be fixed," he said, his voice flat. And Mother turned, walked away toward the house.

The upshot was the decision that next day we would all drive down to Tiger in the Hupp and see Daddy off on the train. Blainey was delighted. Her sour mood sweetened. At least she would have him that much longer. But Mother and I were afraid—she because of the drive alone back up the steep grade, I because of the train itself.

There was no real railway station, just the mustard-colored little shed outside of Tiger. There you had to flag down the train, or it went thundering past on its way to Tallulah Falls. We had done this last year, Mother and Blainey and I, to save Daddy the long drive to Cloudacres at the end of summer. George and the bulk of our summer paraphernalia had gone back to Atlanta earlier with Daddy. It had been arranged that Uncle Frank would drive us and our remaining luggage down to catch the train at Tiger.

The memory chilled me of the overpowering iron monster as it roared down the track. Uncle Frank semaphored, the engineer raised his gauntleted hand. The side bars, those great churning elbows of steel that powered the grinding wheels, slowed. Metal screeched on metal, shattering my sense of time, place, self, as the locomotive braked to a steamy, fiery stop. This was nothing at all like waiting for a train in the big Atlanta station.

Here on Tiger's narrow platform, the great beast was

close enough to touch. A turmoil of wind threatened to snatch me under the wheels. Surely the Devil himself manned the throttle, for steam and smoke swirled around and about, we were showered with cinders, while the reflection of the stoked fire reddened the fireman's face, turning it malignant as Beelzebub's. The roar and the clangor drowned the sound of my desperate crying.

Maybe it was the thought of Daddy's foot in its neat black sock that made the racketing train such a nightmare. Daddy's big toe was gone completely, and where it had once been, the vacant sock sagged, somehow to me terrible and obscene. Daddy had told us the story a long time ago of that childhood mutilation.

"When I was a boy, I went exploring through a train yard with two friends of mine. At one place, a long line of motionless boxcars blocked our way. It seemed a simple matter to climb up and over the coupling between two of the cars."

"What's a coupling?" Blainey had asked.

"Great steel contraptions holding one car to the next," Daddy said, then continued. "The other boys went first. I was last through. For a minute I balanced there, barefoot, on the coupling. There was no way for us to know, but far down the track, an engineer had started the line moving. Suddenly, with no warning, the cars jerked, bounded, rebounded. I held on, clutched with my toes. The jaws of the coupling smashed together and neatly bit off my big toe."

Blainey and I had covered our faces, groaned.

"Not so bad," he had reassured us. "It might have been a whole foot."

Those words summoned up a picture that doubled my horror, a horror I could never shake.

On this Sunday, though, we didn't have to leave Cloudacres before midmorning. Daddy had been up since dawn. He was busy with something under the hood of the Hupp. We had awakened early to the clank of tools outside, and every once in a while there was the roar of the motor as he would start it and listen attentively.

Blainey and I finished breakfast and went outside to watch. He was still so preoccupied with the machine he seemed oblivious of us. And we were certain he had not noticed that Mother was serious and pale when she had packed a lunch for him to eat on the train. There was no diner on the Tallulah Falls Line, and the connection with the Atlanta train would be after noontime.

Mother came outside once, looked in our direction, hesitated, then disappeared indoors again.

I whispered to Blainey, "She looks sick."

"She's just worried about driving back up the mountain alone," Blainey said.

"But we're coming back with her."

Blainey laughed. "A big lot of help we'll be! Besides, she'll make us walk up the steep part." But presently she said, "Don't worry, Magpie. Everything'll be all right. Let's go swing."

But everything wasn't all right, and, suddenly cross, I said, "I'd rather pick huckleberries."

"We can't. Mother said to stay clean. Let's play Parcheesi."

"I don't want to."

Blainey sighed, shrugged. "Daddy's through fixing the motor anyway. We'll be leaving pretty soon."

She was right. Presently we were wheeling out of the gate, with the fresh morning air blowing through the open auto. There had been showers during the night, but already the red clay of the roadside was drying in the early sun. The pines were dark and shining. In their shade the dogwood and azalea spread their lighter lacy green. We passed the Jefferson place. None of the Cowans was in evidence. The fenced field and the shed that had once housed Lucifer were empty. My eyes searched the upper window where I had caught a glimpse of little Henry Cowan the day of our visit here. This morning it looked as vacant as field and shed.

But Daddy seemed in a hurry now and we sailed past. After another turn or two of the road, there was the beginning of Hayes Field on the left. The little half-wild pigs were out rooting beneath the ancient abandoned apple trees that had once been the mainstay of some forgotten farmer. Forgotten except that his name was Hayes. Come fall, the mountaineers would gather in their pigs, pigs that never seemed to grow to any size at all. But there would be small hams, and pork meat, and meager fatback to help tide the families over the cold winter.

Pauly John had once told me how he helped slit the pigs' throats, and how he and his papa hoisted the little porkers to hang by their pointy-hoofed, dainty hind feet

to drain the blood. I was glad we were vegetarians. Today I tried not to think of the fate of the free-roaming
little summer pigs.

After passing Hayes Field, the road began the drop
down the steep grade, descending to Tiger. Daddy
shifted to low gear. He handled the wheel expertly
around the tortuous bends. There was no room for passing, except at the infrequent turnouts. But very few
autos or trucks came this way. Still, some thought of
this danger struck Mother, for she gave a stifled moan,
and said to no one in particular, "I hope there's no car
coming down when we make the return trip. I always
forget who must back up."

"The one coming down, because it's safer to back
uphill than down," Daddy said without looking at her.
"So you'll be all right even if you meet someone."

Then, as though the thought had just come to her,
she asked, "You'll be up the end of August to drive us
back to Atlanta?"

A long silence while he negotiated a hairpin bend.
Finally he said, "I'm not sure. I may stay over in England
a little longer than I planned at first."

"Why?" The word leaped out as though it had gotten
away from her.

"Arlene wants me to help her in the purchase of a
piece of property over there. She's thinking of starting
a finishing school for young ladies."

We were out on the easy slopes near Tiger when
Mother said firmly, "I'm not going to drive the auto
back myself. I'll just leave it here if the girls and I must
make the trip alone."

"Don't worry about that, Mase." Daddy flushed, his voice turned gentle. "George is getting to be an expert driver. You'd be surprised how he's taken to it. I'd have brought him this trip, but Nora's auto was too crowded. He'll come up on the train and drive you back. You'll be perfectly safe with him."

"George will come *if* you're not home from England?"

"Yes. Yes, of course. If I'm not home by then."

The rest of the summer without Daddy. On this sunny first day of August, despite the soft bright air, the world turned bleak. Blainey became very quiet. As we flew along the easy road she stared out at the blur of blackberry thickets and offered me no assurance. But when we finally pulled up near the siding, she sprang out and onto the narrow board platform before the bilious yellow, ugly little shelter, open fronted, dusty. And vacant, as it probably was most of the time.

She bobbed in, grabbed the faded red flag from its holder, then popped out to stand ready to flag down the train.

Daddy smiled at her. "That's my little trooper." But there was something in his face I couldn't read.

When he said "trooper," it came to me that I had not conquered the swing for him. Before I could say a word about it in these last minutes, the train's whistle sounded, plaintive and sweetly dissonant, from far down the track. The swing was instantly forgotten. Even the thought that Daddy was leaving barely surfaced. Instead, all of me concentrated on standing stiff and silent as the train appeared around the curve of track. This day, no tears. Seven, too old to cry, no matter how monstrous the locomotive.

Daddy said his good-byes now, while there still was ample time. In my rigid resolve, I hardly felt his hug and kiss.

I scarcely heard Blainey when she said, suddenly intense, "Do you *have* to leave, Daddy?" Or his, "Yes, sugar, I do have to," as they clung together for a long moment. It made little difference to me then that he and Mother did not embrace.

The train grew rapidly in size. Its sound and fury swelled in the quiet air. Blainey needed no prompting. She flashed a smile at Daddy, her eyes bright and bold. With great vigorous thrusts she waved the flag. The locomotive's side bars slowed the mighty wheels, metal flanges screamed on rails, the shrill exhaust of steam began. Finally, with a last jar and belch, the behemoth jerked to a stop. Station house, platform, and we stood dwarfed. It was some strange child, not me, that Mother's arm encircled while the wrench of linkage against linkage diminished down the line.

A conductor stuck his head from a passenger-car door. He reached down, set portable steps to bridge the gap to the low platform.

"All 'board, suh," he said.

I saw Daddy's feet, neatly shod, nimble, spring up the steep steps. It wasn't until the train started, with almost as much noise as its stop had made, that I forced my gaze upward. The windows of the passenger car slid slowly by. Then there was Daddy's face, framed above us. At first the imperfect glass made him waver. He seemed to be crying. But the flaws shifted as the train picked up speed. It was plain then that Daddy smiled and waved. Blainey smiled, returned the wave, but to conquer my tears I had used all my will, and for this moment, none was left to raise my hand or the corners of my mouth.

The train rocked with its gathering momentum, the fury of sound gradually diminished, and when, at last, the sinuous line of cars leaned round a curve far down the way and disappeared, the day turned silent. Into this silence came the sound of a blue jay, scolding somewhere off up the mountain. It was then I felt my neck hurt where Mother gripped me tightly to her side. Presently her hand loosened and slipped around my shoulders.

"You're getting so grown up." She smiled down at me. "You didn't cry this time."

She straightened a little and turned, walked down the platform toward the Hupp. I saw her shoulders lift twice as though she had snatched herself a couple of big breaths of the sun-fresh mountain air. For a moment I thought it was she who was crying, but her voice was steady as she said, "Come on, girls. We've still got to get the Hupp back up to Cloudacres."

"Would you like for Margery and me to walk?" Blainey's words were subdued now.

Mother laughed shakily and smoothed Blainey's hair from her forehead, trying to coax a smile from her suddenly somber child.

"Not yet," she said. "Only on the steepest part. You know, the grade just below Hayes Field."

We climbed into the back of the auto and settled. Alone, on the high front seat, Mother gripped the wheel, but today her hands weren't trembling. How strange to see her there instead of Daddy. Briefly I wondered if she felt less a lady. As we rolled forward with only a jerk or two, I said to Blainey, "You've got smudgy places under your eyes."

She didn't look at me.

"Mind your own beeswax," she said softly.

꣩

Maybe the walk up the steep road did us good. It took longer than it should have. We dawdled, picking blackberries, ate them sweet and warm from the sun, dusty after the long wait from green nub to this juicy, dark fullness. They stained our fingers and our tongues. Mother wasn't cross when we reached the flat that bordered Hayes Field. Perhaps she was only pleased to see us less hangdog than before. She had edged the auto off into a wide space beside the fence. Once there had been a gate here; now only a few makeshift rails closed the gap.

Immediately she said, "Maybe, if we find enough apples, we can persuade America to bake us a pie tonight. Or dumplings."

We were through the rails, quick as scat. She tried to follow, struggling a little to get her plumpness through the narrow opening. We ran back and pulled at her until all the black mood of Daddy's leaving evaporated. When, finally, she popped through like a released cork, we collapsed on the grass together, laughing, breathless; then Blainey and I were up one of the trees while the skittish pigs dashed here and there, half bold in hopes of apples thrown down, half frightened for fear we had come to catch them. Did they sense their autumn fate?

Blainey and I didn't question then, but now in recent years we've often wondered why the Hayes trees always seemed to be amply hung, even in summer, with the small mountain apples streaked with red and gold, so juicy they squirted when you bit them, so sweet-tart they made your jaws ache. But you had to watch for worms. That day, by the time we had thrown down dozens of apples for the little pigs, and enough to fill Mother's caught-up skirt, we were starved and turning cranky.

"Get off my branch," I yelled at Blainey. "You almost made me fall!"

"Baby! Baby!" Blainey taunted and shot me one of her looks. "Babies ought to stay on the ground!" She gave the branch an extra jounce before she climbed higher. I shrieked again.

"Come down, little chicks," Mother said. "Let's have lunch."

"I'm going clear to the top." Blainey tilted her chin and climbed higher.

Still angry with her, I turned sweetly docile and slid to the ground, smiling like an angel.

Mother's voice firmed. "Come, Blainey. This minute."

From her lofty perch, Blainey peered down through the leaves and branches, rebellion flashing in her eyes. The sun glinted behind the halo of curls. I was disappointed when Mother suddenly smiled.

"Come down, chicken little," she said softly. "I packed a lunch this morning. It's in the auto. We'll picnic here. And there's watermelon for dessert. Beau brought it yesterday."

Mother knew her own. The lure of food was too much for Blainey. She descended instantly, agile as a squirrel, the rebellion gone. She looked as angelic as the cherubs in our framed sepia prints of Asleep and Awake.

When we had finished the tomato-and-lettuce sandwiches, the deviled eggs, the thermos of lemonade, the cookies and watermelon, Blainey and I liked each other again. Stuffed, we lay back in the grass in the shade of our tree. Presently, though, recovered, we leaped to help Mother pick up the litter we had made.

The little pigs, who had watched from a wary distance, came squealing when we threw the scraps. In their eagerness, they forgot all fear of us. In the glory of gulping down their feast, they seemed no longer to sense the tragedy that awaited them in autumn. And we were only delighted with them, admiring their tissue-thin, pointy ears, their busy, rubbery pink snouts; the quickness of stiff legs; the throatiness of greedy grunts.

Oh, ye little pigs of summer, heedless and happy in your gluttony!

16

Blainey's Disaster

Our second day of August proved to be shadowed by some strange blight. One natural explanation for such a congregation of mishaps could be that roguish spirits ruled that day. After all, the ancients were convinced that a certain number of their gods were mischievous; and our Salem forebears credited witches for unexplained disasters. There are countless other historic precedents to support this psychic view.

One mishap forced Mother to drive the steep grade down to Tiger again, then back the next morning. Still, Blainey, not puckish spirits, quite directly caused that. I suppose, in a more circuitous way, Blainey was also the cause of my learning more about love than I wanted to know. It would be unfair, though, to lay the whole blame at Blainey's door for all of our August second miseries.

The day started deceptively well. This despite the gloom left over from Daddy's departure.

"Come, little chicks." Mother made her voice brisk. "We have a whole morning full of things to do. First we'll go berrying. America says she'll make jam if we pick enough."

Blainey's face did not brighten. Resolutely Mother continued.

"We can save a few jars to take back to town with us. You know how Daddy loves blackberry jam."

Blainey looked up at mention of Daddy. Her gloom lifted a fraction.

"There are zillions of berries along the fence between here and Pinewood," she said.

Mother brushed a curl from Blainey's forehead.

"You can show us where they grow thickest, sugar," she said. "We should be able to fill two buckets. But it's going to be a hot day. When we've finished picking, let's hike down to the spring and wade. I've already packed a basket lunch to take along."

Even I perked up at this prospect. Some of the desolation of August without Daddy lifted.

"Let's go clear down where it's dark and mossy," I said. "Maybe we'll find a salamander."

"That would be fun," Mother agreed. "Salamanders are magic creatures. Or so mythology tells us." She gave a laugh and hugged me. "This afternoon Ellie wants us to come for tea. By the time we get back here, we'll be ready for our nap. Tonight, instead of dessert after supper, we'll invite America to toast marshmallows with us. And then, about eight o'clock, when you're both tucked in bed, we four can see what happens in this week's episode of 'The Covered Wagon.' The *Post* should come today."

She smiled brightly at us. We could detect no sign of sorrow or worry. She had planned this busy day to crowd out sad thoughts.

All went well until midafternoon. The berries were picked, then washed, sorted over for leaves or stems, and finally sugared down ready for America in the morning. Today she was gone to tend to some urgent need of her family. Work finished, happily we trooped down to the creek that ran from our spring. We splashed and waded, Mother with her skirt hiked above her pale dimpled knees. Refreshed, we were off to Ellie's.

Dear Ellie, gay and loving at teatime with us, had baked sugar cookies shaped like boys and girls. Only as we were ready to leave did she tell us Uncle Frank was sick in bed upstairs.

"I'm terribly worried about him, Mase. He really feels very poorly."

"Something he ate?" Mother reached a quick hand of sympathy.

"I hope it's only that. But he had chest pains last winter. At first, the doctor feared it might be his heart. The symptoms disappeared, though, and they decided Frank was fine. Nothing serious at all. Then yesterday his chest hurt again, and I saw him rubbing his left shoulder and arm."

"Oh, Ellie, you've been so sweet with the girls and

me, all the while hiding this worry over poor Frank—"

"You brightened my day." Ellie's voice lifted. She put an arm about Blainey, stroked the top of my head.

"America is with her family today, or I'd send her right over to help you," Mother said.

"No, no. We're fine, dear. You mustn't concern yourself. Really."

"I certainly shall concern myself! You and Frank are family to us." She hesitated then as though fearful she might be meddling. "Frank really should see a doctor, shouldn't he?"

Ellie's voice was earnest but unaffronted as she said, "There's a doctor who lives just outside of Tiger on the road up from Clayton. His name is Jarren. Dr. Jarren. Maybe you've noticed the name on the mailbox."

"Yes. Yes, I think I have. But is he good?"

"I understand he's very good. He treats the locals now, but used to practice in Atlanta. I've heard he came to live up here because his little daughter was ailing in the city. If worse comes to worst—if Frank doesn't seem better tomorrow, I'll have someone go down in the wagon and bring the doctor here to Pinewood. There's no one can drive the Packard but Frank."

"I can go down in the Hupp if it becomes necessary." This offer cost Mother something, but then she brightened. "America will be back late this evening. Tomorrow morning we'll come right over to see how Frank is doing, to see what needs to be done."

Gratitude rose through Ellie's words. "It *would* be sustaining to see your friendly face in the morning."

"I'll certainly be here, bright and early."

"I become frightened when Frank is ill, or even if he's away for a while. I don't know what I'd do without him. He takes care of everything, but *everything*. Including me!" She tried to laugh.

"Of course. We know how it is." And I knew Mother was thinking of summer without Daddy. Without anyone to take care of us.

"But you're so staunch, Mase. So strong and—well"— Ellie searched for the right word—"independent." Then she hurried on to add, "Independent, but in a nice way."

For a moment I puzzled over what kind of independence was unnice.

"I?" Mother laughed in disbelief. "No, not I. You, Ellie dear, are the independent one. We both know that. You even managed that awful Mr. Cowan."

That memory made Mother laugh again. Ellie joined in and we left on a wave of reassuring merriment.

Later, as I looked back, it became clear that Uncle Frank's chest pains were the beginning of our strange series of circumstances that day. Uncle Frank, himself, recovered fully. By the next morning, his chest pains were gone and it was decided they were only indigestion as before. But by then they had already served their purpose of launching the disruption of our day.

After the walk home from Pinewood, the rest of the afternoon might have gone well but for naptime. This lull gave Blainey a chance to make her own special contribution to the disasters of the second of August.

With the living-room shades pulled down to act as a buffer against the heat, Blainey and I reposed on the floor. Folded quilts padded us from the hard planks.

The floor seemed cooler than our beds. Mother dozed on the couch. How peaceful she looked beneath the bright silk throw. She never slept without a cover.

"Unladylike," she always declared. "Besides, one is certain to catch cold from a draft if one sleeps uncovered. It never fails."

As soon as Mother's eyes were safely closed in sleep, Blainey and I kicked off our light muslin sheets. Now the corners of Mother's mouth belied the cheery face she had worn all day. They drooped in an expression of infinite sadness. Lines from nose to mouth, frown marks above her nose, made her look suddenly old. Her momentary peace seemed disturbed as her fingers twitched slightly from some unpleasant dream.

Blainey tossed, restless, wide awake. But I, tired from our busy day, drowsed. A cicada buzzed in the distance. A fly bumped monotonously inside our screen door. The slight sounds underscored the silence.

"Magpie," Blainey hissed.

My voice, dragged back from some far world of sleep, was loud in the shaded room. "What?"

Mother stirred. Blainey scowled at me, pressed a finger to her lips. Mother resettled, slipped deeper into sleep. Blainey arose, pushed through the screen door, stood waiting for me on the porch. Reluctantly I got up, followed, squinting at the golden light.

"It's too hot for a nap." Blainey brushed the hair from her damp forehead.

"*I* was almost on the A.P.," I grumbled.

"Let's *do* something."

"Like what?"

"Oh, anything, except just lying there thinking. I hate that."

"What were you thinking?" I drooped against the porch rail, disinterested in the answer.

"None of your beeswax," she said, but then she smiled, coaxing me from grumpiness. "What can we do that's fun?"

"You could read to me."

She groaned, then brightened. "I know what. Let's see how far we can walk on the porch rail without falling off. I'll bet I can balance all the way around."

Her eyes sparked at the challenge of this feat.

"I don't want to," I said.

"You can just watch if you're scared." But she put no meanness in the remark.

"What if you fall off?"

"I won't. Besides, it's not far to fall."

"It's far from here."

I went to peer over the rail at the end where the land dropped off into a draw. This shallow declivity led down through the dell where we had waded a few hours before. Now a quick livening of air brought the distant endless tappity-tap of the pump pulling water from our spring there.

"It's awfully far down here," I repeated.

The hard red clay waited at least ten feet below. A line of stones marked the edge of an old flower bed. Nothing grew there this summer.

Blainey shrugged. "So what? I won't fall anyway. Just watch me, Magpie."

And she bounded to the other end of our long porch

where the rail stood a moderate three feet or so above both porch floor and outside level ground. Hooligan, snoozing on the bench swing, gave a little start, raised his head as she rushed past, then sighed, dropped his head heavily back in place. His eyes, half shut, showed green slits.

Up Blainey scrambled, crouched, stood erect, wavered, caught her balance. With delicate step she began her walk along the rail. A coiled snake could not have held me as riveted, as hypnotized. I watched in fascination while Blainey teetered along the two-by-four beam. I tried to smother the dread anticipation of that final turn onto the end railing, tried to forget the hard ground with its edge of stones so far below.

"See, easy as pie." Blainey's glance flicked at me, then back to the rail. "Quit squinching your eyes, Magpie, for heaven's sake. I'm not going to fall, I tell you."

It is true, she was nimble of foot, steady of balance, and surely a trooper if there ever was one. After negotiating half the distance of the long side of the porch, she stopped, smiled at me, wavering only slightly now.

"Aunt Arlene did our horoscopes, remember. Capricorn. That's me. Capricorn. The goat. Goats are surefooted as all get-out."

She proceeded once more. The tension had stolen my sleepiness. Aunt Arlene had told me I was Leo, but at this moment my lion's heart thumped, heavy and afraid, afraid for Capricorn on that final high rail. Still, Blainey would have been perfectly right in her confidence, and Capricorn would have won out, truly as agile as a mountain goat. Yes, Blainey would have been perfectly right, except she hadn't figured on Hooligan. If there had been someone to play the witch that day, surely Hooligan would stand charged as a witch's familiar.

Blainey laughed when she turned the corner onto the dangerous last stretch. With great aplomb she covered two thirds of the distance. Victory was within reach.

"I told you—" she began triumphantly.

In that instant a lizard scurried from below the rail to do push-ups on the sunny top. Blainey wavered slightly. Hooligan's eyes slowly opened. They shot green fire. Relaxed body imperceptibly stiffened, magically flowed to crouch. Claws, unsheathed, gripped wood swing slats. Lizard, heedless, whisked inches more atop rail. This quick movement further unbalanced Blainey. She wavered again, regained balance, took another precise step.

Then Hooligan made his move. Tabby lightning streaked from swing to floor to rail. Lizard popped from sight. Hooligan hit the rail, overshot by a hair, hung by frantic claws, lost his hold, plummeted to ground, landed on feet, flashed away unhurt. Cat and lizard. Too much for Capricorn. Nimble goat wavered violently, then in silence went the way of cat.

Unlike Hooligan, Blainey did not land on her feet. I heard the thud as she hit the ground. No other sound. Fearfully, I peered over the rail. Fear turned to terror. Dread certainty shook me. Blainey, dead from her own daring. For an instant, transfixed, I stared down at her still form. The next, I ran screaming to Mother.

Blainey had come to, before Mother reached her. But a thin line of blood trickled down her neck when she sat up. Its source, a huge knot rising where the back of her head had hit a stone. And something was very wrong with one arm. Her eyes looked blank, unfocused. She turned her head a little to one side, leaned over and threw up Ellie's sugar boys and girls. She touched the back of her neck, then stared at the red stickiness of her fingers, wiped them down her coverall leg, began to quietly cry.

"Concussion?" Mother whispered to herself.

For a moment her fright quivered in the warm air, but when she bent to Blainey she spoke firmly.

"Sit still, little chick. I'll get something to brace your arm. We'll have to have the doctor take a look at it. Don't worry, honey, you'll be all right."

She arose, ran to the back door. I could hear her inside, opening, closing doors and drawers. In a minute she rushed back with a short length of broken bed slat, some strips of cloth, a large bandana.

"If only Allen were here—" she murmured, "if only America would come back sooner—" and she continued talking, at one moment reassuring, at the next breathless with her own hidden alarm, "—be brave, little chick—" "—your arm will feel much better once we keep it from moving—"

While she talked, deftly, gently she splinted the arm, folded the bandana for a sling, settled the awkward limb in it. Though Blainey moaned several times and I cried in sympathy, presently the arm was secure. The swelling on her head pushed through the matted curls, but the bleeding had stopped. Mother, with some difficulty, managed to pick Blainey up, carry her to the porch swing. Eyes still unfocused, lids at half mast, Blainey drooped heavily against the armrest.

"Don't go to sleep, sugar." Mother gave her a sharp shake and Blainey's quiet tears began again.

"You're mean!" I cried at Mother.

"Sh-h-h, little chick," she said, distracted. "It's not good to go to sleep with such a lump on the head." She seemed on the verge of tears herself when she said, "I'd give my right arm to have phone service on the mountain right now." Then she squared her shoulders. "Well, never mind. What's good enough for Muhammad is good enough for me."

"Who's Muhammad?" I asked.

Mother seemed to ignore my question.

"If we can't call the doctor to come to us, then we'll go to the doctor," she said.

"What doctor?"

Even I knew that Dr. Baird, in Atlanta, was too far away to help us. Dr. Baird who had saved us through the years, coming quietly through our front door with his magic black bag. Dr. Baird, like God himself, but reachable and friendly.

"There's the doctor who lives outside of Tiger, the one Ellie mentioned. Dr. Jarren, she said. Uncle Frank can drive us down—" Then she stopped. When she went on, she sounded breathless again. "No, not Frank. His heart—"

She stood there, uncertain.

"Beau could drive us—" I began, remembering how good he had been at helping me the day of the swing accident.

"Beau can't drive. The Woodalls and the Tulleys only have wagons. A wagon would be too rough, take too long. No, it will have to be the Hupp."

She stiffened her spine, her voice firmed, and the look in her eyes was new to me.

"I'm the only one here to drive it," she said. "*I'll* take Blainey down to the doctor, myself. There's no reason I can't. After all, I got the Hupp safely back up from Tiger yesterday when Allen left—"

But she was really talking only to herself again, bolstering her courage, and there was nothing for me to say.

Shortly, the Hupp stood in the drive, its motor running. Mother had on her hat and coat. She put a shawl around Blainey's shoulders, for the heat of the day was giving way to the cool of late afternoon. The sun slanted low in the sky. Soon the day would fade to dusk. The thought came—Mother behind the wheel of the Hupp and darkness swallowing the steep narrow road. But urgency was in her every move now, for Blainey still kept drifting into sleep, and shaking her did no good.

When I started to climb into the Hupp, Mother said sharply, "No, Margery. I want you to scoot down the road to Ellie's. You're a big girl now. Seven, remember. You can manage that short distance alone."

"I want to go with you."

She smiled at me, softened her tone. "Two of us in the auto is enough this late in the day. You'll be safer here. Just tell Ellie that Blainey took a tumble and got a bad bump on the head. Tell her we're down at Dr. Jarren's. She'll understand. Oh, yes, you might tell her,

too, that I'll ask Dr. Jarren to come up tomorrow to
see Frank. You stay with Ellie and I'll come for you
when Blainey and I get back. It shouldn't take too long.
After all, Tiger isn't Timbuktu."

"But—" I began frantically.

Mother fixed me with a stern eye. "No argument,
sugar. Do as I say."

Suddenly she seemed as unyielding as Daddy.

"If America was back—" I tried again.

"But she isn't. You'll be safe at Ellie's," she repeated.

And I knew she was thinking of the steep grade below
Hayes Field, the steep grade and the darkness of a moun-
tain night that would overtake her before she reached
Tiger.

"Scoot now, little chick." Her voice was adamant. "I'd
take you myself, but it would mean another half hour
by the time I stopped to explain to Ellie."

She reached, shook Blainey again, waved at me in a
distracted fashion, shifted gears with only a small clash-
ing sound, drove down the driveway, out the gate. Rapidly the Hupp disappeared along the road. I remembered
how Daddy's fast driving used to scare her.

17

Likin' or Sweetheartin'

Long shadows stretched from the trees across the road to the west. They swallowed the yard. Swallowed me. It was a comfort to see Pinewood down the way. The sun still touched the second-story roof there. Even as I watched, shadows engulfed that too. The road seemed to lengthen, Pinewood growing small with the distance.

For a second there appeared to be a movement of someone halfway between Cloudacres and Pinewood. Maybe America was coming down the pike to save me the long walk alone. Whatever the movement had been, though, it was quickly gone, and the road lay empty once more. I wondered if any of the huge, bony-hipped mountain cows had strayed so late in the day.

Maybe Beau would come even if America didn't. I

stood for a long time in the yard. Even the kudzu was
silent, even the tree frogs did not sing. At last I moved.
There was no America, no Beau. If I didn't get a move
on it would be completely dark before I reached Ellie.
Already the dim glow of lights shone from Pinewood's
front windows. Sudden fear rushed me out of the yard,
along the road.

But somehow, the thought of Beau had fixed itself
in my mind. He was probably at the cabin, the cabin
that had been George's in other years but now was
Beau's. Perhaps that had been Beau moving across the
road a while ago, moving across this main road and
going down the narrow track that led to the cabin. Of
course. That was why the movement had been so quickly
gone.

As I trotted along toward Pinewood, the thought came
of how fine it would be to bring Beau back to our house
instead of going all the way to Ellie. I could fall asleep
in my own bed and Mother wouldn't have to come for
me. She would be dead tired after piloting the Hupp
through the night.

Yes, with Daddy off to Arlene and England, with
Blainey hurt and Mother on her way down to Tiger,
it would be unusually comforting to sleep in my own
bed at Cloudacres, with a man about the premises to
scare the night frights away.

If some gleeful and wicked spirit had not tucked this
idea in my mind, maybe I would have gone straight
off to Pinewood with no further difficulty on that dis-
tressing day. Instead, when I reached the cabin track,
I stopped, peered into the thickening dusk. As though

to answer my urgent need, there far back through the trees a light sprang to life. That would be Beau lighting his kerosene lamp to tame the darkness.

On impulse I turned from the main way. At first the forest was open, the lamp, winking in the night to guide me, easy to see. Confidently I rushed along. Presently, though, the stands of pine thickened, trees began to crowd in on either side, touch together over my head. Huckleberries flourished here, hedges of growth making a black tunnel of my path. A curve in direction suddenly stole my light. In panic I stopped with the darkness trapping me before and behind. Gathering my courage, I moved ahead, slowly now. As instantly as it had disappeared, my light came on again. When the narrow road curved once more, I did not panic. But it was farther to the cabin than I remembered, or perhaps the darkness only made it seem so.

Again the cheerful lamp glow disappeared. Holding my fear at bay I edged forward. Then a sound came from behind me. The sound of lightly running feet. In terror I dodged into the thickets. Was something chasing me? The *pat-pat* of the feet came marvelously quick. Something or someone was in a frantic hurry. I thrust farther away from the track, farther away from my pursuer. Back and back until the sound grew faint, and presently became no sound at all. For minutes I sat frozen there.

Ah, wretched, roguish sprites to lead me astray. Path and light and runner all lost in the darkness. And I lost from everyone. I cast here and there, looking for the track. Brambles scratched my face, tore my clothes, bit at my ankles. The heat of the day was long gone. My chambray coveralls did nothing to thwart night's chill. It took forever before my feet through tennis-shoe soles felt the almost-smooth and open track. By then I was shivering, held-back sobs choked me. But wild gratitude filled my heart. I had at last found the way.

It was some time before I decided I had missed the cabin and must turn back. The road, I knew, led through the forest for some miles. Eventually it came out again onto the main way not far from Tessie and Pauly John's place. Somehow I had passed Beau's cabin while fighting thickets and trees.

All sense of time was gone when the light flickered once more to guide me through the dark. Relief released my tears. They were gone in one wild rush. I wiped my sleeve across my face to blot the flood, trotted along secure again in the thought of Beau.

As I came up to the cabin, a sudden burst of laughter leaped out into the night. A woman's laugh, and presently Beau's. Suddenly I knew, those lightly running feet that had sent me plunging off the road belonged to the owner of the feminine laugh. There was something in the intimate tenor of Beau's words, spilling from an open window, that stopped me dead in my tracks.

"Noni, sweet thing, you be as spirity as a wild pasture filly in springtime. What would your pa say ifn he knew you come flyin' through the dark and jumpin' in Beau Tulley's bed, like it were your own?"

"You talk an almighty lot." Noni's hot voice warmed the night.

"You tellin' me you didn't come a-runnin' for talk?" Beau chuckled, pleased with his own teasing. "Why, girl, talkin' is just about the most fun, 'specially bed talk."

Noni sounded as pouty as a child when she said, "You don't love me no more, Beau Tulley."

He laughed again. "I don't love you no less, sweet thing," he said.

I raised my hand to knock at his door, but something held me from it, something that told me I shouldn't be standing here in the dark listening to this talk, talk that Noni didn't want.

What did she want? Why had she come flying through the night then? Was she alone and scared of the dark, too? Why would her pa care? It seemed a certain thing that Mother and Daddy would not mind if I came to Beau, if I took him by the hand back to the house to watch over me and perhaps to talk with me until Mother returned to make me secure once more.

But words were no longer coming from the cabin. There were murmurs and small stirring sounds for a few minutes. Loneliness grabbed me. It was a long way back to the main road, longer to Ellie's. I wished my crazy idea about Beau had never snagged me off the main track on this foolish excursion. The sounds from within made me want to cry with my solitariness. It was then I noticed in the dim reflected light that a crate stood, upturned, near the open window. It is only a short step from eavesdropping to peeping, and desperation numbs the conscience.

The words began again. This time Noni's.

"Beau, honey, no man in hollerin' distance of Rabun Gap got hands like yourn." She sounded breathless.

"You been checkin' up on all them hands?" Beau's voice teased again, muffled but delighted.

"Oh, you devil, Beau!" But she was not displeased. Then, "Touch me right here, Beau, darlin'."

There was another silence. Beau's words came so softly, they barely spilled out to me. "Bees don't give no honey sweeter."

"You be about the mostest fella I ever *did* know." Noni's whisper was so intense every word came clearly. "All the girls go wild over you."

"Every single one?" He was cool, bantering again.

"Every single one, and some that ain't, or my name ain't Noni Maryjean Shattock. *All* the girls go wild over you. Old 'uns, young 'uns, even little-bitty ol' runny-nose gals. I even seen them little city gals shinin' up to you, a-swingin' on your hand, a-battin' their eyes at you."

"You be about as crazy as they come, Noni, sweet thing."

Soundlessly, I managed to lift the crate below the window. Up I stepped, rose until my eyes just topped the window's lower rim. Inside, the steady soft light of the kerosene lantern half revealed, half concealed what went on there. At first I could see neither Beau nor Noni. Then in the dimness on the other side of the room, beyond the wooden table and iron cookstove, I made out the shape of a bed. There was a movement there beneath the covers. The covers slipped.

My horrified gaze took in a length of soft white back, the wide pale beam of bottom. This was no ladylike dear rear. What lady would expose so much of herself? Unreasonably the thought of Mother and Daddy and their separate bedrooms flashed to mind. It scarcely intruded on the instant of clear shock I felt at how large Noni Shattock's rear loomed without clothes. She had seemed slender and almost dainty that day in the garden.

In this same tick of time, from the other side of Noni, a brown bare arm reached. The hand fastened in the tumble of pale hair. After a moment it released to slide down Noni's back. It reached the awesome bottom. Again, as in the garden, there came a quick, teasing slap. This time a fleshy smack. Then a sinewy leg came up over Noni's white thigh. Even in the muted kerosene glow, I could see each hair of Beau's muscled shank. I dodged back into the darkness below the window, huddled there in misery.

Presently sounds from Noni, sounds with no words, no laughter, sent me running away through the night. Instinct must have guided my feet. I had no way of knowing how I arrived at Ellie's door. No way of telling Ellie why I was trembling and crying. In the end she decided I was in a state of hysteria because for some mysterious reason I had become lost in the night on my way to her. She managed to get from me the story of Blainey's disaster, and the fact that Mother had driven off to Tiger to see the doctor.

"There, there, love." She rocked me for a while. "I know Blainey will be fine. Lots of children have very

hard falls and come out none the worse. Dr. Jarren is
a fine doctor. He'll make Blainey as good as new. You'll
see."

Ellie's words helped soothe my fears over Blainey and
Mother. Her love took away some of the sting of what
I had viewed through Beau's window. I never confided
about that eavesdropping and peeping session, even to
Blainey. I was ashamed of it and mystified as to why
Noni Shattock would run through the night to Beau's
cabin, when her pa would be so set against it, and since
she lived such a distance clear up on the tableland. I
didn't understand what had passed between Noni and
Beau. But my desperate tears were partly from shock
at what I had seen, partly because I knew, somehow,
that Noni had stolen my love from me that night.

Now, looking back, I can laugh. Laugh because of
the knowledge that accumulates with the years. Laugh,
too, with the recognition that not only hope springs
eternal, for it was easy for my love to spring up again
when I overheard America talking to Beau.

"Noni's gonna trap her a man someday. You lookin'
to get snared like a bulge-eyed rabbit, Beau Tulley?"

"You make every'un's business yourn, America?" He
sounded half angry, half amused. "Well, if you hafta
know, Noni's jumped into more beds on this mountain
than you can count. You oughta know, every'un's gal
is no 'un's gal."

I wasn't sure exactly what he meant, but at least the
words carried the message to me that Beau was free
for me once more. For a moment, the thought did pop
into my head: Boys will be boys, but girls must not

be girls. I remembered Blainey's flare of anger over this. But quickly I closed my mind to the injustice done to Noni Shattock. Noni Shattock as spirity as a filly in springtime.

✳

Mother didn't come to pick me up from Ellie's until next morning. As to Dr. Jarren, Atlanta's loss was Tiger's gain. He certainly did know his business. The resplinting of Blainey's broken arm was neat and professional. In the long run it healed perfectly. She did not let it hamper her much for the rest of the summer. Dr. and Mrs. Jarren put Mother and Blainey up for the night so he could be certain the concussion wasn't serious. Thus Mother didn't have to drive the grade in the dark after all.

Dr. Jarren promised to come up and check on Uncle Frank's chest pains. As I said, Frank's difficulty proved to be only indigestion. And Blainey's bodily injuries healed completely. As did my heart, temporarily broken by Noni Shattock.

18

Snapshots and Movies

The whole of that August was a time set apart in memory. Today it seems frozen in a series of still snapshots and short, silent movies. Nothing so tangible as views captured by real shutter and lens, retained on film or paper. Rather, those little flashes in the mind that hold a scene forever for some interior eye.

Occasionally these scenes will ripple in fast series, like a child's game with a deck of picture cards, each picture in the sequence the same as the one before except for some minute alteration. Riffled, they appear to spring to life with quick jerky motion—a Mack Sennett film. Rarely do these invoke a remembered sound. Yet now and then a voice, a laugh, a sigh, does come echoing down the years.

Even more infrequently, that most primitive faculty, the sense of smell, is aroused by some half-forgotten fragrance or odor. When this happens that past scene springs fully to life. The sudden sharp pain of nostalgia twists for a moment, desire flames up for that lost time and place; or if the odor was one tied to terror, the atavistic fears overflow, hands turn cold, palms sweat, there is an instant of trembling panic before the mind dodges away and the recollection sinks back into darkness. Then we laugh, shakily, at our old and conquered fears.

Yes, snapshots and movies . . .

Tea at Aunt Ellie's. Mother and Blainey and I. A lady we do not know. No other children there; we two dressed in clean gingham pinafores; Mother in pale-gold pongee, an amber necklace; Aunt Ellie ethereal in flowered voile. The image of the other lady blurred. Tea and lemon and light perfumes scent the warm motionless air. A still, in color. A Renoir kind of scene. We lean toward each other laughing, pink cheeked, bright eyed; happy that day, as Renoir's women, in our femininity. Aunt Ellie holds the translucent cup with fingers as delicate as china. Mother has laid a hand on Ellie's arm, seems ready to speak.

Tag-Along, our hound pup from last summer. Beau has brought him along on this day to visit. He belongs to Beau now and has forgotten us completely. No longer a puppy, he is bony and leggy, lean and gaunt; and consumed by hunger. He lives, mostly, on what he can forage from the wilds. And on table scraps; but these are scanty where often for humans the pickings are slim. Blainey and I stand at the porch rail, each with a handful of cold biscuits from the biscuit box in the kitchen. America stows them there for us—between-meal snacks. We love them with cheese.

But the biscuits we have today, cheeseless, we throw, one after the other, to Tag-Along. They go down whole with nary a gulp. It is like throwing rocks down a well, for there is a kind of interior echo as each biscuit hits bottom somewhere between those bowed, plain-to-see ribs.

Tag-Along belches, is immediately poised for the next, whip tail motionless, body rigid, saliva glistening in half-open mouth. Blainey's hand has swung forward, the biscuit ready to leap the space between girl and dog. I watch, mouth also half open in sympathy. Beau, head tilted back, is caught in silent laughter.

※

A Mack Sennett film, fast, double-speed movement, but unlike Sennett, this one of horror instead of comedy. Mother flailing with a hoe. Beneath the rising-falling edge, a huge snake, thick as a man's arm, its powerful body yellow with dark splotches. Mother, fierce, protecting home and children and self. Snake writhing beneath her blows, hissing, turning ugly head toward her. Blainey and I motionless, frozen, terror stricken. Mother silent except for primitive grunts as hoe flails, chops, mangles. At last, the snake lies dead, its thick body severed at the head.

Only when Beau finally comes through the front gate for his day's work does Mother revert to ladylikeness. She manages to make the porch, sinks into the swing, fans herself, gasps, feels a trifle faint. Yet I see in her eyes a secret look of triumph.

Later we learn it was a bullsnake she had beheaded, and despite its ugliness no danger to anyone except, possibly, Hooligan. A constrictor, nonpoisonous; useful to man, for it lives mostly on rodents.

The snake's death at a woman's hands a sad Biblical lesson. *The Lord God said unto the serpent, ". . . Upon thy belly shalt thou go, and dust shalt thou eat all the days of thy life. And I will put enmity between thee and the woman. . . ."*

❧

The little scrabble farm where Mr. Govan scratches the soil enough to keep body and soul together. His one really good crop, strawberries. The sweetest you ever tasted. He hates the work of picking them, though. He is very old, cavernous, rangy, thin, still strong, but maybe it is a misery in his back that makes him detest stooping. Sometimes Blainey and I have helped him, careful to pluck only the red ripe berries. Mr. Govan turns grumpy if you bother the pale ones. Our pay—half the berries we pick and the use of Bobby. In equine age he must be even older than Mr. Govan. If Bobby has a misery, our light weight does not stir it.

We are allowed to ride him back to Cloudacres. We always turn him loose there. He crops the rampant vines in our yard, and finally, sated, he moseys on off home by himself. Indolent, he nibbles new grass along the way to keep the kudzu company in his bulging belly—he must have a cast-iron digestion, he never seems troubled by bloat or colic— or sometimes he only stands somewhere along the dusty road, his old gray muzzle almost touching the ground, to catch himself a few winks of sleep.

We love to ride him, though, and it seems his step livens when we are astride his broad back. Blainey sits in front to handle the reins, I behind with arms around her waist, secure in my trust of her to manage Bobby despite his great size.

That August trip to Mr. Govan's, unfaded in a series of stills: Rows of green plants, hung with red berries, lush in the summer sun; two children in blue chambray coveralls, squatting beside a huge bucket that holds their meager pickings; the same two standing beside a bent old man, he ready to divide the berries; the old man helping the children onto Bobby's ample back. One of the arms of the older child is in a sling. She seems unhampered by this fact, balancing to swing into the saddle, handling the single reins with one hand.

The cards flip fast, the stills spring to life.

We have never before detoured to Hayes Field
with Bobby. Now with us astride and out of sight
of the old man, that very idea occurs to Blainey.

"Bobby would love the apples in Hayes Field,"
she says. "Horses love apples and carrots and sugar,
you know, Magpie."

Her light, precise, knowledgeable voice, the confident set of head and shoulders there before me on
Bobby's swaying back, make an indelible picture.
She pulls the reins strongly to the right. The great
old fellow responds amiably enough. We ride along
beside the fence until we find a gap, then through
and on beneath the gnarled bowed branches of the
apple trees. On this day, the summer pigs keep their
distance.

Blainey is right in her judgment of Bobby and
apples. He adores them. They are nectar to him
after the monotony of grass and dry hay. But it
doesn't take us long to decide the detour was a terrible mistake.

Time after time, the drooping limbs of trees almost sweep us to the ground as Bobby nudges
among them. When Blainey gets a nasty crack across
the head from one, we cower flat against the bony
ridge of his spine, press our faces to the old brown
hide. The pungent smells of horse sweat and dust
and hoof-crushed apples and of summer fix themselves forever in mind.

Bobby turns suddenly impatient with the reins.
In Blainey's grasp, they keep him from reaching
a fallen apple that has caught his fancy. With a

fierce thrust of his neck, he yanks the reins from her one good hand. The straps slide down and over his head. We are stranded on our high perch. It is a tremendous way to the ground. We have never mounted nor dismounted without help. Free in this apple-strewn equine heaven, Bobby roams and munches, munches and roams. We can feel the hollow grinding of his molars, the rumble of his strong colic-resistant belly beneath us.

It seems we are doomed to sit, helpless, forever. We will surely never see Mother again. I begin to cry.

"Oh, Magpie," Blainey says, "be quiet, I'm thinking."

With a struggle I manage an uneasy silence. Presently, without a word, Blainey swings one foot up and over Bobby's neck. Thus she sits with both legs on one side of the horse. With some difficulty because of the splinted arm, she rolls to her stomach, hangs there for a moment, then slowly slides off. It is a terrible drop. I hear her grunt as she hits the ground. My sudden wail of fright at finding myself alone on Bobby's back startles even that model of horsy composure. Luckily, his version of bolting is a slow, bumpy shuffle. In a moment, the apples snag his attention once more and he resumes gathering and munching. I have settled to desperate silence by the time Blainey catches up with us.

"Don't worry, Magpie." She smiles up at me, her face pink from exertion, her gaze steady and assured. She gathers up the dragging reins. Bobby,

finally full of apples, is docile. She leads him along
until at last she has him beside the rail fence. Without releasing the reins, she scrambles to the top
rail, maneuvers Bobby sideways, manages to grab
a handful of mane, swings a leg over, and smacks
down astride before me once more. We are saved!
It is clear why my faith in Blainey was strong.

A lizard, large, only a flash as it scurries under the
house and is gone in the shadows there. A repulsive
but strangely beautiful reptile with common gray
scaly back and sides, but underparts an electric
brightness of blues and reds.

"If you ever see a lizard like that again, don't
touch it," Mother warns. "It might very well be
poisonous."

But Hooligan has shot under the house in pursuit
of the fast-moving lizard. We stoop and peer after
him, call, but with no results. There is, eventually,
a faint scurrying, a short squall from Hooligan.
Then silence. Finally we give up the vigil. Later
in the day we see him, asleep on the shaded corner
of the porch. Only by nightfall do we realize that
he has been mortally wounded.

There is no way to know if it was the horribly
beautiful lizard, or perhaps a snake's bite, but Hooligan's head swells grotesquely. He seems unable to
eat or drink. His thickened tongue protrudes from
his mouth. He is stoical in his last hours, squinting
off at some far horizon, making no sound, waiting

for healing or death with equanimity.

Brave Hooligan. None of the rest of us are so heroic. We bury him in the petunias, his coffin a sturdy Sears, Roebuck shipping box that had once brought Daddy a pair of stout boots. We cry, the three of us, off and on, for a week. But even after we are cried out, the rest of the summer is blighted, at least during our quieter moments, by regrets over Hooligan's sudden and untimely demise.

"He had a good life with us" is the only consolation Mother is able to offer, for she is as stricken as Blainey and I.

Oddly enough, the two vivid memories that remain of Hooligan come from an earlier time. A kitten's wet head thrust from Daddy's overcoat; and Hooligan in June, at the beginning of this strange summer, riding his last ride to Cloudacres in our new Hupp. . . . Memory brings again his claws fastened in the thick wool shoulder of Daddy's coat . . . striped body sleek and pampered from its winter indoors, that day turned primitive and predatory. . . . Again in memory, he leans forward at an angle, braced against the blast of air as the Hupp picks up speed . . . again, eyes squinted, nose aquiver, whiskers streaked flat along his masculine jowls, he is as bold as a dog against the wind and the elements. . . .

✄

A happier day. Tessie and Pauly John and Beau and Blainey and Mother. And me. We have gone for a hike. The trail leads down through rocky, water-filled dells. There are ferns and mosses and pale little salamanders in the quiet backwaters of the rushing stream. Finally, we climb out of the defile into the sun and steeply up a ridge. From the top we can see Tallulah Falls off in the distance. The real falls, not the town. But they are too far away for even a whisper of sound to reach us. The day is clear and dry. A light wind has swept away the smoky blue haze that sometimes softens our mountains and gives them their name.

Returning, I grow tired. Beau swings me to his shoulders. He is careful not to knock my head against overhanging branches as we plunge down through the dark woodsy gorge. Once he slips, I grab across his eyes, he says, "Hey!" blinded, and I shift my hold to his lightly moist forehead, snug my crotch closer to his neck. The feel of his shoulders moving beneath me is exciting. I squeeze with my legs. There is a sensation of the swing at full sweep again. I squeeze more tightly. Beau laughs, but presently sets me down, telling me that the rest of the way is an easy walk.

He is still laughing. Even in the gloom I can see him shake his head, and his face is flushed. For some reason I do not understand, I am hurt and embarrassed. But my love for Beau, though temporarily rejected, is undiminished. The still shot in my mind's collection: Beau's back, his full stride as he steps off down the sun-dappled trail before me . . . his worn chambray shirt snug across his back . . .

the sleeves rolled into narrow, tight, ropy cuffs
around his biceps . . . the frayed jeans, white on
each sinewy cheek, so even in shade that part of
his anatomy seems highlighted in the old scene. . . .

⚜

Glorious triumph! With Beau coaching, I pump
high in the swing.

"That's it!" he encourages. "Don't you let them
old ropes go lazy. Keep your arms straight. Give
a real push with them pretty little legs of yourn.
That's the way! That's the way!" Then his laugh,
full and deep and joyful. "You done it! Whack-o!"
he shouts as the high branch lightly thwacks my
dear rear.

The beautiful, bright, triumphant scene swings
forever in memory.

⚜

The morning we went for honey at the Shattocks'.
We hardly ever went as far back in the mountains
as the Shattock place. Old man Shattock and his
old woman have three milk cows. And a bull. That
way they keep the whole Shattock clan—there must
be forty or fifty scattered in the glens and uplands—
supplied with milk and butter, and have enough
left over to slop the six hogs they fatten every year
to help carry them all over the winter. Unlike the
other mountain families, the Shattocks do not depend on the little summer pigs. They keep chickens
and bees, too. Their clan is better off than most.

As America had mentioned on the day of my party,
". . . Them highfalutin Shattocks."

People for miles around know about the Shattock
bull. Old man Shattock calls him Charley-boy, or
more exactly, Cholly-boy. And Cholly-boy is mean
as all get-out. Anyone on the mountain lucky
enough to own a cow brings it to Shattock's bull
from time to time for stud service.

It was Pauly John told us this. Said it kept the
bull's meanness down to a tol'able level. Whatever
stud service is, Cholly-boy must not get enough of
it, for tol'able level or not, twice he almost gored
old man Shattock to death. But it was Cholly-boy
who taught me that you can't judge the whole of
a person by what you hear from others, or even
by what you abhor in that person yourself. Cholly-
boy taught me that people aren't that simple.

This day we go the whole distance to the Shattocks', Mother driving the Hupp carefully around
the bends of the almost-flat upland mountain road.
It isn't until we drive into the Shattocks' yard that
she sees the Cowans' black Studebaker.

"Oh, my goodness, gracious," Mother says, but
cuts the motor and climbs out. "We've driven so
far to buy honey, and I just won't go home without
it. You wait here," she murmurs to Blainey and
me and the Hupp.

Left alone on our auto's high seat, Blainey and
I have a good view of the yard—the hog sty off to
the left, the small dilapidated barn some distance
behind the one-room cabin, and Cholly-boy's corral

off to our right. We can see Cholly-boy behind his
bars, and he can see us. He glowers and rumbles
a little, but we know the fence keeps us safe. Besides,
we feel invincible in our lofty Hupp.

Blainey nudges me and rolls her eyes toward the
Studebaker. It is then I see Cora Jane and Una Lynn
peering in our direction from the backseat of their
own car. They have their heads together and are
whispering. We display great interest in Cholly-
boy, a good excuse to turn our backs on the Studebaker. We both see little Henry Cowan at the same
time; we both hear Una Lynn's voice, suddenly loud
and sharp with irritation.

"Now where do you suppose that no-account boy
has gotten to?" she says. "Papa told you to watch
him, Cora Jane!"

"Me!" But Cora Jane's outrage is lost on us, for
we are frozen, watching Henry flirting with doom.

He sits straddled on the lower stringer of Cholly-
boy's corral, one foot inside, one out. His legs look
smaller, more delicate even than I remembered. Below short black pants, knees and shanks are tiny
bleached drumstick bones, thrust into miniature
patent-leather oxfords.

"We ought to—" I start in a whisper to Blainey.

But she has already slid toward the car door. Then
she turns to me and breathes, "Don't yell at him,
we might scare him right in with Cholly-boy."

The next instant, though, we see she is too late
to have any hand in Henry's fate. He swings the

outside foot over the lower rail, stands upright inside the corral. All unaware of any danger, he starts across the bare, dusty ground. An old oil drum, halved lengthwise, rests, cut side up, in a makeshift cradle not far from where Cholly-boy stands motionless with massive head lowered. But the bull's small dark eyes do move, following Henry's slow progress across the corral. A rusty pipe leaks into one end of the oil-drum trough. Water spills languidly from the other end. It is this that has caught Henry's eye. Only as he reaches the center of the corral does he seem aware of the bull, for Cholly-boy has come to life.

He lowers his head further, paws at the ground, shuffles, backs up a step or two, paws again, sending dust and debris against the water trough. Henry freezes. The whole world freezes, including Blainey and me, and even the Cowan girls. Suddenly the day has turned terribly silent. Cholly-boy raises his head. He peers across at Henry. Maybe it is true that bulls are nearsighted. He looks puzzled, as though he can no longer see the static child.

Memory's film, a still shot of cabin, yard, Hupp, Studebaker, girls, small boy, bull. The single shot slips immediately to another and another, the still scene flips to motion again. A bulky man appears from behind the cabin. Ethan Cowan. He sees boy and bull. His mouth opens, he is shouting. But all sound is lost in time past. Awkwardly he springs forward, races to the corral. The child hears him,

turns. With this move, little Henry is no longer
invisible to the bull. The child starts to run. Cholly-
boy lowers his head, charges. The man flings himself up and over the top rail of the corral. He falls
as he lands, heaves himself up.

Mack Sennett would have shown it hilarious:
Cholly-boy thundering from one side of the corral,
Ethan Cowan lumbering from the other. In frantic
terror, the man looks wildly about for some weapon,
stops, yanks off one of his own shoes, throws it
full in Cholly-boy's face. Heel smacks gray, soapy,
tender nose; bull swerves; man snatches up child,
runs; bull wheels, charges again. In the end, it is
old man Shattock who wards off Cholly-boy with
a pitchfork, as Ethan Cowan thrusts Henry between
the rails, scrambles to safety himself.

All freezes to a still shot. A father clutches his
child. A look of leftover terror muted by painful
relief is caught on the man's face. One of his pudgy
hands covers the boy's back, the other holds the
pale little head tucked under the jutting, aggressive
chin. Strangely now, a voice comes winding from
this scene.

"Oh, my son, my boy . . ."

Only a breath, yet it carries a terrible weight of
tragedy.

But for Cholly-boy, I would have been much
more comfortable purely hating the Grand Dragon.
And, later, other dragons. Life is simpler when
wicked is wicked and good is good. It was a long

time before I forgave Cholly-boy for this revelation.
It was easier to forgive him his meanness.

※

At last, at last! George!

He jumps off the train onto the Tiger platform.
No one sets a step for him as the conductor did
for Daddy. George does not seem to expect it.
He lands nimbly, smiling. He has ridden, not in
the passenger car, but in the caboose, and must have
made friends among the crewmen, for two wave
at him and at us as the train pulls away from the
platform. Through the real and obvious joy of seeing George again, for me there comes another hidden pleasure. The noise of the locomotive no longer
triggers my tears!

I remember the illustrations in one of the Theosophical books at home. The particular page that
fascinated Blainey and me: line drawings of men
and women, with little detail of anatomy, no clothing, but each figure filled and encircled by a lovely
cloud of color. Pink or red or blue or yellow or
gray. These various auras depicted states of the emo-
tions or of being. In anger one's aura turned red.
Yellow was happiness. Blue was love, misty lovely
expanding blue.

As George jumps down on the platform beside
us, it seems certain to me that all of our auras must
surely be blue, all touching and combining with
love. George straightens from his leap, one hand

raises in farewell to his traveling companions, but his face turns to us.

Dark eyes sweep Blainey, Mother, me, something hidden there but the glad greeting itself open and plain to see. He is dressed in one of Daddy's last-year's suits and a silk shirt. He carries a small carpet-bag with his other belongings. Daddy's castoffs hang loosely on George's narrow frame, but he is the best sight in the world to us.

He is concerned over Blainey's arm, still in its cast, until we reassure him. Then Blainey and I each grab, swing onto a hand, and he says, "I come to drive you-all back to Atlanta, safe 'n' soun'."

Blainey and I don't say anything more, but we look at each other, delighted, relieved, happy.

We have loved Cloudacres. Except for missing Daddy, Blainey's terrible fall, and the tragedy of Hooligan, the weeks of July and August were good ones. But somehow we are glad that George has come and that summer is over.

19

A Konclave of Kluxers

The last day of August. One of those hot, heavy days
when only the cicadas seem able to make any effort.
So we waited until afternoon to start down from the
mountain. If we had set out earlier, we would have
reached Atlanta before dark. In daylight we might not
have taken the wrong turn.

Mother and America had been busy the past week.
The house had been thoroughly cleaned, the windows
shuttered, the furniture sheeted, the porch swing and
chains unhooked and stowed in the garage. Beau had
raked the yard and beaten back the kudzu one more
time. The afternoon before leaving, we said a sad good-
bye to America. But she and we lifted our spirits with

promises of next summer, and other *Saturday Evening Posts*.

She turned and called back from down the road, "Don't you 'uns forget ol' America Woodall. I'll just be endurin' the time. . . ."

So, on this last day, Mother gave everything a final appraising look.

Beau, who had come over to see us off, said, "Are you 'uns fixin' to go on along down now?"

"Yes." Mother smiled but looked distracted. "I don't think we've left anything turned on or unlocked. Allen usually does all of this."

"Don't you 'uns go pesterin' your head about how the place is gettin' along. I'll look in any time it happens I'm passin' by here."

"I don't know what we would have done without you this summer, Beau." Mother touched his arm, pressed an envelope into his palm. Curious, he opened it, then fished out some bills.

"You 'uns already settled up," he said, "first a the week." And he held the money out to her.

"Something extra." She gave his arm a friendly little shake. "You took such good care of us all." When he started to press the money on her she said, "Buy something for some of the Woodall children. Maybe Tessie and Pauly John. School is starting soon. They'll need some store-bought things."

At this Beau grinned. "Now that would truly pleasure them. Thank you kindly." And he thrust the money into his pocket, shook Mother's hand, poked his head into the Hupp, kissed Blainey on the forehead and me on the neck. "You keep my little ladies safe, drivin' all that way back to the city," he said to George.

George, serious with the task before him, did not return the smile, but bobbed his head. Mother tied the streamers of her hat, climbed in, exclaimed, "Oh dear, the pump down at the spring!"

"I'll turn it off," said Beau. "You better get a move on. Storm's a-comin'."

George started the motor, adjusted the spark. As we drove out of the yard, I looked back. Tag-Along had come from his foraging to stand beside Beau, who was throwing us a final kiss.

And so farewell, handsome Beau, my first love. Goodbye, Tag-Along, our hound who forgot us in one season. And adieu, brave Hooligan where you rest in the petunias.

Blainey and I both knew that Mother was nervous about this auto trip without Daddy behind the wheel. She was worried that George could not handle the Hupp, especially if the storm that Beau had mentioned descended upon us. Black clouds had bulged in through Rabun Gap, thunder muttered off in the distance, the air was oppressive.

But she shouldn't have worried about George. He had spent his entire summer driving Daddy's construction trucks, far more difficult to handle than our Hupp. So, even after it started to rain and the red clay became treacherous, George eased the auto around the curves with great skill. He thwarted each incipient skid with a deft turn of the steering wheel.

Mother finally said, "You're very good at this, George.

It frightens me to drive. I've had my fill of it this summer. I'm never going to drive again. I'll just leave that all to you."

"I likes to drive," he answered quietly. "This big old Hupp is like ridin' to heaven on a cloud. Nothin' atall like truck drivin'."

But the trip down the muddy difficult grade took a long time. After a bit the rain became so heavy, George stopped the auto, got out, leaned in to fish the storm curtains from under the backseat. He turned them end to end and upside down, then back again.

"Now le's see," he kept saying softly to himself. He was soaked to the skin when, at last, he had them in place.

By the time we stopped at Cornelia on the main highway, the rain had stopped. The sun swung free of the clouds to touch the western horizon. George got out, began unsnapping the storm curtains.

"Oh, dear," Mother said, "we'll be way after dark getting home." But when she glanced back at Blainey and me, she smiled and said as heartily as she could manage, "It will be fun to drive after dark. There should be a full moon tonight."

George, never talkative, said nothing as he finished with the curtains. The air was hot and still, and as oppressive as it had been earlier at Cloudacres. Uneasy weather. Maybe that was why George's apprehension reached out and infected us, too.

When he climbed back in and put the Hupp in gear, and we rolled forward, he said, "I never done no night drivin'."

"You will do very well, George." Mother kept her voice steady and calm. "It's just like day driving, except one goes a little more slowly. Besides, we know the road right straight to Greenwood Avenue, and the moon will light us along the way."

She sounded so certain that Blainey and I settled down to enjoy this after-dark adventure.

But night driving proved to require more than going a little more slowly. Darkness overtook us halfway between Cornelia and Atlanta. And the lowland moon cast far less light than had the Cloudacres moon. As we approached the city's outskirts, traffic increased, and the oncoming headlights made the surrounding night seem more impenetrable.

At the end of half an hour, though, we decided we had taken a wrong turn, for the other traffic had mysteriously disappeared and we were alone in the night. Maybe it had happened back there after an approaching auto strayed to our side of the road. George had swerved the Hupp, the two cars rushed safely past each other, each on the wrong side of the way. But suddenly another pair of headlights blossomed immediately ahead. The only escape, farther left. George twisted the wheel. We all braced for the ditch. Miraculously the Hupp continued upright and steady along a paved surface. Now the road, overhung by trees, was midnight black. After a bit we decided we had truly lost our way.

"Why don't we stop at some house and phone Daddy?" Blainey asked. "He'd come out and find us."

"We'll manage," Mother said. "We can't really be lost this close to Atlanta. We've probably driven out here dozens of times. It's just that everything looks different and strange in the dark."

"Anyways," George said, "it wouldn't do no good to call Mr. Standfield. He's gone. Nobody to answer at the house."

"Of course," Mother said. "He would have come for us at Cloudacres himself if he were back from England."

George hunched closer to the wheel, peered into the night. He said nothing.

After some distance, the overhanging trees were left behind and we were rolling along through bright moonlight.

Suddenly Mother exclaimed. "There. That's Stone Mountain, off to the left. Now we know where we are."

"You're sure right, Miz Standfield," George said. "That's sure enough Stone Mountain."

His relief spread to us, but it was short-lived, for Mother spoke again, this time uneasily. "Something's going on over there tonight."

Blainey and I glanced at each other, both dredging up what Una Lynn had told us. I could see Blainey's face flicker in the reflection of a bonfire blazing in the night. It must have been a huge fire to cast its light so far.

Blainey leaned forward to Mother. "Una Lynn told us there was to be a Grand Konclave here at the end of August. That's why Mr. Cowan had to come back to town."

Mother twisted to look at Blainey. "The Ku Klux

Klan is gathering tonight? You're sure that's what Una Lynn said?"

"She just said a Grand Konclave," Blainey answered.

"A Grand Konclave of Grand Dragons," I chimed in.

"Silly," Blainey said. "There's only one Grand Dragon, and that's Mr. Cowan. He bosses everybody else around."

I wondered how Blainey always knew so much about everything. But George was not listening to us; nor was Mother now, for she had turned back to him.

"Don't worry, George," she said. "You're with us and everything's all right."

George did not answer. Instead, in great haste, he started to turn the Hupp in the narrow road.

"No, no," Mother said. "Go on a little way. There's bound to be a turnout that will give more room. We don't want to get stuck here."

The flames lit up the night, but in moments we were again swallowed by the darkness beneath branching trees as George rushed us along. Uneasy fear had turned everyone silent.

At last Mother said, "Here's a wide spot."

But George had seen it more quickly than she, for already the headlights were scribing a circle on the surrounding curtain of trees and shrubs as he wheeled the Hupp about.

In that instant, halfway in the turn, the lights picked out a shadowy figure. It crouched below the three-foot bank of the road cut. Only the eyes showed clearly in the light, wide, staring. They reminded me of Lucifer's white-rimmed irises. The face must have been black as midnight, for it was almost invisible. The Hupp, turn incomplete, jarred to a halt.

"Somethin's caught the wheel," George breathed. His voice choked, and sounded not at all like George.

He flung out of the car. Ignoring the crouched figure, he began to struggle with something heavy and difficult. We could see him bend in front of the auto's lights. He grunted with the effort. The figure at the edge of the road detached itself from the dark. We saw, then, that it was a man. He came forward and helped with the fallen sapling that had wedged itself between road bank and one of the front wheels, cramped for the tight turn. At first, George seemed scarcely aware of this help. Then, there in the headlights' glare, we saw George's face change with surprise. He said a word or two, but immediately, with the obstacle removed, he lunged around the auto, leaped back into the driver's seat.

For the first time we could hear him speak to the man. "You better light outta here, Uncle Franley. Ain't a good night for colored folks. Most 'specially for muley colored folks."

Uncle Franley stepped a little closer. "Come on, you're not gonna leave me here for the Kluxers, George? I just now give 'em the slip. They're comin' right on my tail. What's the matter with you, boy—"

He reached for the door of the Hupp. When his other hand thrust in and grabbed George's arm, it was the first time he could see there were others in the auto. Now he yanked his hand away, dropped again into a crouch, ready to flee, as George said, stricken, "This family ain't about to take a chance, Uncle Franley. They's two little girls—"

"Wait." Mother's voice trembled. She sounded more frightened than on the day when she had learned to drive. "George, is this man your uncle?"

"He is that. The Kluxers been givin' him a peck of trouble. But I knew you-all wouldn't let him come climbing in with—"

"Get in." Mother spoke directly to Uncle Franley. "Hurry." She kneeled on the seat, reached back, struggled with the mass of cover packed level in the back. "Girls, let him lie under your feet. Help me lift up the pillows and blankets. That's it."

Without a word the black man crawled over the side into the back of the car with us. I could feel the cold fear sweat of his back as he brushed my leg. His shirt was gone. He slipped in beneath the raised blankets, dark and silent as the night. He sank away into nothingness. Mother arranged the cover, smoothed it, said, "Stretch your legs over it again, girls." Her eyes were a little hard with her resolve, but she managed a smile at us. "Don't look so glum. If anyone stops the auto, pretend you're asleep."

George had to back and fill to get the Hupp around. Before he could complete the turn, on the bank above the road cut a dozen white-robed, hooded figures loomed out of the dark. They must have come directly through the woods from the fire. Now Blainey's hand had mine, she pulled me close, whispered, "Play 'possum, Magpie."

Despite my racing heart, I settled against her, closed

my eyes, let my mouth droop slightly open, tried to breathe deeply, easily. But before I had closed my eyes, there was a glimpse of men's feet and the swinging hems of white robes, clear to see in the glare of headlights. The skirts seemed ludicrous with the heavy old brogans or the street shoes, worn and cracked, protruding beneath the hems.

Several of the Kluxers jumped down and blocked the Hupp's turn. They flashed a light into George's face. One said, "Well, we've caught us some niggers," but as the beam of light swung to Mother, the muffled voice from under the hood said, "Oh, beg pardon, ma'am, we thought some uppity niggers was drivin' round out here to meddle with our business of the evenin'."

The light swung to the back of the car, passed briefly over our faces. I squinched my eyes and stirred a little.

"Don't wake up the kiddies," one voice said. For a moment it spoke kindly enough, but hardened when it asked, "Have you seen anyone as you was drivin' around hyear, ma'am?"

"No," Mother said. It was the only direct out-and-out lie we ever heard Mother tell, except social lies for politeness' sake. "But we did see the reflection of a fire over there near Stone Mountain. We didn't want to get mixed up in any nighttime gathering, so we were trying to turn around. We seem to be lost. Maybe you could tell us which road goes to Atlanta."

"Sure thing, ma'am. Just turn 'round like you was doing, go back about a mile, maybe a mite more, bear right, and watch for Ponce De Leon. That'll take you straight on in through Decatur."

His voice diminished, so I knew he had backed away from the car. Relief flooded me, and Blainey silently squeezed my hand. Then suddenly, another voice came striking through the dark.

"What you got there, boys?"

And despite the fact I was still supposed to play 'possum, my eyes flew open. It was Mr. Cowan's voice. The Grand Dragon, himself. The boss of all these white-robed men, men more frightening than any Halloween bogies.

The familiar and awful voice went on. "Did you catch our nigger? Wouldn't you know that uppity black bastard would have cronies with a auto." And Mr. Cowan's head came thrusting in at George. But he must have seen Mother immediately, for he said, "My Gawd!" There was a moment's silence, then he blurted, "What's a lady doin' out here this time of night?" As before, the light came stabbing into the backseat. "I see you got two little girls with you."

It came to me at that moment that Mr. Cowan thought he was unrecognized behind his white hood. Except for that first *my Gawd* of recognition, he now spoke as though he had never seen us before, his words and tone rough, with none of the polish he had assumed that night at Pinewood, or even the day when Lucifer had bitten me. For some reason, it was terrifying to hear the voice, familiar but changed, issuing from behind the pointed hood. The elongated pallid dunce cap of cloth came down to snugly blend with the chunky sheeted shoulders. Why was it so frightening that the eyes were blank slits?

"This your nigger?" he asked Mother, and again shone the light full in George's closed countenance.

"He's our chauffeur," Mother said, icy and aloof.

Ethan Cowan felt safe in his anonymity. His tone turned to a bullying sneer.

"You seen any other nigger boy running around the road, here, Miz High 'n' Mighty?"

His gallantry was entirely gone. The beam of his light stabbed here and there inside the car, as though, somehow, he owned the night and everything in it. Did he remember we had snubbed his girls? Had he read that note of Mother's refusing the invitation to their tea party, that note as coolly aloof as Mother's voice now?

"We have seen no one," she said.

Blainey and I huddled together. The light found us. Mr. Cowan's hand reached and pinched Blainey's cheek, his tone eased a bit when he said, "Don't you two little ladies be scared. I won't let none of my boys hurt you."

For an instant the picture of Ethan Cowan holding little Henry Cowan to his chest floated in my mind. But it was replaced the next moment, as I imagined that round face with its hairy nostrils smiling inside the hood. Despite the words, meant to reassure us, now Mr. Cowan reached in with one hand that grasped an ugly metal-tipped pike. The pike punched at the blankets under our legs, probing, thrusting.

I began to cry. Blainey rose up next to me. "Stop that. You're scaring my sister. Besides, we have our dolls packed in the blankets so they'll ride safe. You're liable to break them."

A chuckle issued from the hood. "Now you're really

somethin', little missy," the voice said. But the hand gave another vicious punch with the pike.

Blainey pushed at the mean cudgel while she knelt on top of the blankets and glared at the faceless hood.

"If you don't go away and leave us alone, Mr. Cowan," she said in a voice that had begun to shake, "I'll tell our daddy and he'll see you get in trouble for bothering ladies at night."

In the glare of the flashlight, held-back tears glistened in her eyes. Even I could feel the fright that lay behind her outrage.

Instantly, the Grand Dragon, shorn of anonymity, backed away a step, stood staring in at us. The flickering light from that faraway bonfire made me wonder if Hades were something like this so that fear itself became a torture and a horror. It cut off my breath and squeezed my stomach. The only thing that moved for a moment was Mother's hand, which reached for Blainey's arm, held it firmly. It was difficult to know if Mother meant to restrain or to protect her wayward child.

George had not moved a muscle since the Kluxers had surrounded the Hupp. His hands still strangled the wheel, he seemed frozen, hunched a little forward. His eyelids were lowered as though he watched something on the Hupp's floor.

The silence grew terrible and long. The Grand Dragon was weighing our fate. Except for us, no one would know for sure that Ethan Cowan had been at Stone Mountain this night. At last, with a lunging motion, he thrust his head and shoulders back into the auto. He leaned across George and spoke directly to

Mother. Something of his demeanor at Pinewood returned. You could hear it in his quieter tone, in the
sounds of ingratiation that went with the words.

"I'm just puttin' on a little show here to keep the
boys stirred up. We've got some more huntin' to do
tonight. Don't want them to cool off too much. If I'd
recognized you quicker, we wouldn't have held you and
your young ladies up. You headin' for Atlanta?"

"Yes. We came this way by mistake." Mother's voice
had a distant quality, but she maintained her calm. "One
of your men gave us directions. We'll be on our way,
if you will all stand aside and let us pass."

The Grand Dragon backed off, saying loudly. "Okay,
Miz Standfield, you can go 'long now." And turning
to the crowd of robed men—there must have been two
or three dozen by now—he said, "They're okay. Neighbors of ours this past summer." Then harshly to George,
"Get a move on, boy, before we change our minds."

It was then in the glare of the flashlight that George
looked squarely at the slit-eyed hood hovering behind,
beyond the circle of light. It came as a shock to me,
that one glimpse I had of his dark eyes. I had thought
him frozen in deadly fear for the last several minutes.
Instead, his eyes gave me the first glimpse I had ever
had of pure hate. He was no longer the George I knew.
Surely the Grand Dragon would destroy him on the
spot. Instead, there came an ugly laugh, muffled by the
hood, a wave of the flashlight. We finished our turn
and drove off with the flames lighting up the night behind us.

That taunting laugh and the memory of those vicious

thrusts of the pike made me certain that Ethan Cowan was as cruel and wicked as any dragon in my story-books. The picture of Henry Cowan was blocked from my mind, little Henry saved from Cholly-boy by his awkward, frightened father; little Henry's fair head tucked beneath the man's aggressive chin; Henry's fragile back shielded by the stubby-fingered hands.

Aunt Ellie's words came back to me, "—some good in even the worst men—" words that did not console me. Then, as now in later years, this sparse good lent a human face to an ancient evil, and thus chilled the soul.

It was easier to purely hate Mr. Cowan when George stopped the auto at the edge of the colored district.

Softly, he said, "C'mon out, Uncle Franley. You only got a short piece to walk to Emmet's house. You're safe, tonight anyways."

Mother reached back and helped pull the blankets aside. She gave a little moan when Uncle Franley sat up. One of the pike thrusts had caught him across the side of his head. There was an oozing furrowed gouge through the tight black hair.

"You're hurt," she said. "We must get you to a doctor. Is there a colored doctor near here?"

"We could take him to Dr. Baird," I said, but no one paid any attention to me. Dr. Baird had treated all of the Standfield family ailments for years. Dr. Baird had no colored patients.

But Franley crawled from his cocoon and out of the auto in seconds. "No'm. No doctor. That's a nothin' cut. Just a little wool and skin. But my back done bled on your blanket." There was apology in his tone.

"The blanket doesn't matter," Mother said, and now her voice was trembling, the voice that had stayed so cool during the confrontation with the gathered Klan. "You really *must* have a doctor. . . ."

But the shirtless figure had backed away. We could hear a murmured "You-all, thanks," as he turned and hurried out of sight down the dark rutted street. It was nothing like Greenwood Avenue's paved surface; the dilapidated shacks, crowded in on either side, were nothing like our secure and comfortable home. There was only a glimpse of Franley's torn back as he disappeared into the night. Una Lynn's voice sounded in my head, and I remembered the looks of Lucifer's scarred sides. "Like Daddy says, niggers and horses do better with a good whipping. . . ."

When we finally turned into our street, Mother said, "Greenwood Avenue has never looked so good! I don't think I'll ever leave it again."

Blainey and I, too exhausted with the day to say anything, both rolled into bed already half asleep. Mother's and George's voices scarcely wound down into my consciousness as their talk filtered from the kitchen to our room.

"Why don't you fix us both a cup of coffee, George," she was saying. Then, "Why were the Klansmen after your uncle?"

"He has a no-'count piece of land south of Atlanta. Not sharecropped. He owns it hisself. Just a little old scrap of land. But it's hisn. He scraped his whole life to get it. The Kluxers is tryin' to take it over now."

"But why would the Klan want such a place?" Mother sounded skeptical. "Maybe your uncle is in some other kind of trouble."

"No'm." George was quietly positive. "They wants his land, 'cause there's talk of puttin' through a paved road out that way. Some of the Kluxers is buyin' up any piece they can get their hands on cheap. You couldn't buy a hog jowl for what they wants to pay. Besides, they know scarin' a nigger off is cheaper even than buyin'. But Uncle Franley is a muley man. He'll hang on until they kill him."

Over the years, I've thought of Uncle Franley and his no-'count piece of land, wondered if the Kluxers got it away from him, if they bought it cheaper than a hog jowl, or scared him off. Or killed him.

20

Ellie's Magic

The morning after we returned from Cloudacres, a Saturday, we slept late. It was nine when Blainey and I bounced out of bed. In our nighties, we raced for the dining room. At last, one of George's good breakfasts with our family whole again.

"Daddy came home last night," Blainey told me as we scrambled down the hall. "I went out and found him in the dining room. Mother had already gone to bed. He grabbed me up and kissed me and told me to be quiet and to go back to bed, too."

We were both laughing when we tumbled into the dining room. Mother sat at the table alone. She sipped a cup of steaming coffee. Her plate of eggs and biscuits and grits was pushed aside, untouched. She held a page

of notepaper in one hand. The paper quivered as though
it had a life of its own.

"What's the matter?" Blainey said, and the joy of our
rush died in her voice.

Suddenly I was afraid. More afraid than anytime in
this past uncertain year. All the hidden uneasiness of
the summer surfaced, congealed into oppressive terror.
Mother, white, stricken, silent, tried to speak. Her chin
trembled. Tears were rising and spilling as though from
some bottomless sad spring. No words came.

"What's the *matter?*" Blainey's voice scaled up and
it was clear that she was as frightened as I.

At last Mother said, "Daddy has left us."

"For how long?" Blainey tried for the straight of this
incomprehensible news.

"For good," Mother whispered.

Ridiculous. Impossible. How could she think this? It
was almost a relief to know that Mother was upset over
some colossal mistake. Daddy would no more leave us
than we would leave him. Daddy, as constant as sun
and stars and sky. No doubt entered my mind. A glance,
a shrug from Blainey confirmed this certainty, but we
threw our arms around Mother and cried with her, sorry
over her terrible mistake, sorry it made her so devastat-
ingly sad.

It was Blainey who finally jerked upright. She asked
in a muffled tone, "Did—did Daddy die?" The last word
was a whisper.

"No, no," Mother said, her voice thick and unnatural.
"He just won't be living here anymore. He's taken a
room at the club."

That would be the Atlanta Athletic Club, where he
worked out to stay trim and fit. Mother sounded as
though staying at the AAC was every bit as bad as dying.

"He was here last night." Blainey made her voice rea-
sonable. She used the same tone she would to explain
something very clearly to a very small child. "He can't
be gone. He wouldn't want to live anywhere but here
with us. He never has. It was very late when he came
in. He's probably asleep in his room. I'll go and wake
him up so he can eat with us." She turned toward the
door, but with a helpless motion of the hand holding
the notepaper Mother stopped her.

"He *was* here last night, then," Mother said. She spoke
in a numb way, worn out from her crying. "I heard
him and waited for him to come to my room and tell
me about his summer in England, about Arlene's finishing school. This morning I realized I fell back to sleep
waiting. The drive down from Cloudacres, the Klan,
and George's uncle, his back cut to ribbons . . ." The
words trailed away. It was easy to see that she, herself,
could not understand how she had fallen asleep without
seeing Daddy.

She finally went on again, "I found this on the table."
A listless wave of the hand holding the note. "When I
looked in his room, all of his clothes were gone. He
must have moved out while I slept. The note says he
meant to sit down and tell me face to face, but he just
didn't have the heart for it. That's what it says." And
she looked at the lines of strong up-and-down writing
and began to cry again.

Only in looking back is it clear the terrible shock

she had suffered. Mother, who had always protected us
from life's harshness, revealing to us the depth of her
painful despair; Mother, who had always winked or
smiled in the face of minor disasters, now devastated
and unaware for the moment of the effect on her chicks.

But Blainey, with the fear gone that Daddy might
have died, rallied, looked relieved, then leaned against
Mother and rejoined the crying over this temporary sorrow. Somehow, part of my own fright dissolved. On
that bright morning at the edge of autumn, it was clear
to me that only death could permanently remove Daddy
from us.

Still, by noontime, Blainey and I began to realize that
there was some element of truth in what Mother had
told us. It was Marian Pickett's visit in the middle of
the morning that helped to convince us. Marian Pickett,
still Mother's oldest and best friend in Atlanta. She and
Mother settled in the sitting room. Their voices were
quiet, but Mother was crying again.

"Mase, you poor dear." Marian sounded distressed.

Blainey and I crouched at the crack of the door. We
could see a slice of the room. There sat Marian and
Mother. Marian had one arm around Mother's bowed
shoulders.

"You're certain he's left you?" Marian's usually crisp
tones were gentled on this day. "Maybe it's just one
of those little spats."

"Allen and I seldom spat."

"Spats do clear the air." Some of Marian's crispness
returned.

But Mother's attention was on the note again. "There

was just this, propped against the sugar bowl this morning." She began reading again. " '—differences talking won't settle, differences in the way we look at life. I need my freedom, now—' Oh, Marian, I don't even know what differences we had. Nothing of any real importance. As I told you, Allen and I didn't even have those little spats you mentioned."

"When did you get back from Cloudacres?"

"Last night."

"Did Allen say anything then about leaving?"

"I haven't seen Allen since July, since Margy's birthday party. I heard him come in last night. Then it seemed I must have been dreaming—he was supposed to be in England."

"Oh, Mase." Marian put her cheek against Mother's bent head, got out her handkerchief as though to dab her own eyes.

"He went to England to be with Arlene."

"With Arlene!" Marian straightened, gave a scornful laugh. And the handkerchief went unused. "Arlene must have had a hand in all of this."

"I don't know." Mother sounded helpless. "She and Allen were always very close. Anyway, George drove the girls and me down from Cloudacres yesterday. Such an ordeal, Marian. We got lost and became mixed up with the Ku Klux Klan in the dark over near Stone Mountain. I was exhausted when—"

Marian interrupted. "Good heavens! What in the world were you doing clear over at Stone Mountain? And after dark, too."

"We took the wrong turn."

"Well, I guess. The front page of this morning's *Constitution* said that the Klan held a Grand Konclave at Stone Mountain last night. That means every Klansman in Georgia who could get there would have been over at the mountain. The paper said a colored boy was found out there about dawn. He had been lynched. About eighteen years old, the paper said he was. Hanging dead from a tree." Mother moaned, but Marian went on as though she were reading from the remembered page. "A message was scrawled in paint on the stone at the mountain's base. It said, 'This nigger hung for touching a white girl.'"

I tried not to think of someone hanging from a tree, someone no older than George, someone not as lucky as Uncle Franley had been. I wondered if anyone but us knew for certain that Ethan Cowan was at Stone Mountain last night.

Mother mentioned neither the Grand Dragon nor Franley. She did not breathe a word about Ethan Cowan. Instead she was saying, "Oh, Marian, everything is too much, just too much."

Blainey started to pull me away from the door. I was frozen, immovable. Mother, still visible through the narrow crack, lifted her head, blew her nose, wiped her eyes. She had heard our struggle. Her voice reached out and nabbed us.

"Girls?" She put her grief aside for the first time that day, and there was the old velvet authority. "Ladies don't listen at doors. You may ask George for two biscuits with jam. Then go down and play in your playroom. You can have lunch with Marian and me in about an hour. At lunch you can tell Marian about your summer at Cloudacres, the party and all."

We started to leave. I was strangely relieved to escape the weight of sorrow and the reminder of last night's terror. It was even a relief to hear the authority in her voice as it caught us again. "Girls, please close the door, then run along."

Without a sound, we shut the door.

In the kitchen, George lightly touched our heads as he gave us the biscuits. There was sympathy in his eyes; and uncertainty. It was obvious he knew about Daddy and that his own future was threatened by this split in the family. But he said nothing.

We were settled in the playroom before Blainey spoke to me.

"Daddy will be back with us pretty quick, you'll see, Magpie. Don't you worry about that."

She tilted her chin and her bright gaze dared anyone to disagree. She got no fight from me. Blainey should know about Daddy. After all, he and she were very close.

Suddenly, Marilyn Louise Carstairs arose in my mind, the way she tossed her head and pranced along, the airs she put on. The memory came of how certain I had been at the beginning of summer that her daddy had left her because she was so uppity.

What hidden flaw did I have?

That night and other nights dreams awoke me, and I lay in the dark trying to find the answer to this terrible and shadowy puzzle. Blainey slept on, but she cried out in dreams of her own, or twisted beneath the cover as though her body did not rest. In daylight, the question receded from my mind; I talked to no one about it. Once, though, in the middle of a moonless night I crept down the hall to Mother's room to find comfort from my guilt, but through the door came sounds of crying. I sat for a long time in the dark, but the crying did not stop.

Slowly the house sank into silence, and September would never end. Mother came from her room each morning, weary, pale, and unmoved by the clear air of autumn or the turning leaves of our woods. She would gather herself, manage a smile at Blainey and me, send us off to Greenwood Avenue School with lunch and books and sweaters. We no longer came home at noon to eat in the comfort of the kitchen with George for company, no longer came home to Mother's middle-of-the-day hug and kiss.

And Blainey no longer spoke of Daddy's return. There was no word from him. Once Marian Pickett told Mother, "Mr. Pickett saw Allen last night. The two of them still play basketball once a week with the Y team, you know. Mr. Pickett said Allen is very quiet and withdrawn, and didn't say a word about why he is living at the AAC."

Blainey had started a stamp collection. She spent hours bent over the colored squares, sorting, putting the extras in little transparent envelopes, pasting others into the thick album someone had given her last Christmas. I spent an equal time with spool knitting, turning out long brightly colored ropes of woven wool, but I was uncertain as to their final use. Solitary play in a solitary house. We did not think of tomorrow. All the tomorrows were gone. What was tomorrow without Daddy? Houses, children, wives, died without a man to care for them.

During the month of September, the house sank more deeply into silence. Mother only picked at her food, and her plumpness began to melt away. Through the dark of each night, the sound came down the hall of her feet pacing, pacing, pacing behind the closed door of her room. In the daylight hours she sat staring off into space, dozing from time to time, the sleeping and waking of the same joyless quality. She still saw to the things necessary for Blainey's and my welfare, but she had forgotten how to smile or laugh.

It was Marian Pickett and her husband who came by on the last day of September to persuade Mother that the three of us should join them at the Annual Theosophical Bazaar. It took some earnest urging on Marian's part to convince Mother.

Finally, in exasperation, Marian cried, "You just can't stop living, Mase! It's not fair to the girls. *Or* to you."

So, at last, Mother, unsmiling, reluctantly agreed to go. She gathered up a few things to donate to the bazaar. *A lady always does her part in community efforts.* Perhaps it was the tenets that really pulled her from depression.

At the Lodge Hall, we pushed through the double doors, and the rush of sounds and sights stunned us after our solitary weeks. Chatter and lights. The hustle-bustle of shifting buyers and sellers and lookers and talkers and laughers. The clink of change, the rustle of bills. Decorated tables laden with homemade cakes, pies, jams, jellies, cookies, pickles. Other tables displayed guest towels with tatted edging, embroidered dresser scarfs, hand-sewn baby clothes, crocheted bonnets and bootees and soakers.

The largest offering: a collection of dolls, one from each state in the Union. The Georgia doll had a basket of tiny cloth peaches on her arm. The California doll was no doll at all, but a golden teddy bear, sporting a royal-blue knit vest. Someone had gone to a lot of trouble for that collection, and the prices were fancy.

Almost every Atlanta Theosophist, man, woman and child, had contributed something. Mother had brought along two potholders from Blainey and me, Blainey's square and strongly made, mine a little lopsided and fragile. Mother had gathered them from our kitchen where they had hung, carefully unused, since we had made them. Her own donation—a coverlet pieced together from Daddy's old silk ties. She had worked on it most of the summer. Now it glowed in the bare-bulb lights, as gorgeous and flamboyant as a peacock's tail. While I watched, someone bought it.

At that moment, Frank and Ellie Benton joined us. Presently, Uncle Frank was off on his own, touring the booths, and the Picketts were swept away on a tide of shoppers. But Ellie herded Mother, Blainey, and me toward the meeting room so we would be sure of seats for the program that would start soon.

Tonight, Ellie held me on her lap during the short performance put on by the Theosophical Society children. This year we did not join in. Last year Blainey had sung "Watchman, What of the Night?" with Mother at the piano. Blainey had been a real hit, because she had a clear, true voice and ample stage presence. I had read from *Mother Nature's Children*, a long-ago gift of English verse from Arlene. I was a hit, too, because, small for my age, I looked too young to sit there gravely reading page after page. But my performance smacked of hoax. In reality I had recited each quatrain from memory, for Mother had read the book to us a thousand times, and we knew every page by heart.

Tonight, after the program, I leaned motionless against Ellie's kind bosom. I remembered the magic she had performed for Lucifer. Should I ask her to use her magic to reveal my unknown flaw? Then the thought came—maybe the flaw would scare beloved Ellie away, too. Yes, safer not to ask at all. Instead, I used my wish left over from my birthday at Cloudacres. After all, it was an overdue wish, one owed me for blowing out the candles with one breath. It was not granted now; no miraculous light was shed on the problem of the flaw. A delayed wish must be forever lost.

It was Ellie speaking to Mother that brought me from my reverie. The four of us sat apart from the rest of the people in the busy room. Ellie still held me, and Blainey had tucked herself under Ellie's other arm.

"Mase, you must pull yourself out of the doldrums," Ellie was gently saying. "It's not good for you or the girls to sit around moping about what can't be helped."

Mother must have remembered Marian saying almost the same thing, for now she looked directly at Ellie as though really seeing her for the first time this evening. She gave a faint smile.

"Nothing makes sense to me anymore, Ellie," she said.

"You do understand that Allen is not of a nature to do something with no thought given to it. His summer with Arlene must have firmed his mind on some idea he had."

"Arlene won out after all," Mother murmured.

Ellie ignored this and went on. "Even if we don't understand his leaving, Mase, at least we must accept that it is done."

"Yes, I suppose so." Mother's voice was scarcely more than a whisper.

Ellie plunged ahead. "Have you ever thought of a change of scene, a new life for you and the girls?"

"A new life?" Puzzled, Mother aroused herself a bit. "I can't imagine one. Besides, where, Ellie? Where? Cloudacres . . ." Her voice faded, the effort of thinking this bold thought too wearisome to sustain.

"No, certainly not Cloudacres, dear Mase." Ellie spoke with kind firmness. "An entirely new location. That would be the ticket. I've been giving it some thought. At first I wondered if maybe Virginia, your hometown. Lynchburg, isn't it? But no, I told myself, that would just dig up old feelings, old memories, there would have to be explanations to family and acquaintances."

Mother flushed, looked at her own tightly clasped hands, said nothing. I remembered the disgrace of Marilyn Louise at school after her daddy left her, remembered that Blainey was reluctant to play with Marilyn Louise after that descent from respectability.

But Ellie was rushing on, determined to lay out all of her cards before Mother could close her mind to the new ideas. "Cloudacres, of course, is impossible too, for it would only keep painful scenes alive. So, the logical and hopeful plan would be an entirely different, new, exciting, stimulating place."

For the first time, Mother seemed aware of everything that Ellie was trying to say. For a moment, Ellie's enthusiasm caught her and brief interest flickered in her eyes.

"Now where in the world could I find a place like that? How would I make my way and take care of the girls?" The interest began to wane. "Ellie, Ellie, your heart's in the right place, but—"

"Krotona. The ideal solution for you, Mase." Ellie leaned forward, clasped one of Mother's hands, intent on her own eagerness to help. "Yes, Krotona. The girls could go to The School of the Open Gate. A wonderful, wonderful school, they say. I'll bring you the Open Gate brochure and a booklet all about Krotona, itself. They came in the mail to me yesterday. I wrote for them. You see, I've been concerned over you, but not wanting to intrude. I should have brought the leaflets along to-night—"

But suddenly Ellie broke off as Mother quickly arose. For a moment the change in Mother's face frightened me. Even Blainey looked alarmed. It seemed that something had instantly snapped shut in Mother's mind to block this outrageous suggestion of leaving Atlanta and friends and everything she knew. She looked for her purse as though she intended to run home and hide in her room and never come out again.

"Oh, Mase," Ellie cried softly in distress. "You know I'm only trying to help. You're my dearest friend. You know I wouldn't suggest your going away if I didn't think it might help." All of Ellie's assurance fled on her own tears, discreet tears, for one must not make a public display.

Ellie released Blainey and me, began to search frantically in her purse. All the while, the anxious, sorry words poured out.

"I don't know what I'd do without you, Mase. I'd miss you so terribly. The girls, too, they're so very dear to me. Almost like my own would have been." And finally she found the handkerchief she was looking for, blotted her eyes, very quietly blew her nose. "It isn't as though we'd never see one another again. Frank and I could visit you at Krotona." She blew once more.

Suddenly Mother's lifetime of ladylikeness rose up and saved the evening from complete disaster. Truly the tenets lent her a saving strength, for with Mother they went beyond the surface to the heart. *A lady would never distress a friend and make her cry in public.*

"Oh, Ellie, dear Ellie," she whispered, sinking down beside her friend. "How beastly I am. How selfish and unbearable I've become. Of *course*, you are right. There is certainly something in what you have been telling me. It *is* an idea. Don't cry, dear Ellie, please. Oh, please. It *has* become terribly difficult here in Atlanta. Our friends are so dreadfully kind. Everyone feels so sorry for us."

Mother sounded a little breathless, as though it was hard to get enough air in the warm, brightly lit room. But her words rushed on as she reached to touch her friend's hand. "Oh, Ellie, now, now. You *do* help, you know. You know you do." And Mother had to ply her own handkerchief to her nose, then briefly to Blainey's, at last more thoroughly to mine, for now we had all dissolved in quiet tears of ladylike distress.

"Oh, what a mess we all are," Ellie finally gasped, looking from one to the other of us, at our red eyes, our streaked faces, our runny noses.

She sniffled, then gave a choked giggle. For a moment she and Mother stared into each other's eyes. Then they leaned forward, each against the other's shoulder, laughing. Weakly they clung while the strange merriment welled up as uncontrollable as the tears had been before. In huge relief, Blainey and I joined in, all of us laughing, laughing like four children together.

So Ellie had worked her magic after all. At least in part. Even I had no illusion that our problems were solved. We had turned serious again by the time Mother spoke.

"Yes, Ellie, do send the brochure about the school, and any information you have on Krotona. At least I'll consider it."

"I know several people there," Ellie said, tentative now, fearful of another deluge. "Hannah Davenport is one of the leading lights. Frank and I stayed at Krotona for four or five days when we visited California last spring. It's a lovely colony in the hills right above Hollywood. I'm sure we could help arrange it for you, so you could stay right at the Theosophical Center. You'd be protected there, dear, and you'd love the Ternary Building. They've divided it into three apartments. The

Ternary looks like something from India with acres of rolling, landscaped grounds around it."

India. A tremor of excitement seized me. India. And the memory of those stories read to us arose again in my mind. "Rikki-Tikki-Tavi." "Mowgli and His Brothers." And the strange little girl from India who walked through the pages of *The Secret Garden.*

"Would there be room for the three of us at the Ternary Building?" Mother sounded uncertain.

"I'll write to Hannah tonight, if you like. There just might happen to be a vacancy. It would be a perfect place for Blainey and Margery."

The excitement of India died. Fright crept into my heart. A perfect place for Blainey and me. And where would Mother go? The terrible uneasiness that had filled me at Pinewood last summer when the name, Krotona, had been mentioned came back to haunt me. Krotona, so far away, so foreign. The impossibility of Daddy leaving us had become a fact. Now, I realized nothing in life was certain.

Mother did not reply to Ellie. Was she thinking of the years here, and of all the friends like Ellie and Marian she'd leave behind? Was she thinking of Mrs. Hewitt and their fine old arguments about the Revolutionary War? Was she wondering how it would be to have all the familiar places and old friends supplanted by strangers' faces and unknown scenes?

Krotona, a whole world away from Daddy, from Greenwood Avenue, from George. Forever away from Cloudacres.

It was Uncle Frank who really saved the evening for me and for Blainey. When he came back to us from touring the displays alone, he had bought a baby doll with hand-sewn clothes, and hand-crocheted bonnet and bootees, from one of the needlework counters. He stooped and gathered Blainey to him.

"For you, sugar," Uncle Frank said.

The doll was wide of bottom, soft of body, sweet of face. Her hair was painted on, but her eyes, larkspur blue, opened and closed and had thick real lashes. She gave a plaintive "Ma-ma" when bent a little forward. Blainey, who cared nothing for dolls as a rule, swept this one to her.

"I'll call her Peggy. Baby Peggy," she said with decision, and cradled her new child to her breast.

"How good of you, Frank," Mother said. It was plain that she no longer clung to her own closed world of utter despair. "It looks like an honest-to-goodness baby," and she managed a smile at him.

Before she could prompt, Blainey said, "Thank you very much, Uncle Frank," and kissed him on the cheek. He laughed and hugged her again.

"You're my—" he began, then stopped to kiss her, so that for an instant it seemed he might say little trooper. Instead he finished, "—dear child."

Blainey ducked her head against Peggy's sweater. Only I could see she was crying again.

It was the golden California bear for me. How could Uncle Frank have known it was the only thing in the whole evening that had really warmed my heart? The silky bear with the black button eyes, so far from his home. California. California, a world away. Beneath his handsome and jaunty vest, surely his bear's heart was breaking with loneliness. I held him, rocked him.

"I'll take care of you," I whispered in his beautiful round ear.

Mother started to say something, but Uncle Frank interrupted her. "Never mind, Mase. It's enough thanks that Margy loves it. Don't make her toe the mark tonight."

He was still stooped beside me when I kissed him. The suggestion of stubble along his cheek made me think of Daddy. Uncle Frank kissed the top of my head, hugged me. He seemed unaware of any secret flaw I might have. Greatly relieved, I kissed him again. His good smell came to me, a little like cloves or cinnamon, a little like the trees of his beloved Pinewood. I hated to let him go.

21

Oh, Susanna!

Oh, Don't You Cry for Me

The brochure for The School of the Open Gate came in the mail on Friday, the first week in October. There was a second booklet with the magic word *Krotona* across the front. The brown letters raised on the tan cover were in an angular and exotic script, very handsome. Mother was perusing the pages when Blainey and I pushed through the front door at quarter past three.

"Come here, little chicks." She smiled at us.

The ghostly weeks of seclusion were over, the days of open weeping had passed. Now Mother bravely turned a pleasant face to the world. Her eyes were still shadowed, bewildered, but when she looked at us she would give her wink and a little twist of her head that told us life had not ended after all, that somehow a family could survive without a man. As we came in, she held out the booklets.

"Look what Aunt Ellie sent us." She fanned through the pages and eagerly we settled, one on each side of her.

The Krotona brochure opened to a splendid picture of a building—a storybook palace. The photo showed lower walls and a tower, a flat-roofed two-story central building with arched, pointed windows that made me think of India and cholera and mongooses. Yes, a palace for some legendary potentate. It was set on a rise of ground with shrubs and trees and gentle slopes falling away toward the bottom of the picture. Behind rose a hill with open land and groves of strange trees, and stone steps leading up and up until they dwindled to nothing.

"Is that the Ternary Building?" I asked.

"How in the world did you know that, sugar?" Mother put one arm around me.

"She read under the picture," said Blainey.

"I didn't read. It's just that Aunt Ellie said the Ternary Building looked like a palace from India. She said it would be a good place for you and me, Blain, remember?" The fear leaped up again, the fear that had hidden at the back of my mind since Ellie's words.

When I turned to Mother, my voice sounded muffled. "Wh-where are you going to live?"

"Oh, darling"—she drew me close against her—"we three are inseparable." Her other arm reached for Blainey, and for a minute it seemed Mother might start to cry all over again. Even more unbearable than having

Daddy gone would be for Mother to retreat to her room once more and shut us out.

"Absolutely inseparable," she whispered.

"Like the Musketeers?" Blainey said, breathless from the fierce hug to Mother's warm bosom.

Instead of crying, Mother started to laugh. "Yes, just like the Three Musketeers." Then for some reason we were all laughing together. The world leaped to life, we knew the silent weeks were gone for good, and suddenly everything became possible.

When Mother said more soberly, "Or like Ruth," the loving, warm vitality had returned.

We knew she was talking about the biblical Ruth, the one shown in the painting on our dining-room wall, the one who talked with the beautiful Naomi. In fine script below the picture was written, "Whither thou goest, I will go. . . ."

After we finished the Krotona booklet, Mother asked, "Would you two like to go to California? Ellie does say we can get an apartment in the Ternary. An apartment for the *three* of us." She gave me a comforting squeeze. "There are lots of Theosophists in Krotona, so we'd have friends to help us in our new way of living." She went on, half to herself, "Besides, women are much more independent these days, and this will be our great adventure together."

Again I thought of "Rikki-Tikki-Tavi," of "Mowgli," of *The Secret Garden*. And finally of "The Covered Wagon" and its trek westward. Our great adventure together! One far greater than I had envisioned at the beginning of last summer in our new touring auto with

its storm curtains. Adventure. This time real. And I
remembered the bold flash of eye, the brave smile of
my Suffragette.

"I'd go to The School of the Open Gate?" Blainey
was asking, the question cautious, tentative. But her
voice held a hidden excitement, too.

"Yes," Mother answered, "you and Margy, both. Let
me show you the book about it. You could study marvelous things that aren't even taught at the Greenwood
Avenue School. The Open Gate school is what convinced me we should really go to California. Such an
opportunity for you girls."

In the brochure there were pictures of the school
buildings, standing separately like cottages in a setting
as woodsy and inviting as the one of the Ternary Building. Mother turned the page and there was a view of
children with their kind-faced teacher, gathered together beside a feathery bush.

" 'Nature Study Class and Acacia Trees,' " Mother
read the caption.

"That would be fun," I said, "to go to school outside
underneath—what kind of trees?"

"Acacia trees, little chick."

"Under acacia trees. Unless it was raining. What do
they do when it rains?" Acacia. A lovely word.

"They go in one of the buildings." Blainey's easy logic
made me angry, and stole my pleasure in acacia.

"You're a smarty-pants!" I cried, wishing we were
allowed to hit. It surprised me, my secret pleasure in
yelling at Blainey again.

Mother smiled, unperturbed. "It doesn't rain much

in California. It's sunny and warm most of the time. And there are fields of wild flowers everywhere all year long."

The imaginary scene, filled with color and sun and sweet breezes, stole my anger. We turned pages and looked at every picture. There were classes in Literature and French and Art and Music and The Dance. And, of course, Nature Study. Our existence on Greenwood Avenue suddenly paled by comparison. How dull our life had been. Besides, there was no Daddy to anchor us here.

Mother drew a deep breath. "I think we shall go to California." She lifted Blainey's chin with one hand to look into her eyes. "Would you like to travel to California, honey?"

Blainey was silent for a while, but her gaze was steady on Mother's face. I wondered if she was thinking of "The Covered Wagon" and the dangers we might face. Another thought angled into my mind. Blainey no longer insisted to me that Daddy would be back with us. For the first time, it came home to me that our life had truly changed. My Suffragette, almost a whole year ago, had warned me. *Get ready for some changes, little girl.* Again I saw the streak of blood across her cheek and the brave raising of her banner. *Remember . . .* she had finally called. And I had.

In retrospect, it is easy to see that, with Daddy gone, Mother had begun to lean on Blainey when she felt that decisions needed an agreement from someone.

So she had asked, "Would you like to travel to California, honey?"

After silent and due consideration, Blainey said, "Yes, let's go tomorrow!" Her cheeks flushed, her eyes began to shine with the thought of this coming adventure.

Mother looked almost happy. "We'll have to pack and settle things here first." When she turned to me it was clear that her own mind had been made up with Blainey's agreement. But she asked, "And you, chicken little? Are you game for such a trip?"

"Whither thou goest . . ." I solemnly said, and wondered if we would truly travel by covered wagon. She laughed and kissed me.

But, even with the booklet closed, the Ternary Building sprang clear in my mind. What a grand thing it would be to live in an Arabian Nights palace. It just might be worth the risk of the wagon trek.

When Mother told George we would be leaving for California in about three weeks, his face lit in a free and genuine smile.

"California! I reckon that's just about as good as heaven," he said, laughing. "Folks say it's nothin' but sunshine and flowers and easy livin'. And we're goin' there!"

"Oh, George." Mother's voice broke. "I've given you the wrong impression. Only Blainey and Margy and I are going. We can't take you with us."

George's laugh died. He seemed suddenly smaller, younger, frightened. "Miz Standfield, I feel safe livin' with you-all. If you goes, I'm goin' too."

"Mr. Standfield will be moving back here when we're gone. There will be a place for you with him. He'll *need* you."

"You-all needs me more'n Mr. Standfield." George's face closed with stubbornness. I remembered that George's Uncle Franley was a muley man.

"It's impossible." Mother's voice hardened in a way we had never heard before. She sounded as stern as Daddy. But she looked as though she wanted to cry. Instead, she set her mouth in a firm line so it stopped the trembling of her chin. She told George, "Mr. Standfield has promised to send a certain amount of money to me each month so the girls and I can live decently in California. He will keep the house, the Hupp, Cloudacres, everything." Her voice broke again.

In a moment she went on, bolstered now by reasonableness. "Allen wrote me a letter. He said that a monthly check is only just and fair since we accumulated all we own together. He is a good and decent and fair-minded man." Her chin did tremble then, but she controlled herself and went on. "It will be expensive for him to keep up two households, and there won't be enough to allow for servants of any kind in California. We will have a place just barely big enough for the three of us. So, you see, it's simply impossible for you to come along." Abruptly she turned and walked from the room.

I started to follow to plead George's case, but Blainey grabbed my arm, hauled me off and down to the playroom.

"Magpie," she said seriously. "Mother has enough trouble without us pestering her. We've got to *really* behave like ladies now. Like grown-up ladies, and not fight with each other, or make trouble, or argue with her about every little thing."

"Look who's talking." I glared at Blainey. "It's you almost got a spanking from Daddy for arguing with Mother. I bet you're just about the world's biggest arguer."

The mention of Daddy turned Blainey silent for a moment. Then she said, softly, "That was ages ago, way back right after Easter."

But a shadow of my fright on that day returned when Mother had wailed to Daddy, "I just don't know what I'm going to do with Blainey and her everlasting arguments. She's resisted everything I've asked her to do for the past month."

It was the end of the day, and Mother had run entirely out of patience. Maybe things hadn't gone well for Daddy at work. In any event, grim faced, he turned to Blainey.

"You must want a paddling, young lady," he said and without another word marched her off to the bathroom.

Daddy had never spanked either of us, despite his threat of it last November after Blainey's fall from grace at school—a threat unfulfilled. This present offer of paddling seemed more than threat, and terrified, I had crept into the dark hall and crouched outside the door. Behind its panel, the low steady sound of Daddy's voice went on forever. When they came out, Blainey was subdued and silent. They passed me by, and I could hear Blainey in the sitting room. She, who hardly ever cried, was crying, telling Mother she was sorry to have caused her so much trouble.

Presently, that day in the hall's dark, I knew Daddy was standing above me.

"Why are *you* crying, sugar?" he asked, his voice gentle.

"I-I thought you were going to paddle Blainey. I was scared."

He swung me up. "I just gave her a talking to."

I laid my head on his shoulder. "Will you give me a talking to?" And through my fright came the quick and urgent longing for that closeness with Daddy behind blank and secret doors.

He hugged me. "You're a good child. You don't need a talking to," he said.

Suddenly I had hated being a good child.

So again Blainey had not been paddled, and now it was too late. Now Blainey no longer needed it. These weeks had changed her. Had changed us all—Mother, Blainey, me. And most certainly Daddy. Somehow I knew the changes were not over.

"It wouldn't be any use to argue with Mother about George coming with us. You can see she's made up her mind, Magpie."

"It's not fair," I began.

"Sometimes things can't be fair. She's right about the money, you know, about not having very much. I guess we won't even own an auto in California."

"She's still afraid to drive anyway. So what if we owned one, who would drive it?" Auto and Daddy were tangled in my mind. One without the other seemed impossible.

Blainey shrugged. "Besides no auto, she'll have to do all the housework and cooking herself."

Instantly contrite that I had almost added to Mother's troubles by arguing, that I had given no thought to the terrible difficulties she faced, I said, "We can help."

"Let's start helping now, Magpie," and Blainey gave me a little hug. "Let's pack some of our own things, ready for the trip."

So we snatched up our most precious toys from the playroom, among them Baby Peggy and the golden California bear, and flew upstairs. There, from the sleeping-porch closet and from the dresser drawers, we dragged out what we wanted to take with us.

As for George, it seemed certain to me that Mother would relent. We just couldn't do without him.

☙

The day before we were to leave, Marilyn Louise came prancing down the street toward us. She tossed her long, glistening mane of hair out of the way. I half expected her to whinny. Strange, that since she reminded me of a horse, I still disliked her so much.

She said, "Our teacher told us that you won't be going to Greenwood Avenue School anymore. She told all of us you're moving to California."

Marilyn Louise's eyes were not equine like the rest of her. Instead, they were as hard as a jay bird's looking for a nest to rob.

"Yes. That's right." Blainey did not flinch beneath the dissecting gaze.

"You don't have to run away just because your daddy's

left you. Good riddance, my mother says. *We* get along just fine, me and my mother. She makes him pay a lot of money every month."

Blainey's chin came up. "What *you* do has nothing to do with what *we* do. We're going to California so Margery and I can go to a very private school. We will take Literature and French and Art. And study The Dance." Blainey turned and marched up the steps, across the porch. With finality the door slammed behind her.

Marilyn Louise giggled, then her gaze came to rest on me.

"You better watch out when you get to California," she warned, her voice turning soft and ominous.

"Why? What's so scary about California?" I tried to sound as high-and-mighty as Blainey.

"There's lots of Chinamen out there. I've heard tell they like to kick little girls. Especially if you say, *Chink, Chink, Chinaman, Sittin' on a fence, Tryin' to make a dollar Out of fifteen cents.* If you dare to say that to one, he'll come up and kick the stuffing out of you."

"I wouldn't say *that*." I was horrified at the awful results the rude lines would beget. My high-and-mightiness had fled.

Marilyn Louise leaned closer. "You just better watch out anyway, Margery Standfield." She straightened, tossed her mane, cantered off down the sidewalk.

There was to be no covered wagon for us after all. The huge Peachtree Street Station in downtown Atlanta sounded hollow, echoing, eerie. Even Mother looked small and somehow ineffectual in the great busy chamber. George had come to help us aboard the Southern Pacific Pullman train. Mother hadn't relented after all; this was George's last act for us. We had overheard her telling Marian Pickett on Marian's last visit before we were to leave, "I don't know how we'll manage without George."

"Why don't you take him along?" Marian asked, as though George were only another suitcase or trunk.

"Oh, Marian, I only wish I could, but there's no room for him at the Ternary. We'll have a one-bedroom apartment. Scarcely enough for us three. Besides, I hear that colored people are very uppity in California. I'd feel so responsible for George. And what would I do with him if he got uppity way out there?"

Somehow it consoled me, thinking of George and uppitiness. I remembered the look in his eyes as he had glared at the hooded Grand Dragon. Remembered that he had a share of Uncle Franley's muley streak. Beyond that, he had escaped from the chain gang. Yes, the thought of uppitiness lifted my spirit. I could not have borne our parting without the strength of the knowledge that George, like the rest of us, had changed. He was no longer so young and frightened, no longer dependent on us for his safety, his life. Instead he stood there in the terminal building, a new, a stronger George, one with a man's ableness, ready to do what a man must do. I decided, anyone who could throw hate from his eyes into the face of a Grand Dragon could move mountains if he had to.

There in the Peachtree Street Station, it was George

who looked after us. He had seen that the two steamer trunks with all our worldly goods were safely stowed in the baggage car. Now he handed Mother the claim check.

"When you-all winds up in California, you can't get back your steamer trunks lessn you show that," he warned, and he picked up our hand luggage, scorning the redcap who came hurrying up. "I'm takin' care of these folks," he said, his voice steady, firm.

"Maybe Daddy will come down and see us off," Blainey said, her voice subdued with disbelief, yet hope bright in her eyes. "Does he know we're going this afternoon? Does he know when our train leaves?"

Quickly Mother said, "He knows when we're leaving, but it would be just too painful for us all if he were to come here—" She broke off, sounding a little breathless, and began to search in her purse. "I was saving this for the train. We have a few minutes, don't we, George?" She turned to him as though she needed reassurance, yet already she was settling on a waiting room bench.

"I guess—" he murmured, but worry creased his forehead.

Mother brought out an envelope. On the front of it was Daddy's plain, firm writing: *Blainey and Margy.*

"He enclosed this in a letter to me. It came yesterday afternoon," she said. Her hand shook a little as she handed it to Blainey. "You read it out loud to Margy, sugar, it's for you both."

Blainey snatched the folded sheet out, opened it, sat down, spread it on her knees, began to read immediately.

My darling girls,

You are about to begin an adventure. An adventure even better than the ones in the books we have read together, for this one is real. I only wish we could be together. Since I can't go with you, I will tell you here what I want you to do for me. Keep your eyes open and see everything that is to be seen. When you get to California sit down and write me a letter telling me all about it. That way we can be together even though we're apart. I'll write to you often, telling you what is going on here in Atlanta and on Greenwood Avenue, and next summer about Cloudacres if I have time to get up that way. I'll be busy earning money to take care of all of us, so maybe I will stay in town next summer.

I've sent along some traveling money for each of you. Mother will give it to you when you need to buy something special. I hope you will use some of it to buy writing paper or a notebook to jot down all that goes on so you can tell me everything in your letters.

Now, my two beloved children, help Mother all you can and be good little troopers. Don't forget your Daddy, who sends you hugs and a world of kisses, and wishes for a good and adventuresome trip to California and Krotona.

Love,

The note was signed *Daddy* with such a bold flourish that it seemed he reached right off the page to touch us.

At that instant, there came the cry, "Bo-a-a-rd!" from

outside on the platform, then a jumble of words, and finally, "—Kansas City!"

"That's us!" Mother sprang to her feet, grabbed my hand.

"We don't want Kansas City!" Blainey cried.

"Yes, yes. Kansas City. Out of our way, but the best route with only one change and a very short layover. There's a train directly to Los Angeles from Kansas City." Mother had already started off with me in tow. She looked back at her reluctant child. "Come *along*, Blainey!"

Blainey, Daddy's letter still clutched in her hand, leaped after us. George had already snatched up our luggage and now led us through Gate 10 and out onto the platform. A train stood waiting there, far larger, far grander than the Tallulah Falls train. Down the way the locomotive was giving tentative little puffs and sighs. Once, the line of Pullman cars gave a subdued jerk as though it were anxious to be off and away. But then the locomotive let out a great sigh of steam and everything settled to quietness again.

"We got lotsa time," George said, for even the conductor who had called "Bo-a-a-rd!" had walked off along the train's length. Now, neither he nor the train seemed in any hurry to leave Atlanta and start the long haul to Kansas City.

"You-all got your tickets now?" George asked Mother.

"Yes, yes." She fished frantically in her purse, sighed with relief when she found them in the same place they had been each of the half a dozen times she had already looked while inside the waiting room. Now she turned to George, said uncertainly, "We might as well get on board, I suppose." Then in a rush of words, "Oh, George, we shall certainly miss you. You've been one of our true blessings there on Greenwood Avenue, and summers, too, at Cloudacres. Oh, dear"—she struggled with tears— "what will become of you? No, no, how foolish of me! You'll be with Mr. Standfield, of course, safe and comfortable with your own room as always."

Suddenly George smiled. He looked Mother directly in the eye with no shy sidelong glance now.

"Safe ain't enough for a man." How strange to hear these words from George. We had always thought safe and comfortable was all he wanted, safe from the chain gang, safe from the Klan, comfortable after all the pain and hardship he had endured. What more could a young colored boy want from life?

But now he was saying, "Safe ain't enough for a man, not enough by a long shot. You've been mighty good to give me breathin' time, but don't go fussin' your head about me, Miz Standfield. I'll stay with Mr. Standfield for a stretch, but once he's settled down from all his upset, I'm goin' on along."

"Wherever to?" Mother sounded despairing, unable to imagine George any place but secure in his basement room.

"I got me some irons in the fire. One is a cousin got a jazz band. Uncle Franley's boy. The band's headin' for up north. Maybe New York, maybe Chicago. That'll be in a coupla months." His eyes lit with the joy of anticipation. "You-all don't know it, but I blows a mighty mean clarinet. I been makin' myself a little money nights, playin' with my cousin's band. I done saved up enough to bankroll myself for goin' north. Maybe after I gets more cash ahead, maybe I'll even go on to school some more. A man's got to think ahead."

We had never heard George say so much all at one time. Mother was studying his face. For a minute I wondered if she thought he had already turned uppity.

Finally she said, "I had no idea."

But she sounded relieved, and plainly amazed that George had a side to him she had never guessed. Then, despite the tears that were rising, she smiled and said, "I'm so very glad for you, George. Blainey, Margy, and I will miss you terribly though."

"I'll miss you-all, too," he said softly in genuine sorrow.

Now Mother repeated, uncertainly, "We might as well get on the train, I suppose." Then before George could answer, she straightened her shoulders, firmed her voice. "Yes, we'll get on and settle ourselves."

But when her hand brushed my face, it felt as cold as last January's snow. She clutched one of her Irish linen lace-edged hankies. "I always cry at good-byes." She flourished it, laughing as though this oddity were amusing. Nevertheless, she caught an early tear with it.

George swept Blainey up. They gave each other a great hug. He was so small, himself, that Blainey's feet reached down to his knees.

"You-all be good and help your mama, y'hear, and don't give her no sass," he said, his voice as gruff as it could get with us. He set her down, wiped his nose with an oversized handkerchief from his hip pocket. In a moment he picked me up and we mutually squeezed. I could feel the bones at the back of his thin neck.

"And don't you-all cry, all that long old way to California," he admonished, trying to laugh.

"Just while we say good-bye," I promised, for there was no way to stem the tears that had already begun.

The whistle blew, a conductor stuck his head from the Pullman door.

"Bo-a-a-a-rd!" he shouted, the word drawn out so long it curled through the great station, a winding serpent of sound.

Now no time for tears. Mother and George bundled me and my California bear up the steep steps. Blainey, with Peggy under one arm, leaped up after. Mother, puffing and pink, managed the flight. Then George slid our hand luggage in after. We pushed through the hard-to-open door, made our way along the aisle between the high-backed green-plush seats. The conductor brought our luggage, stowed it in a compartment above the windows.

The train jerked. We collapsed on the green plush. There came the muffled rattle and crash of linkage. Outside the window, George, small on the endless platform, slid slowly backward and away. He had his handkerchief out again. He swiped at his face, then flourished the white square at us. Blainey and I waved, Mother fluttered her little handkerchief.

The platform picked up speed. George disappeared. The station buildings slipped by, were gone. A phalanx of gleaming rails appeared beside our train. These raced past, faster, faster, until everything streaked in a dizzy blur. At last we rumbled out into the early sunshine of October. The dingy back streets of Atlanta flew past.

There was a snatch of view down one of Atlanta's boulevards. Sun glinting from a windshield blinded me for an instant. And suddenly I heard an echo, reaching forward from almost a year ago, of John Philip Sousa's "Washington Post March." In imagination, the flash of light that blinded me glinted from the flared bells of golden horns. Remembered music blared up and the Marine Corps Band turned the corner onto Atlanta's Peachtree Street. The tubas and trumpets and slide trombones and flutes and fifes, the cymbals, the rattling snare drums, the booming bass drums, oompahed and beat and fanfared and sparkled. The sound faded and there, from a year ago, was my Suffragette waving, calling only to me.

"Get ready for some changes, little girl. Remember . . ."

And here we were, we three ladies, rushing forward to a new future. Presently we rumbled across the Chattahoochee River bridge. The train's whistle gave a long banshee wail.

"We're on our way, girls!"

Mother's voice held a note of triumph, the same kind of triumph that had secretly shone in her eyes last summer after she had killed the snake at Cloudacres.

Now two small rivulets of moisture were released by her glasses. She took them off, briskly polished the lenses with her linen square, wiped her cheeks. She resettled her glasses, smiled at us. As we left the Chattahoo-

chee behind, she started us off to sing a short snatch
of song.

> *Oh, Susanna!*
> *Oh, don't you cry for me.*
> *For we're goin' to California,*
> *With a banjo on our knee. . . .*

On Greenwood Avenue, the past three weeks, whenever our spirits had sunk low, this had been our theme
song. In its own way, it was as jolly and soul lifting
as an Armistice Day band.

Some of the other passengers peered out from behind
the high green-plush backs, smiled at us as we finished
the song. Mother tucked away the lunch basket she had
packed, rummaged in her handbag, discreetly powdered
her nose, touched up her rouge. Blainey got up, went
exploring down the aisle.

I held my golden bear to the window so he could
see we were truly on the way, leaving our Atlanta, traveling to his California.

"You're going home, Teddy," I whispered into his
round ear, and wondered how soon we could come
to the open plains and wild lands of the covered
wagon.

Mother took my hand and winked at me. With a little
shock I realized she was as changed as George. When
she spoke her voice had a confident ring.

"Really on our way, little chick, headed for our great
adventure!"

My own laugh startled me. It pleased Mother. She
gave me a hug.

"How nice to hear that," she said. "Yes, heading for adventure with our spirits high."

I leaned against her, resting, as secure in her strength as I had once been in Daddy's.

Blainey, returned, caught the last of Mother's words.

"Adventure, just like the Three Musketeers!" Her chin tilted, her eyes sparked.

Then, together, in perfect unison we said, "Whither thou goest . . ."

Suddenly we laughed, the three of us, linked little fingers for a wish.